ECHOES FROM THE PAST

Echoes From the Past

Cheryl Leach Cairns

Copyright © 2004 by Cheryl Leach Cairns.

ISBN :   Softcover   1-4134-6503-X

All rights reserved. No part of this book may be reproduced or transmitted in any form or by any means, electronic or mechanical, including photocopying, recording, or by any information storage and retrieval system, without permission in writing from the copyright owner.

This book was printed in the United States of America.

To order additional copies of this book, contact:
Xlibris Corporation
1-888-795-4274
www.Xlibris.com
Orders@Xlibris.com

CONTENTS

ACKNOWLEDGEMENTS 9
CHAPTER ONE: DREAMS 13
CHAPTER TWO: SARAH'S VISIT 21
CHAPTER THREE: MISTER BUCK'S BUCKSPORT 29
CHAPTER FOUR: SARAH 35
CHAPTER FIVE: THE COMPANY EDWARD KEEPS 48
CHAPTER SIX: SECRETS 61
CHAPTER SEVEN: THE POKER GAME 75
CHAPTER EIGHT: THE ARRESTS 86
CHAPTER NINE: BUCKSPORT HEARING 100
CHAPTER TEN: HEARING CONTINUED 113
CHAPTER ELEVEN: ENTANGLEMENT IN SURRY 124
CHAPTER TWELVE: STRANGE HAPPENINGS 132
CHAPTER THIRTEEN: ALMENA'S ENCOUNTER 139
CHAPTER FOURTEEN: SUPERIOR COURT 148
CHAPTER FIFTEEN: TRIAL CONTINUED 166
CHAPTER SIXTEEN: STATE CONTINUES 177
CHAPTER SEVENTEEN: CRUTIAL TESTIMONIES 193
CHAPTER EIGHTEEN: DEFENSE 214
CHAPTER NINETEEN: IS THIS
    THE CONCLUSION? 236
EPILOGUE: SARAH'S FREEDOM 249

This book is dedicated to Catherine Denning.

ACKNOWLEDGEMENTS

Material for this book came from sources of the Bucksport Historical Society, Articles in the Bangor Commercial Newspaper and Boston papers of the time, Bucksport Memorial Library, Augusta State Archives and recollections from other people. I wish to thank the History Channel for the interview with me concerning my book, 'Echoes From the Past,' in the year 2001. Also, many thanks to the ladies of the Clerk of Courts in the Ellsworth Courthouse, who allowed me to spend many hours doing research. I am grateful to my family and friends for the support they gave me, without their encouragement I probably would not have pursued the writing of this book. I wish to give personal thanks to my daughter Tammy, who was involved in the origin of my book. I wish to thank Alexandria Stubbs, my professional Physic; Joy Hundermark, who had remarkable insite; Carol Shultz, authoress and friend; Amy Dunn, who transferred the manuscript to disk; Gerry Spooner, Librarian at the Bucksport Library who helped with research; Barbara Schannon and Sharon Gray for their excellent drawings. My sincere thanks to my dear friend, Jimmy Sweet, for his newspaper articles.

Also, my ad infinitum thanks to my editor, Alice M. Motycka, M. Ed, C.A.S. (Language arts) for the endless hours she took copyediting my book.

PLAN SHOWING BUCKSPORT DISTRICT WHERE SARA

LOCATION of the BODY

PLAN OF PART OF BUCKSPORT

...ARE IS ALLEGED TO HAVE BEEN MURDERED.

Three ladies of Bucksport

CHAPTER ONE

DREAMS

I see myself sitting in Mrs. Emily Lemerson's kitchen on Main Street at her small oval shaped maple table. Two other prominent ladies are there, Mrs. Mary Moss and Mrs. Elsie Finn.

'Is that me?' I ask myself. Why am I taking on this personage? My name is different. My clothes are different. I even feel different, but it's me, as Dr. Lemerson's wife. What am I doing here? I am about fifty years old, with grown children, still having the delicate small figure of a woman half my age. I have long chestnut colored hair. I am wearing it in a neat round bun at the nape of my neck. The dress I have on is dark blue with a high neck. It has long full sleeves with small round gold buttons at the cuffs.

Mrs. Elsie Finn is sitting at my right. She has a creamy white complexion, the palest of blue eyes with light brown hair. The silk shirtwaist blouse, cerulean in color, compliments her eyes. Her hands, long and slender, show a noticeably large beautiful diamond ring. Sitting behind the sparkling diamond is her gold wedding band signifying her marriage of thirty years. Mr. and Mrs. Finn own an emporium on Main Street, which is located in the center of town. It is across from Mr. and Mrs. Samuel Pall's grocery store on Main Street in Bucksport.

Mrs. Mary Moss is seated to my left. Her sharp tongue and quick wit are as noticeable as her flaming red hair. She wears her mother's striking ring, consisting of two extraordinarily large diamonds surrounded by large rubies the color of deep red roses. The powerful Mrs. Moss chose not to display her unique wedding band. She seemed to take pleasure in showing all the ladies her many pieces of exquisite heirloom jewelry. She has chocolate brown eyes that pierce right through you. She wears a Victorian tan linen dress trimmed with deep brown velvet piping. This dress always looked stunning on her and she knew it! She and her husband James Moss own the Robinson House Inn, which they purchased around 1860.

Mrs. Harriet Pall, wife of Selectman Samuel Pall is sitting across from me. She has hazel eyes and dark brown hair. She wears a black satin skirt. Her blouse is wisteria blue with white hand stitched lace at the neckline. The lace accentuates the blouse to perfection. The back of the blouse has pearl buttons down to her waistline. A cameo brooch sits proudly at the front of her neck. The only other piece of jewelry is her gold wedding band. Most of the citizens know Samuel Pall as a storeowner as well as Town Selectman. The elected position involves many duties, including overseeing the community's government officials such as the Sheriff, Deputy Sheriff Genn and Constable Danvers. This prominent position requires him to hold town meetings with the other elected officials.

We are playing our weekly game of bridge. I slowly look to see what is around me. At a small glass kitchen window are soft beige lace curtains. The curtains are an intricate lace pattern and on the table is a white tablecloth edged with the same lovely lace pattern. The gray slate sink has a hand drawn pump. The sun's rays filter through the small glass panes and I feel it on my face. I sense we are afraid of something. What is it? Why do our conversations inevitably always come back to the same subject?

The conversation is about a murdered woman whose name is Sarah Ware. She was a gentle caring woman. Sarah was a woman definitely ahead of her time. Townspeople were aware that Sarah lived alone without her husband for ten years before her death. Why he suddenly left would surface at a later date. I recall what she looked like. Sarah was a pretty looking woman in her youth. Her nature was one of low self-esteem. Her fawn brown hair had turned gray in her later years. She also wore her hair in a bun on the back of her neck, it was the fashion of the time. Those once large emerald green eyes always looked sad. Her head became detached from her body when she was found two weeks after her murder. The conversation continued about her detached head, which had been placed in a wooden box and stored in a vault at the Ellsworth Court House and later viewed at the 1902 trial.

As the dream continues, I see Mrs. Willey a large, coarse, rough looking woman with an abundance of ignorance. She owns and operates a local tavern in her Summer Winter Hotel, which is in the Emery Block brick building on Main Street, constructed in 1873. This building is situated near the town office and other business establishments. In the building besides Mrs. Willey's Summer Winter Hotel there is an insurance company; stock company; shoe store; Mr. Page's drugstore; and Mrs. Robbins millinery store. Although rooms are rented mostly to traveling salesmen, Mrs. Willey also rents rooms to many of the workers from the shipping vessels owned by local captains. Her tavern is a place where you would rather not be seen!

She disliked Sarah because she perceived her as competition to her barmaids. Mrs. Willey chose to believe the gossip spread by Mrs. Moss and Mrs. Bolder a few years after Sarah arrived in Bucksport, Maine. Mrs. Bolder told Mary Moss she suspected that Sarah had had an abortion and that Mr. Bolder, her husband, had arranged this because he believed he was the baby's father. Mrs. Bolder childless and older than her husband was jealous of her husband's friendship with Sarah.

Mrs. Willey employed her own daughter as a barmaid in her hotel. The females Mrs. Willey employed appeared to have all the grace and beauty necessary for their profession. Mrs. Willey, jealous of Sarah's natural grace and beauty, was heard saying to more than one male customer "Well what's wrong with my girls, I bet you're going after that sweet young thing up on the hill." Mrs. Willey enjoyed tarnishing Sarah's reputation, much the way Mary Moss did.

In my dream, while playing bridge, my female companions and I discuss the dark cloud surrounding the death of Sarah Ware. We also confer how unnerving her death has been to the community. To have such a brutally alleged murder happen to a person in this quiet family-oriented town was unthinkable. Rumor, suspicion, and innuendoes ran rampant throughout Bucksport. We thought of our town as being one where everyone knew practically everyone else, full of forthright citizens of honor and integrity. Certain people chose to ignore rumors of murder.

Before this murder occurred Bucksport was a thriving community. How could this happen, we ladies ask ourselves? It is all very shocking! Is it possible that we know the person or persons responsible? What a horrifying thought! The town is about to enter the twentieth century. An incident like this could surely ruin the town if it was confirmed that one of its own citizens had perpetrated such a ghastly crime.

In the dream, I know what is going to happen next. With excellent manners, I suggest we take time from our bridge game and conversation to taste the delicious cake and tea. I also know within one hour the game will end.

Since it was a lovely day, I decided to take Miles Lane on my way home. The lane was peaceful. The late fall afternoon sun is warm on my face as I walk past the oak and maple trees. After arriving at Angela and William Bogg's dry goods store on Central Street, I purchase a cigar for my husband and inquire if the new shipment of dress materials from Boston has arrived.

Angela Bogg is a pleasant middle aged shopkeeper's wife with two grown sons one they call Joe Jr. at times and a younger son Thomas. Angela grew up in a family of what people sometimes called backwards. Her family had a history of mental instability. This is evident in her son Joe Bogg as well as herself.

Her husband William was sad because people thought Joe was not his son. His cross to bear in life was that of his son Joe, whom he calls Jr., and who looks more like his Uncle Joe Mank, Angela's brother. It was rumored Joe looked like his uncle because Angela's brother Joe had been having sexual relations with his sisters by force.

When Angela and William were courting, things got a little out of hand. Angela became pregnant with their son Joe. Since

William had been out of town on business, he could not get back in time for the marriage to take place before the pregnancy became obvious. The speculation of William not being the father was always in the air. It seemed to be on people's lips continuously. That was a shame Angela felt she had to bear.

Joseph came two months early. Angela named him "Joseph," giving their son her maiden name Mank since she was not married. When William returned home, he and Angela married as planned. In the eyes of the law and the pious citizens, who felt William should have married Angela before she conceived, caused William to feel he must adopt their son and give him the name of 'Bogg.' Angela could not accept herself as an upstanding citizen. She carried her inner childhood traumas of abuse and feelings of worthlessness into her adult life compounded by her illegal son.

There was always negativity from the town concerning Joe's birth. Was it really all a matter of just bad timing? Was Joe Jr. the product of incest, or was it simply a matter of having his mother's coloring? He did have darker colored skin and dark brown curly hair, but his eyes were a dark blue, suggesting he was William's son!

Angela's father was a minister in Orland and his occupation often required him to be out of town. Contrary to his profession he pretty much had a woman in every port that he meandered through. Occasionally Mr. Mank would take his son, Joe Mank, along with him on these out of town trips. Joe's father with his genetic deficiency thought that was what all men did; sought women to service them. In his and his son's minds it was all right. Angela's father often left Joe in charge of his sisters while out of town. When unexpectedly returning home from one of his trips, he caught his son with one of his daughters. He tried to keep this hushed up, but the secret of the town was quietly voiced among the men. It was around the same time of Angela's pregnancy!

Growing up, Joe Bogg would hear rumors of his uncle being his father. Joe would hear people whispering, "His mom is . . . . his daddy is . . . . his Uncle . . . ssh here comes Angela." This irritation was compounded by the fact he knew he didn't look like his father, William Bogg. Joe stood about six feet tall, having the natural dark color complexion from his mother's side. In Joe's warped uneducated sick mind he at times believed William was just a good guy who wanted to do the right thing by his mother. Joe always felt he was not good enough. These feelings came from the way his mother treated him. It really messed up his paranoid schizophrenic mind and he was not able to accept his condition. He had no medication to help him, so he did what he had to do in order to survive. People saw many different personalities in Joe.

Angela, Joe's mom was able to somewhat keep her schizophrenia at bay, because of her age and being a woman, along with her husband who would defend her. In one of her sudden and unreasonable bursts of anger her husband would say, "Oh Angela is just being Angela", or "Angela is having one of her moments."

William had sincere feelings for his wife Angela. She was an attractive woman when they married and still was. He had heard stories and rumors of her family's history when they were courting. William knew he and Angela were not upper class people. He also knew he was not a handsome man and believed that he himself was not a great catch, but that maybe he could help Angela. Perhaps they could have some sort of life together.

Several times when Joe was separated from his wife and not working on Captain Calder's shipping vessels he rented a room at Captain Calder's home. Joe had more brawn than brains and was therefore suited for menial work on shipping vessels. His grandfather, the Reverend Mank, had performed the marriage between Lillian Bosey and Joe Bogg when he was twenty-six and Lillian was twenty-two. Lillian had light brown hair and sky blue eyes. Their daughter Julie-Ann had dark brown curly hair and dark brown eyes, with skin that looked as though Julie-Ann had a year round tan. With this complexion she in many ways resembled her grandmother Angela, Joe's mother. Everyone knew there was black blood in Angela's family. Julie's grandfather, William Bogg, thought the world of Julie-Ann and it was evident to everyone.

Joe Bogg more than once manifested his warped personality. On more than one occasion, he accused his wife Lillian of being unfaithful, saying that their child was not his. Humiliating Lillian in the privacy of their home was something he enjoyed doing.

Thomas, Joe's younger brother, tended to be a selfish self-indulgent person. He tended to look more like his father with the lighter complexion and blue eyes. He lived in South Carolina, making periodic trips home for extended visits. He lived in South Carolina out of embarrassment due to lack of respect for his family. One time when Thomas was at home visiting, he had his way with a black girl in the nearby town of Orland and got her pregnant, but claimed no responsibility!

I chat with Angela and William Bogg for a few minutes. Angela and I discuss when Sarah previously boarded in a room over their store. Angela stated, "Even though Sarah was there for about four years before living at Mrs. files, I did not know her well, she kept to herself. She continued, the only thing I ever saw her do was buy cheroots for herself." Angela also mentioned that Sarah and William Bogg had shared religious beliefs. When Sarah came in the store they would talk about her Catholic faith. Sarah told William she did not feel the need to go to church to be close to God.

Upon awakening from my dream, it was hard to realize that I was one of those ladies, in another time period. This recurrent dream is so real! Did this really happen? Why would anybody want to harm Sarah? Why are these women in my dreams? Is this truly the town's history? Did these families really exist? Was Sarah's murder ever solved? As my dreams continued, I tried to process all of this information I was receiving. I was determined to discover some of the answers to my questions.

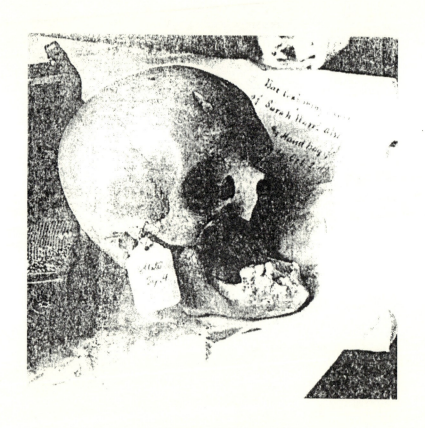

State exhibit #4 (Sarah's skull)

CHAPTER TWO

SARAH'S VISIT

On the following Saturday morning after I awoke and went into the kitchen, to my surprise, I discovered my daughter also knew the identity of the murdered woman.

Saturday mornings everyone usually slept late. I had decided to make a breakfast of hotcakes and bacon. I was up before anyone else, sitting at the kitchen table enjoying my cup of black coffee. Living seven miles out in the country I found it a treat to watch the wildlife through the large sliding door in the kitchen. The bacon was snapping and sizzling in the black iron skillet. The aroma of fresh coffee brewing floated throughout the house.

Tammy, my daughter of seventeen, wandered into the kitchen. The delicious smell of breakfast must have awakened her and her sister, Nicole. While Nicole was freshening up, Tammy asked, "Mom can I help you?" I told her she could put the basket of freshly baked bran muffins on the table. As she placed them on the table she asked me, "Mom have you ever heard of a woman who lived in our town in the late 1800s by the name of Sarah Ware who had allegedly been murdered?"

I asked, "How do you know she was murdered? Why do you want to know about this woman? What makes you think any of this is true? Perhaps it is only a dream."

Tammy replied, "No Mom, it is not a dream, she came to me in my room again last night while I was sitting on my bed. Sarah told me about her mysterious death and asked me to help her!" I asked Tammy, "What do you mean, how long has this been going on?" Tammy went on to tell me that when Sarah first started to come to her, she was afraid. Tammy said, "Sarah made me feel uncomfortable until she put me at ease by saying she meant no harm."

Nicole entered the room saying, "I wish I could join in on this delicious breakfast, but I have a book debate at the school library in twenty minutes."

With a soft and sincere voice Tammy continued saying to me, "Mom we have to talk about this woman. I don't know what's happening or why she is in my dreams, but she is! Mom, Sarah started to come into my dreams about a month ago. I just dismissed it as a silly dream, but Mom she is now in my room! Sarah became frustrated at first when she thought I did not take her seriously. She began to get my attention by sliding my silk scarf, which was hanging on the bedpost, across the room behind her! I sat on my bed; my eyes wide with disbelief watching my flowered scarf as it floated in the air. One time I tried to pretend it was not happening but the radio kept getting louder and louder! My bedroom lamp kept going on and off! I knew it was Sarah, she told me it was she and that she meant me no harm!"

Tammy continued to say, "Sarah at first came to me as a faceless woman, but as she began to feel more comfortable she began to reveal what she looks like. She looks as though she is in her forties with light brown hair and emerald green eyes. She always wears the same old-fashioned black dress with buttons open at her bosom. When she appears in my dreams I feel as though I've known her before. She said she lived in the 1800's. This is 1988. She always says the same thing to me. She wants you and me to help her. Mom, please help me find out who this woman is and how can we possibly help her. We have to find out. Something is terribly wrong, we have to help her or she won't leave us alone. She must feel that she can trust us! In my first dream of this woman she was underwater. In this dream I reached out to grab her hand, but I could never touch it. We couldn't seem to reach one another." Sarah told me, 'The past involves the present, one day you both will understand.' Tammy went on to say, "What does she mean?"

How could I answer this question? I did not know the answer myself. I sensed, however, that this meant something was about to happen. What was it we were going to learn? Why was there such a strong need to help Sarah?

We were two women of the present who had many questions ahead of us that could only be answered by going back in time. Sarah needed or wanted us to solve the suspicious circumstances surrounding her death. I didn't know how we were going to help her and why it was going to have such a long lasting effect on my life!

My daughter and I, feeling somewhat apprehensive took on the challenge. We must help, but can we? This started our journey into the world of the past. It revealed the most twisted entangled mass of information imaginable! Articles in old newspapers, the Bucksport Historical Society and Town Office supported what we thought was only the imagination of our dreams. The information we uncovered made us more determined to help this woman, bewildering and confusing as it was. The first of many echoes from the past was about to begin.

I went to work and Tammy went to school. She went to her classes as usual, then to her after school activities. That evening, Tammy and I briefly discussed what we could do about this situation. I said, "Tammy, I feel strongly that we should call our local minister. How do you feel about that?" I asker her.

Tammy responded with, "Well mom, there needs to be a starting point somewhere, so why not with the minister? Maybe he will have some knowledge we are not aware of."

I phoned our minister and made an appointment with him for the next evening. When we finished explaining what was happening he agreed to bless Tammy's room. He said to us, "Things should be better now!" However, we both knew our work was not over!

In the morning it was clear to us that Sarah was not going away! Tammy said to me, "Mom, Sarah came into my dreams again last night. She said there was more work we needed to do and that we had to find another way. We would have to do this by ourselves.

There were reasons why she chose us. We would know what they were at the appropriate time. Sarah trusts that we will find the information we need in order to help her."

It wasn't until evening when Tammy and I had time to talk. We discussed and agreed to take on this challenge and how to put our investigation into action. Where do we go to get the information to see if this woman really lived in Bucksport? Why is it important to her that we get answers?

The following morning we decided the first logical place to look for our answers would be at the Silver Lake Cemetery which is in two sections divided by a road and a lake. I decided to take the Silver Lake Road, stopping at the upper half of the cemetery first, thinking it may hold the burial site of Sarah Ware. We were drawn to our first clue, unbeknownst to us at the time, which was a huge monument with the name of John Bolder. His monument location provided a view of the entire lake and ultimately was a view of the pauper's burial site of Sarah Ware.

Without stopping to look around at this cemetery we proceeded down the road to the lower part of the cemetery which was adjacent to Silver Lake. It had a path that led to a small dam, which the paper mill in the town of Bucksport still uses as their water supply. We did not know why we came, only that we felt compelled to stop. We followed our instincts and looked through the cemetery for a gravesite with Sarah's name on it. We did find a headstone with the name of George Ware on it. Unbeknownst to us at the time, George Ware was Sarah Ware's brother-in-law.

Not finding her grave, we followed the foot-path down to the dam. We sat at the water's edge for a rest, both of us were fatigued after all the walking we had done. Feeling somewhat frustrated by what seemed to be a very long day without answers; Tammy began to skip rocks across the water. It was then that another clue was given to us but we did not realize what was happening. Without much thought she picked up a small branch at her feet and tossed it into the lake. Normally the branch would have floated away but this time it did not. The branch made a couple of small circles that seemed to move on its own back to the person who tossed it. Tammy turned to me with a look of utter surprise. She said, "Mom, why did that stick come back to me?" I did not know what to say. Through research we learned Sarah's child, that was miscarried, was buried near this site.

Between wandering in the cemetery and our short rest at the water's edge it seemed as though time had flown by. The warm spring air had started to get chilly. We then decided to make our way home.

It was the next weekend while trying to fit the pieces of this fragmented puzzle together that we thought we had found some answers. Fortunately for us the Bucksport Historical Society had changed their hours and decided to open earlier than scheduled. In the museum we found treasures of the past that we could use to help Sarah. We found several newspaper articles, which contained photographs of Sarah's rings; pocketbook; key; earrings; waterproof; and Sarah's skull. At this point we didn't know these items were going to present themselves again and again but in different ways. The newspaper articles that carried the story of this alleged murder triggered what seemed to me unsettling memories from my past. How can this be? I didn't live in her time period! Still I felt as though I had some knowledge of what I read. Why did seeing her rings, purse, earrings and waterproof give me such an ill-fated feeling?

Tammy said, "Mom, listen to what this newspaper article says about Sarah; now I understand why I saw Sarah underwater even though I did not tell you at the time. It says here that her body was kept in a crypt at Silver Lake Cemetery before they buried her in a pauper's grave. In 1929, the lake was flooded and enlarged to accommodate the Maine Seaboard Paper Company, which was under construction. The newspaper articles say that her body was moved at that time to the Oak Hill Cemetery on McDonald Street in Bucksport along with other bodies, but maybe hers didn't make it! Mom, maybe it got left behind and is now part of the lake. Mom, it also tells about the trial and that her skull is still in a box in the Ellsworth Court House. The case was never completely solved. That means that she was buried without her head! Her head was used as evidence at the murder trial in 1902."

Excited that maybe we had discovered one answer, I said, "Perhaps Sarah just wants us, or you, to go to her grave and pray for her. Lets go to Oak Hill Cemetery to find Sarah's gravesite and pray for her." Tammy picked a bouquet of wild flowers, then took them to Sarah's headstone where she knelt down and said a silent prayer. We then went to Ellsworth to see Sarah's skull. The skull was crushed in on one side with a piece missing. The jaw-bone was partially missing. The thing that I thought was odd was the one strand of her hair that was still in a slight crack in her skull.

* * *

Many years have gone by, Tammy is now married with a young daughter of her own. She has a job she thoroughly enjoys. She works in the Court System as a Victim Witness Advocate in Ellsworth. *Was it a connection between Tammy and Sarah because Sarah did not have anyone to advocate for her; she was dead. The State Attorney General was concerned with convicting the alleged murderer, but did he succeed?*

I have had no visits from Sarah for a long time, but her past life drifts through my dreams to let me know that my work is not completed. It is all a learning process; one that I am about to embark on that will take me further than I ever imagined possible.

I was about to learn what Sarah wanted of me. No matter how many years go by, serious abuses whether they are physical, emotional, or psychological still need reconciling. Sarah never had reconciliation and neither did the men who were involved in her alleged murder. These echoes from Sarah's past keep calling to me. I feel their need to be set free.

Strange things happen which compel us to do or complete a task. It was in a summer recently while I was sitting on a rock with my shoes off at the water's edge of Silver Lake. My friends were sitting on another rock close by. The sun was making my feet feel extremely warm, thinking the water would cool them I decided to walk in up to my ankles. Gradually, without knowing why I had done so, I had walked out to my knees. It made me felt very serene.

The birds that had been making their presence known earlier had suddenly gone quiet.

This beautiful bright yellow winged butterfly, which had been fluttering around back and forth from the water to the rocks where we had been sitting, appeared in front of me. That was when I began to feel this tingling sensation in my toes, slowly at first, then more noticeable. I did not move, as I felt numbed, almost glued, to where I was standing. I looked down at my feet.

A white mist began to appear very slowly at first. The vapory nebulous was very distinct in the clear water. It seemed to be coming from between the small rocks slightly in front of my feet. I couldn't believe what I was seeing at first. I said, "Barbara, Adriane, come here, you have to see what I am seeing. Don't disturb the water. Walk very slowly." Jumping up from the rocks, where they were sitting they slowly walked out to me. "Look down at my feet. Do you see it?" I asked. By this time the white mist, slightly beneath the water, had begun to grow larger and take on a formation of its own without ever coming apart. "Yes, I see it," said Barbara softly. "I do to," replied Adriane quietly, "It's moving over and around your feet." I replied, "Yes I know, but I don't feel afraid, only peaceful, and the tingling sensation has gone away."

It appeared as though it was about to touch my ankle. I noticed the tingling feeling was leaving my feet as it moved closer to me. Then the white mist began slowly to rub against my ankles, as a kitten would nuzzle and rub against you to get your attention, and let you know it was contented. We all looked at one another not speaking a word. We knew what had happened!

At this point, I decided it was definitely time for me to make a commitment to Sarah Ware.

Tekworgy's Residence and Store

CHAPTER THREE

MISTER BUCK'S BUCKSPORT

Colonel Buck was known to have settled the area in 1762. He had come from Haverhill, Massachusetts with his family. He was sent to this area by the military to help make a settlement. The Colonel was known for conducting a kangaroo court of a young woman accused of being a witch. Some citizens believed he was having an affair with this young woman and some thought he fathered her son. Having been found guilty of witchcraft she was sentenced to hang by her neck until dead. Prior to her demise she threatened to leave her mark on his tombstone and obviously she succeeded! The outline of a boot, to the present day, cannot be eradicated. (It is noted as a 'must see' if you ever travel to Bucksport, Maine.)

Bucksport was a small shipbuilding town with a prominent shipping port situated eighteen miles up the Penobscot River. In the town were two barbershops, one owned by James Innis and one by Mr. Sweet.

Rose Calder and her husband, Captain Calder, who shipped out from time to time, lived on Pine Street. Rose Calder owned a millinery shop in their home. Her customers were the prominent citizens of Bucksport. The millinery shop was adjacent to the house with a separate entrance. The Calder's home resembled a cottage with a stream flowing in their back yard. A footbridge over the stream connects Pine and Mill Street several yards up from their neighbor, Mr. Dorr. Rose rented extra rooms in her home to overnight boarders, some for extended periods of time. Rose hired Susan, a local girl with learning disabilities, to do the laundry and cleaning. For these services Susan was provided with room and board. Her room in the back of the house was small but adequate and overlooked the footbridge with a view of Mill Street. When Joe Bogg rented his room it was also on the second floor. His room overlooked Pine Street with a limited view of Main Street.

Mr. Tekworgy was a general store owner who had a prominent business on Pine Street two houses down on the same side as the Calder's. Joe Mank, Joe Bogg's uncle, occasionally stopped and would visit Mr. Tekworgy at his place of business.

Bucksport also had a well-known carriage and sleigh manufacturer owned by Mr. George Bailey. It was on Main Street housed in a fairly large three-story building. Mr. Bailey employed about twelve of the town's citizens. Bucksport had other business dealers such as, horse harness makers and carriage makers, several blacksmith shops and livery stables that were continually active. There was also the Doggett Tanning Factory, which employed many local Bucksport citizens.

Dr. Lemerson was a dentist and physician when needed. His office could be found three doors down from the town office. He was also Bucksport's health official. During town meetings he would update Selectman Pall on the health status of the school children in Bucksport. Working close at hand they quickly became friends and cohorts.

As mentioned, the town had a prominent Inn, The Robinson House owned by James and Mary Moss. They accommodated famous personages such as President Grover Cleveland amd Commander Perry, who went to the North Pole on the ship the, 'Roosevelt', which was built on Verona Island. Their son Fred and daughter Nellie were nine and five when the Moss' purchased it. The family lived at the Inn. There were oak French doors leading into the parlor on the second floor where Mrs. Moss spent most of her leisure time. The room was decorated with the most beautiful Queen Anne furniture. The wallpaper of elegant gold brocade met the molding at the edges of the ceiling. James Moss preferred to be in his greenhouse, although when he had guests of importance he really came alive. He entertained with a courtly grace and dignity and wore his smart costume of a swallowtail coat with brass buttons which was accompanied by a tall beaver hat when outside.

Bucksport residents shared the rumored news that James Moss kept illegal items hidden among his roses. It was rumored that under cover of darkness he waited for the liquor to be shipped on the schooners going to and coming from Boston. Captain Calder also frequently made this run. Then there were those nights that he and his male friends stayed out most of the night doing who knows what?

The Moss's son, Fred, married Isabelle Bernard. Isabelle was a descendent of Colonel Jonathan Buck, the founder of the town. In 1891 Fred started Rose conservatories much like his father's conservatory. He often brought his shipment of roses to Boston and brought back packages or other shipments for some of his male business friends, including his father. Fred owned two greenhouses and his father owned one greenhouse behind the Moose Head Printing Company on Federal Street.

The local newspaper office, The Moose Head Printing Company, was unique in certain ways. Although beautifully decorated with a comfortable sitting area; was there an ulterior motive in this construction? Perhaps there was. In this room one could see who was walking the streets from every direction long before one decided to enter the premises of the first greenhouse, which belonged to James Moss. One sitting in this area could alert Mr. Moss if the law was on its way. 'One hand washes the other,' as some say!

The town of Bucksport had a funeral home owned by Mr. George Ware. He was related to Sarah Ware by marriage, since Sarah had married his brother Edward. There were several real estate developers and insurance agencies in town. 'Self appointed Colonel' St. Barron was one of these real estate developers and Mr. Swazey was an insurance agent. Several other business people such as Selectman Pall, a grain store owner; Mr. Finn, a book store owner; Mr. Britewood, who owned a clothing shop; Mr. Dorr, the local liquor store agent; Mr. William Tekworgy, a mercantile store owner; and Captain Layno, a shipyard owner. These were eight male friends who made up a twelve male secret agreement and would meet over coffee and cigars in the morning hours and discuss their previous illegal activities.

William Tekworgy had his business on 18 Pine Street. Mr. Tekworgy's residence was on number 19 and his stables were number 20. The business contained five different departments, each one containing something for everyone's needs. William Tekworgy was a clever businessman, but his cash flow was insufficient. One department was for groceries; one for furniture and another for clothing; one for jobbing wood, dried sticking, sawdust and shavings; then there was the department of bungs and hardware. He owned two horses. The white horse he used when he did his illegal work for the influential men. His sleek well-groomed black horse and jigger was used for special occasions, such as visiting his influential friends or to visit Mrs. Files for Sunday afternoon dinners since she was a widow and he a widower.

Mr. Tekworgy was a native of Surry, Maine. He was born in Ellsworth the 29th of September 1856 and was motherless by the age of eight. He was a tall man, average looking with black hair. His eyes were almost black in color, round and small, for the size of his face. He wore a short beard. As a child he had never been really cared for. Living with different families, he had been abused, humiliated and even raped as a young boy.

William Tekworgy got his first job in the Ellsworth House, an Inn and Livery owned by George Hale in the town of Ellsworth. William lived with George Hale and as part of his keep he learned the trade of livery until Mr. Hale gave up the business after 10 years. Subsequently, William Tekworgy lived with a man in Surry for about two years who taught him the tin trade business, thereupon he moved to Bucksport and lived with Esquire Wiswell, from whom he learned about Maine laws. He met Paul Buck while he was living with Mr. Wiswell.

Sometime while on his own he met Joe Bogg. They had learned through their personal conversations that they had many things in common. William Tekworgy was motherless; Joe in his simple mind thought that his uncle was his real father. Joe Bogg and Will Tekworgy became good friends.

When Joe Bogg was not shipping, he and William Tekworgy were seen together constantly. They confided in one another. Joe Bogg learned to hide his feelings from years of hiding behind a mask of false happiness. William Tekworgy told Joe Bogg that he knew some citizens of Bucksport that still viewed him as an outcast, even though he was somewhat successful in his mercantile business.

When William Tekworgy came to Bucksport he had a wife Isabel and a young daughter Mary. His second daughter Abby came two years later. William Tekworgy and his two daughters were very close. It was speculated by a number of citizens that Mr. Tekworgy and his daughters kept secrets between them. They were unusually close! Mr. Tekworgy would keep his daughters from associating with other friends. His wife Isabel had died when Abby was three years old.

After Isabel died Sarah Ware watched the girls until William Tekworgy met Olivia from Surry, whom he later married. The two girls became very attached to Sarah and had to make an adjustment when Mr. Tekworgy married Olivia. They began their married life as a family in Bucksport. Within a year their family had grown. Their daughter Grace was born the next year. Olivia and William Tekworgy had a life filled with pain and heartache. Since William Tekworgy was not able to relate to a woman, he found it hard to communicate even to his wife. She tried to make this marriage work not only for herself and her daughter, but also for William and his daughters. Lack of success drove her to take Grace and move to Boston. (Why did she feel the need to move herself and her daughter away from Will Tekworgy and Bucksport? Did she catch Will and one of his daughters in a compromising situation, was she overwhelmed by her husband's illegal activities? Or, perhaps they just were not compatible.) Olivia had told no one of her move. One day she was just gone! Ultimately they divorced!

ROBINSON HOUSE, 1898

Robinson House

CHAPTER FOUR

SARAH

We same ladies are playing our weekly bridge game. It is the late 1800's. I constantly return as Doctor Lemerson's wife. We were talking about the murder of Sarah Ware. The dream seemed to weave in and out. It was filled with new information. It was unnerving to know that Sarah was dead, she had cleaned my house three days before.

Sitting in my secret abhorrence for Sarah Ware, I do not enter into the discussion. I knew she had been with my husband on many Saturday evenings playing poker at Mrs. File's house. This is where Sarah resided! Everyone is discussing who might have murdered Sarah. I have my own reasons for wanting this once happily married middle-aged woman dead. But who could have done it?

As the ladies kept talking it made me remember an afternoon several years before her murder. What I had suspected of my husband and his illegal drug and alcohol affairs was confirmed. It will stay with me for a long time.

I'd had this unyielding, thumping pain in my head. I then decided to leave the game early making my apologies to the other ladies, I started for home. Instead of normally entering through the front door I quietly went in through the kitchen.

Dr. Lemerson was in the parlor with Mr. Britewood, a storeowner; Mr. Pall, Town Selectman; self-appointed title of Colonel St. Barron; Mr. Dorr, the liquor agent; Captain Layno; and Captain Nichols. The men were having a business meeting. Not wanting to interrupt their meeting, I slowly took off my wrap and started up the stairs, stopping halfway when I heard Sarah speaking to my husband.

I remember Sarah being in the adjacent room downstairs dusting furniture since it was her usual day for cleaning. I heard her tell Dr. Lemerson, my husband, that she intended to tell James Moss about the possibility of Sheriff Genn inspecting his greenhouse for liquor. This was not the first time that the Sheriff had inspected the greenhouse of James Moss! The Methodist Church people were always doing this to James Moss. Many times they had unsuccessfully tried to catch him and his illegal sales of liquor to smaller unlicensed dealers.

I heard Sarah say to the gentlemen, "Yes, Mr. Moss had discussed the possibility of purchasing a new bell for the Methodist Church with its board members, since he knew they needed one." Sarah had also said, "Mr. Moss and I talked about a new bell for the church as an appeasement. Mr. Moss was getting tired of all the hoop-la." Then she went on about her business.

I knew the men did not notice me come in. Also, I knew that Sarah could see me from where she was standing, although she did not acknowledge my presence. Sarah just kept on dusting. What was her intent? Realizing that she clearly saw me and chose to ignore me, I promptly ignored her and continued up the stairs. It was clear we had a mutual dislike for one another! My suspicions of my husband's involvement in this kind of illegality were very clear to me now! Sarah's discussion had made that quite obvious!

As the men finalized their business I heard Sarah say to Mr. Britewood, "Tomorrow I will be over early in the morning to do your laundry." Sarah spent long hours at his house cooking his meals, baking and doing his laundry. Some women thought and discussed in private that she and he had affection for one another; feelings they could not show because of the differences in their social status. Mr. Britewood would defend her in a delicate way when he heard anyone saying things of a demeaning nature against Sarah. I remember seeing Sarah leaving through the kitchen door. She quietly left without saying a word. Thinking back on this I felt remorse over my dislike for her.

The story of how Sarah came to Bucksport was speculated by some, and thought to be true by others. It seemed the only ones that knew for sure were those involved. Speculation had it that Sarah was born into a poor farm family from Cape Breton, Nova Scotia, Canada. She had two older brothers and two younger sisters. Sarah was the oldest of the three girls. Because she had to help her family live off the land, Sarah had insufficient schooling, but she was bright for the limited education she was able to acquire. She came from a large family and therefore she had to go to work. Sarah came to Bucksport, Maine, through a member of the Bucksport Catholic Church, John Bolder, a parishioner.

It was Sarah's choice to come when the situation presented itself to her. John Bolder had told Sarah and her family of a working position in the United States, in Bucksport, Maine. He told Sarah and her family of the implied verbal agreement and adoption of Sarah, if things worked out. The work involved was to be a hired girl for an American family. She would also watch their two young children. She would be paid a meager wage, with room and board provided. She would work with the Moss family in Bucksport who owned the Robinson House. Sarah's coming to Bucksport was then arranged.

After taking care of her younger brothers and sisters, she knew she could look after a prosperous family's children. John Bolder knew Sarah's family through his church and knew they needed the extra money. He also told Sarah and her family that he and his wife needed a part time domestic and how Sarah could stay at his house when cleaning. Sarah would arrive at the Robinson house first and meet the Moss'.

John Bolder had talked with James Moss about the possibility of hiring a girl to help his wife Mary with their two children. Mary was a frail woman when it suited her. She did not have time to be with her children. She felt that she was needed in her social circle.

This arrangement would give Mary time for her social activities and allow more leisure time with her lady friends. After much discussion James and Mary Moss had agreed to hire Sarah. Mr.

John Bolder was to relay this message to Sarah and her parents. The contract was verbal! It was hinted to Mr. Bolder that a written contract would be done at a later time to see if the Moss' would agree to adopt Sarah.

With this acceptance of the unwritten agreement in her mind, Sarah said, "Yes," to leaving her family to work elsewhere. Bucksport being an active fishing and shipping port, she thought she would eventually meet and marry a nice young man.

The day finally arrived. John Bolder thought that Sarah should not make the trip alone, so he accompanied her to her new home. It was a crisp fall morning. The year was 1861 when Sarah boarded the stagecoach. She was nervous and the cold weather did not help. With her suitcase on board, her four-day journey began.

Sarah was determined to make the best of her new life. There was no heat inside the coach to warm her hands and feet. The worn wool mittens her mother had made for her provided some warmth. On her feet she wore her boots from the previous winter. Inside the coach was an old gray, scratchy wool blanket that the stage line had provided. It did give her some relief from the bitter chill. The ruts and deep depressions of the hard packed frozen dirt road made it seem like one everlasting trip!

She thought to herself, *this coach has seen better days.* It will be a miracle if I arrive in one piece. This trip is going to take forever! She thought these four days were the hardest and roughest she had ever spent anywhere. She was having second thoughts; even the harsh farm life hadn't been this bad! Sarah began to wonder if she had made the correct choice, but her family needed the extra money. The simple food her mother had packed was long gone. She had not been able to get much sleep. During their long tiring ride Sarah and John Bolder realized a close bond had grown between them.

It was late morning when she leaned forward to look out the small window frame. She saw the tall white building with its long porch and two sets of wide staircases leading to the front door. She knew she had reached her destination when she saw a predominant sign across the front that read 'The Robinson House'.

Sarah saw a man with a kindly face leaning against one of the tall round white pillars. He came down to greet her. With a warm friendly smile he opened the door of the coach and said, "Hello my dear, you must be Sarah. I am Mr. James Moss."

"Hello, Mr. Moss," Sarah answered.

John Bolder looked at Sarah and said, "I will see you in a few days." It was at this point that he said his good-byes and was on his way home.

Mr. Moss took her hand and picked up her one bedraggled suitcase and led Sarah up the stairs. At the top of the porch stood Mrs. Mary Moss. The dress she wore under her exquisite brown fur cape was the most royal shade of blue Sarah had ever seen.

Mary, seeing how young Sarah was with rosebud cheeks and a tiny waist instantly displayed a sober matter-of-fact expression! Sarah was not what Mary had expected at all. Sarah was actually pretty in her own way. Mary's greeting was simply; "You must be Sarah!" Mary had a cold voice and a long icy hard stare. It made Sarah feel as though she had done something wrong. Shuddering, Sarah thought, *What am I in for?* Sarah knew instantly that Mrs. Moss disliked her.

Mary turned in the direction of the stage coach driver and said, "Put the team of horses and the coach in the livery at the back of the inn! As usual your room off the kitchen is prepared. The stable boy will have a fresh team of horses ready for your morning run."

Turning back to face Sarah, Mary sharply said, "Follow me!" They proceeded down the corridor toward the back of the inn and into the kitchen. "Sit," said Mary. Sarah sat on the bench at the long wooden table fighting to hold back tears. Mary walked over to the cook stove and ladled chicken soup into a bowl. Soup sloshed onto the table as she abruptly presented it to Sarah.

Mr. Moss walked from the pantry with a loaf of baked bread on a small cutting board. He pulled a chair to the table and joined Sarah. He looked at Sarah sitting dejectedly by herself with an expression of 'I'm Sorry' on his face, but said nothing.

Sarah observed Mr. Moss. She noticed that his hair was neatly tucked back over his ears. He had a clean shaved face. His eyes, she thought, were different from any she had ever seen. They were almost a midnight blue. Sarah quickly finished her bowl of soup. Mary briskly said, "Follow me!" Sarah obediently followed Mary to the rear of the kitchen, up the back staircase to her room.

Mary stopping abruptly, opened a door, leaned against it and announced to Sarah. "This is your room!"

Sarah politely said, "Thank you, Mrs. Moss."

Mrs. Moss then curtly replied, "Our day begins promptly at 6:00 A.M. I expect you in the kitchen at that time!"

Sarah exhausted fell onto the bed and slept through the night. When she awoke she looked around her room and saw a large writing desk with a clear oil lamp on top. She sat at the desk and started to write in her diary. Writing was one thing that gave her comfort. She could write her private thoughts on paper. Sarah noticed the wallpaper had small pink roses. Matching fabric curtains hung from the window overlooking the livery stable. The small four poster bed had a light pink bedspread. Standing to the right of the bed was a dressing closet where she quickly put her few clothes and hurried to the kitchen for her morning meal.

Mr. Moss sat at the breakfast table and greeted Sarah with a big smile. He then offered her a bowl of warm porridge and hot tea. "Were you warm enough?" he asked.

"Yes, I was, thank you," she answered.

"I am glad to have you here with us. I hope your stay here will be pleasant for you. Now that you have finished with your breakfast dear, let's go upstairs to the parlor; Mrs. Moss is in there waiting for you." As we ascended the stairs Mr. Moss told me some things about his children. "Fred, our son, has already gone to school. He is only a few years younger than you are. Fred enjoys being in the greenhouses with me. Our daughter Nell is younger than Fred; I feel that she and you will get along very well. It is Nell, our daughter, that Mrs. Moss mostly needs help with. She is a bit spoiled since Mrs. Moss likes Nell to have the best. But, never-the-less, she is grateful and very attentive to her mother."

As Sarah slowly went up the wide front staircase her hand felt the smooth white marble inset in the newel post. The hard, smooth, shiny wood was new to her. Her feet were quiet as she climbed the red carpeted stairs fingering the smooth wood all the way up the staircase. Finally, Sarah and Mr. Moss approached the French doors to the parlor on the third floor. As Mr. Moss opened the door for Sarah to enter the room Sarah's eyes opened wide in amazement. The room was the most exquisite she had ever seen. She had never stood in such a luxurious room. From the window Sarah could see the dark aqua colored flowing water of the Penobscot River, which would be frozen solid in another month or two. To the right of the window was a fireplace with a large polished white marble mantle. On each side of the fireplace was a shining brass gas fixture. Facing the fireplace was a large matching marble oval table. Gold brocade Queen Ann chairs complimented the room. Sarah noticed family portraits hung throughout. Sitting on a dark green velvet settee was the stern looking Mrs. Moss.

Mrs. Moss greeted Sarah with a perfunctory, "Good morning. I want to tell you that we expect you to do all your assigned daily chores at the inn. You shall stay here in the capacity of a domestic servant. You must earn your keep while here, by doing the domestic work as well as watching the children. Do you understand?" Sarah nodded and looked down at her feet.

Mrs. Moss went on to say; "Don't you have something more appropriate to wear? We have prominence in this town and I will have to see that you dress the part. I also expect you to behave in a manner that is appropriate for a girl your age. Do I make myself clear?"

"Yes, Mrs. Moss," Sarah replied in a whisper.

"Mr. Moss will review your chores with you later today. As for now, we will go and see what clothes you have brought with you. Come with me. I suspect we will have to replace all of your wardrobe!" Sarah followed Mrs. Moss in complete silence.

Upon examination of Sarah's clothes, Mrs. Moss had them all thrown out! She called her seamstress to come to Sarah's room. Sarah was measured, pinned, poked and prodded, smiling all the time at the thought of a new wardrobe.

Mrs. Moss felt compelled to say to Clara, "Well, I suppose I will have to purchase one dress for Sarah. Clara, give these measurements to Mrs. Bogg! Sarah with your first wages you will have to purchase new shoes as well as new undergarments!"

Sarah then realized that all the measuring, poking and prodding was just for one dress! "I'm leaving her in your hands, James" Mrs. Moss yelled, as she floated down the stairs. Sarah dressed quickly upon hearing Mr. Moss coming up the back stairs.

"Sarah dear," Mr. Moss said, "Come, I will show you around the inn and explain your duties to you." She knew she was going to like Mr. Moss, she just knew it! What Sarah did not know was that he liked her also, in a daughterly way. The rest of the morning was spent with Mr. Moss showing her all the nooks and crannies of the inn.

The chore time of her day would be quite full. Chores included cleaning bedrooms, bathrooms and scrubbing floors. In addition to this daily list, she was to work in the kitchen helping the cook with the meals, and when necessary help with the children!

Mrs. Moss returned to the Inn and quickly went up the stairs and placed several parcels on Sarah's bed. She went to the kitchen where Sarah was eating soup at the kitchen table. Mrs. Moss harshly said, "Sarah, finish your soup, go to your room and hang your clothes in the closet."

Bolting up the stairs and ripping open the package, Sarah discovered a new dress that delighted her. She opened another package and found several dresses and skirts with labels in them that said, "Specially made for Alice Door." Before she could catch her breath, Mrs. Moss burst into Sarah's room saying, "These clothes were given to me by Mrs. Alvah Dorr, a good friend. The clothes belonged to their daughter who has outgrown them. Both she and her husband are well respected in the town. It was very kind of them to offer you these clothes and I fully expect you to send them a thank you note. Did you think you were being measured for a complete new wardrobe? Well, Sarah you were not! That luxury is reserved only for my daughter and myself! You, as a servant, only get one new item which is more than enough!"

Sarah was a bit disappointed, but at the same time she was happy to have a new wardrobe of this caliber. Mary's treatment of Sarah privately made Sarah realize the good life she had hoped for was not going to happen. She felt she was under a cloud of unhappiness; she began to think what a joke life had played on her.

Mr. Moss for a time corresponded with Sarah's family keeping them updated on her progress, telling them that she was becoming quite a lovely young lady. He told them of her progress in her schoolwork that she did very well and has already graduated from high school.

Sarah found some relief from her loneliness in a friendship with young Fred Moss. At times he showed her some genuine kindness. They enjoyed one another's company. Each took pleasure spending spare time in the rose conservatory. They enjoyed watching the tiny buds bloom into beautiful roses. Mary, unbeknownst to them, was keeping an eye on her son, Fred.

Sarah knew there was a public and a private Mary Moss. Sarah remembered how Mrs. Moss would be polite to her, although snobby at the same time when she had her female friends for tea. Sarah recalled one time when Mary said," Sarah, dear, we will take our tea in the sitting room. Would you make sure there are cookies to go along with the tea when things are ready? Oh, do make sure the tea is steaming hot!" Mary had explained to Sarah that the terms of endearment were purely for show and not to expect it in private.

The young people Sarah came to know were children of rich landowners; store merchants and lawyers of Bucksport. She knew them through Fred and Nell. They asked questions about her homeland in Canada. It made Sarah feel inferior and beneath their station in life.

Sarah was dusting the hall at one time, when she heard Nell entertaining her friend Isabelle with gossip. They entered the parlor giggling and laughing at Sarah's expense. Nell was seventeen at this time and home from finishing school in Boston. She heard Nell say, "Well, she is only the servant girl in this house! I know father and mother led Sarah to believe that she may one day inherit a share of the Inn and that maybe one day they might even adopt her, but it was never in a written contract. Father thinks his verbal word should be honored, but mother won't hear of it. They argue over the issue constantly!"

Isabelle asked," Sarah isn't thinking she will inherit a share of the inn, is she? If your mother made it very plain to you that she was not going to adopt Sarah why does Sarah still think she might be adopted?"

Nell replied, "Mother probably wants to please father. He made a verbal agreement with John Bolder to do this. John Bolder is influential with his Church and the citizens of the town. I believe father does not want it to look as though mother has the last say in this matter. You are the only other person besides Sarah, father, mother, Fred and myself, who knows of this agreement. You must never say a word about this!"

Isabelle asked, "Nell, are you saying that your mother pretends she will let Sarah have a share because that is what your father wants to hear?"

Nell replied, "Yes, that is right! Mother has also told me how she has seen Sarah holding her skirts up showing her ankles to father while cleaning!"

Nell and Mrs. Moss did not know that Sarah did this to let air circulate on her right leg because of psoriasis. Sarah had allergies to many detergents, which she used for cleaning. The detergents caused this condition to flare up.

Nell continued, "Mother has told me many times, only the right and deserving will inherit the inn. She has seen the way Sarah is with father, always showing her ankles. Father becomes almost boyish when Sarah is around. I even heard Mother tell Father one day that he was paying more attention to Sarah than he should be. They did not know I was coming up the back stairs. Having heard them, I sat very still so I could hear what they were talking about. Mother was yelling at father having a bona fide outburst of anger! A couple of years ago I heard mother say to father, you're going to disgrace your children and our family! We brought Sarah here to watch the children in the capacity of a servant. I know the children are nearly grown and soon old enough to marry, but your behavior will disgrace them and me. I see how you are when you are around Sarah!"

Nell went on to say to Isabelle, "This was only the beginning of what I heard, there is more! At another time during an argument I heard Father try to assure mother that nothing was going on between Sarah and he."

Mother with her defiant and cold ways told father, "I want her gone!"

All Father could say was, "But dear!"

Mother flared back at him, "I know what you are going to say James, that we both brought Sarah down here years ago when the children were younger. I know what you verbally agreed to, but that was many years ago, I don't care, I still want her gone!" My father then told my mother, that he would think of something in time!

Sarah felt that Isabelle and Nell said all those things so she would overhear them. Sarah knew Isabelle was jealous of the friendship she and Fred shared. Isabelle implied to Nell, that she hoped to marry Fred one day.

Sarah and Mary Moss avoided the adoption subject. Sarah did not know that Mary had told Mr. Bellows, her influential lawyer, to forget the adoption many years ago.

Sarah continually wrote to her sister Catherine and pretended things were going fine. She could not let her mother and father know how unhappy she was. She felt that she was doing the right thing by not telling her sister what was really happening. It wasn't all that bad, at least Mr. Moss wasn't telling her to get out of his way! However, tension between Mrs. Moss and Sarah had not changed. There was little, if any, bonding.

The citizens of Bucksport knew Sarah had come to the Moss' in the capacity of a domestic servant, but did not verbalize it within earshot of Sarah. It seemed the stigma would be with her forever.

Sarah still worked diligently for Mr. and Mrs. Moss and hoped to get papers showing that she would have a share of the inn. She knew the possibility of adoption was not foreseeable but still hoped that Mrs. Moss and she could get along. Sarah secretly would have liked to know the business part of the inn, not just clean it!

Mr. Moss showed Sarah how to make flower arrangements in his rose conservatory. She and he liked putting the flower arrangements together. Sarah had a fast, keen and natural ability with flowers. It was their mutual respect and love of the roses that led them to become intimate friends.

Mr. James Moss wrote to Sarah's parents in Canada less and less frequently. He felt that he did not need to keep them informed of Sarah now that she was older. Besides, she wrote to her parents and told them of her well being and of her life. Mr. Moss did tell her parents of Sarah's development and progress and told them that he was pleased with Sarah's work.

Fred Moss in his Rose Conservatory

CHAPTER FIVE

THE COMPANY EDWARD KEEPS

James Moss and his wife Mary continued to have heated conversations as to what to do with Sarah. Mary still thought that she saw inappropriate situations between James and Sarah. She said to James that she was not going to tolerate this woman being in her house much longer, they needed to do something. Together they came up with some sort of an agreement as to what might be done.

James Moss knew who had recently arrived in town. He told Mary that he pretty much knew who was in the market for a wife. James then started to concoct a plan. One evening, in the privacy of their bedroom James said, "Mary, I have been working on a plan as to how we can get Sarah out of the house, hear me out. Sarah needs to be married and this is how it might work. I have been talking with some people and they have told me that there are a few eligible men in town. After carefully investigating these men, there is one whom I think will marry Sarah. We can present our situation to him. There are certain conditions we can offer him." Mr. Moss continued, "His name is Edward Ware. He is nothing to look at! I have spoken with him down in the bar and we had an in depth discussion. He is looking to better himself. His family is not rich and his older brothers will inherit the family farm and its possessions. I think Mr. Ware might be agreeable to marrying Sarah."

Mary started to interrupt but James continued, "Here is what we tell him. First, I will offer him a job in the hotel, a job with some respect. One, where he will get considerably more money than what he earns at Selectman Pall's grocery store. Also, he won't have to work as hard. When he has been here awhile I will hint that Sarah is like a daughter to you and me and that she is not married. She one day might inherit a share of the inn, and the man who marries her will probably share in that prosperity. Put the right way, I feel he will do almost anything, especially if he thinks he will get a portion of this inn. What do you think?"

"Well James, he'd better not wait too long before he proposes marriage," was Mary's answer. She continued, "James you know there is no way he will get a share of this inn!" James replied, "I know that, but he doesn't!"

It was in the spring of 1874 that Edward Ware became employed at the Robinson House.

Mr. James Moss hired him as a bartender and he proudly wore a long white apron. This meant that he did not have to get his hands dirty. Keeping his hands clean was almost like a fetish to Edward. After being hired at the inn, he became attentive to all the ladies he met. Especially to Sarah, who might be a potential heir to the place!

Sarah continued to work at the Robinson House but also was doing domestic work for more prominent ladies in Bucksport. She valued her independence and enjoyed working for various families. She had been able to save enough money to start her own small dowry.

As the years went by Fred Moss and Isabelle Maynard became closer and closer in friendship and ultimately married. Fred continued working in his father's conservatory and his own conservatories after his marriage as they grew more and more prosperous and needed his attention.

Sarah would stop in at the conservatory and casually visit with Fred. It was almost as though they were brother and sister. Fred had known how his mother felt about Sarah since he was a young boy. He understood how miserable Sarah had felt at times. He truly understood what Sarah had gone through.

Isabelle became increasingly jealous of the time Fred and Sarah spent in the greenhouses. Isabelle felt that she had reason to be jealous of her husband. Before she and Fred married, Isabelle knew that Fred had been serious about another local woman and had wanted to marry her. In her mind, she was sure it was Sarah, because of the closeness they shared.

Isabelle never knew it was not Sarah that Fred was fond of. He never told anyone the girl's father would not allow her to marry him, even though her father knew that Fred came from a prominent family, he did not have enough money. Isabelle always felt as though she was his second choice. She never got past her jealousy of any woman Fred knew.

Nell Moss had married Brandon Smith a few short years after Fred and Isabelle had married. Nell and Brandon lived in Orland. Brandon came from a family of good standing. One, which she knew mother would approve of. Brandon was not her first choice for a husband, but she did not want to displease her mother.

Nell knew how her mother could get when upset. She had seen it often enough when the anger had been directed at her father. Nell knew that it was her station in life to please her mother. After all, she did want to inherit her share of the inn and have good fortune, didn't she? Her mother was a woman who made things happen her way. Nell knew that she had to keep her feelings of unhappiness to herself; always having been a faithful daughter she also chose second best.

Brandon had made a name for him self in the fishing industry and received several awards for establishing a Salmon Fish Hatchery in Orland. Nell, Mrs. Moss and Isabelle were always polite with one another. They all knew the unspoken reality of their marriages, but never openly spoke of them in detail to one another.

Isabelle was reserved when she talked with her mother-in-law and her sister-in-law during social and family gatherings. The subject they did discuss with one another was Sarah. The women agreed that she was good enough to clean their houses, but not good enough to attend any of their formal parties or functions!

Sarah, very knowledgeable, as to who she was, did not care to attend any of their gatherings. In fact, it pleased her just fine not to, she would rather have many male friendships than be associated with those women.

Sarah, still quite lovely in a plain way, did not think much about getting married. She thought she was beyond the age for marriage and also knew that she was in an awkward social position. She kept these feelings primarily to herself, but would share a few confidences with her close friend Abigail Sweet.

Abigail Sweet a farm girl had met Sarah when she first came to Bucksport. Abigail had been employed as part of the working staff at the Robinson House. Abigail had married and moved in town when she was seventeen. This had allowed Sarah and Abigail to keep their friendship close.

One day Mrs. Moss was pleased when she noticed Edward Ware paying attention to Sarah. Perhaps Edward might take Sarah off her hands after all. Had he been thinking more about what James had proposed to him, she wondered? Mrs. Moss had also seen Edward in the bar after working hours talking with her husband James. Why? Was James tired of waiting for Edward to make his move on Sarah? Is that what Edward and her husband were talking about?

Mrs. Moss found herself quite uncomfortable one night after discovering her husband James sneaking into the house late after imbibing with the men in another part of town. Quietly trying to catch him on his return because she thought he might go into Sarah's room, she was startled to peek around a corner upstairs and see him leaning against Sarah's door. His eyes were closed. His hair was in disarray and his breathing quite heavy. This she thought was what she had suspected and she had finally caught James being unfaithful. Now she could use the situation as blackmail against James if there were ever a need! James would have to do something about Sarah. She told no one of this, keeping a close watch on the goings on of Sarah and James from this time forth. Unbeknownst to Mary this was her husband's first sign of heart trouble. Mary's assumption had been totally unfounded and had nothing to do with Sarah.

Mary Moss went to Edward Ware and demanded that he and Sarah get married as soon as possible. His game of cat and mouse was over! She offered to make the deal a little sweeter by offering him money. "Just take this girl off my hands," she told him. Thinking she had her son Fred out of Sarah's grip now that he was married, she needed her husband away from Sarah as well.

Edward Ware put his plan into action. He became more attentive to Sarah. The friendship between he and Sarah grew. Edward gave Sarah the impression that he was a businessman, he chose not to tell Sarah what kind of business. He told Sarah that he had business interests, and that the hotel was his home base. He was working part time in the hotel until his investments came through. Never having told her what this actually meant.

Sarah had no idea what he was talking about. She assumed that Edward had stock in the shipping business. Maybe he was in the transportation of goods. She assumed that the attention he had bestowed upon her must be because he loved her.

Sarah thought that Edward was not the most handsome man she had ever met, but she was still single. She said to herself, I must eventually move out of here. Mary has made that very clear on more than one occasion. I can't stay here forever!

Edward did ask Sarah to marry him. Sarah had severe reservations and did not give him an answer right away. Still, could she do worse? She could set up housekeeping with Edward, and find employment. She had saved some money if that plan did not work out. Once, she saw him get drunk in the hotel and act in a very uncivilized manner!

Edward realized that Sarah was not all that impressed and perhaps wouldn't marry him. He needed to convince Sarah that he had enough money for both of them. "You won't have to work," he said to Sarah. Edward with his persuasive ways finally had Sarah saying "Yes" to his proposal of marriage.

The marriage was in the fall of, October 1878. Sarah's family could not attend, for it was harvest season in Canada and they were preparing the land for winter. Sarah was married in the Robinson House. The wedding was lovely and tastefully done, but small, quite the opposite of Nell's wedding. Mary was in charge of the weddings of both Sarah and Nell. They were married in the Robinson House, of course, with differences!

Nell's wedding was flamboyant while Sarah's was plain and simple. There was a profusion of red and white roses that decorated the winding staircase as Nell descended. The large spacious dining room looked exquisite with Mr. Moss' gorgeous red hybrid roses. Nell's head wreath had been of the best quality, soft white baby roses encased in larger deeper pink and white roses with a touch of greenery added for effect. James and Fred had done their business well. It was no wonder that their rose conservatories flourished, with Fred eventually having a third, forty miles away in Bar Harbor.

Yes, Mary quite graciously had taken care of all Sarah's wedding arrangements, in more ways than one. Sarah looked radiant and happy for she was in love. Edward was smiling, for he thought he could see the road to owning the Robinson House. James was ecstatic for Sarah, since he truly loved her as a daughter. Fred was pleased for Sarah because he felt she found happiness. Isabelle, Fred's wife, seemed as if she did not want to be there, while Nell with her finishing school manners, showed a good front, but could care less. Mrs. Moss was happy, for she had Sarah out of her way, and knew they would never get the Robinson House! She had made sure of it! Mrs. Moss had made everything look as if it were in proper order. Everyone assumed that Edward and Sarah had been legally married. Mrs. Moss had her way again, Edward would not get his hands on any part of the Robinson House as Mr. Moss had indicated, nor would Sarah.

The so-called minister, who came from another town and performed the ceremony, was a fraud. This fraudulent minister was a personal friend of Mrs. Moss' cook. The cook and Mrs. Moss shared many secrets together. They had been exchanging these secrets for many years. For her efforts in obtaining the 'minister' the cook received a pair of ruby earrings. The minister received $100. Sarah received a false marriage certificate to Edward, whom she had learned to love. This was how 'married life' started for Sarah.

Edward and Sarah lived in a small rented house belonging to Colonel St.Barron. It was Buck Street, several streets over from the Robinson House. Although Sarah continued to work at the

Robinson House she was happy to be out from underfoot of Mrs. Moss and content in her married life. It was a pleasure for Sarah to set up housekeeping on her own and purchase a few more belongings, such as another trunk.

Two months after the wedding, Sarah confided to Abigail, her long time friend, that she thought she might be pregnant. Abigail went with Sarah to Dr. Lemerson's office, where he confirmed Sarah's suspicions. She was pregnant, with the baby due in May. Abigail and Sarah giggled happily on the walk back to work. On returning to the Robinson House Inn, Sarah did not know Edward had gone for supplies in the cellar for the evening customers. She wandered from room to room, finally finding Edward in the bar. Having taken his hand, she led him into a nearby closet, "Edward we are going to have a baby, I am so excited!"

Edward looked surprised but happy as he kissed and hugged her. "When?" he asked.

"In May," she responded. "Well, you know Sarah, some people will notice that the date does not correspond with our wedding date," he said.

Sarah replied, "I don't care, that doesn't bother me. You and I know the truth Edward, it's our child."

"And I was happy to introduce you to that truth as you were a virgin," said Edward, "and now my dear, I have to get back to work."

Off they went into their separate corners of the Robinson House. Edward in the bar, and Sarah off to find Abigail and help her dust. Happily Sarah and Abigail incessantly talked as they dusted the downstairs foyer.

Mrs. Moss came into the entry saying, "What are you two up to now? You are talking and talking."

Abigail said, "Tell her Sarah! She will know soon anyway."

Mrs. Moss said, "Tell me what?"

Sarah stood in front of Mrs. Moss saying, "Edward and I are going to have a baby."

"Oh, that is wonderful Sarah," said Mary. "I am so happy for you both. Yes, you are right Abigail, this is great news." Having turned out of the room with her back toward the women, Mrs. Moss said, "And when are you due?"

"In May," responded Sarah."

Mrs. Moss stopped for a moment and then continued walking responding, "I see, very well, continue on with your chores." Mrs. Moss found herself more and more upset with every step thinking about Sarah's baby due in May. Angry thoughts splintered through her head all evening having recalled the scene of her husband leaning on Sarah's door, she was convinced the timing was perfect! Her headache became unbearable, blinding and pounding. She went upstairs to lie down and put a wet cloth on her head, hoping that her headache and those unfaithful memories would slip away. Something had to be done! Something had to be done! These words drew her into sleep.

In the morning, Mrs. Moss with the help of the cook, who now possessed *"A pair of Ruby earrings"* given to her by Mrs. Moss for a former misdeed, devised a plan. The cook and Mrs. Moss discussed a potion that caused Mrs. Moss' earlier miscarriage. They soon put their fiendish plan into action. Mrs. Moss knew what her duty was in a case like this. Sarah and Edward Ware were not going to spoil her social position in this town. James' flagrant behavior and its results would never be known!

Abigail and Sarah came into the large kitchen for their morning tea break. "Come girls there is cake to go with your tea," said Mary conspiringly! The women gathered at the table and the cook brought the steaming teapot. The teacups and saucers were in place. As they chattered away and drank tea it would look all so innocent thought Mrs. Moss as she sat back and watched the ghastly scene unfold. The tea would not harm Abigail or herself, for they were not pregnant, only Sarah's child would succumb to the warm fluid pulling the life away from her womb. This would happen hours later if she made sure that Sarah's cup was filled twice more. The dose would be effective.

Abigail screamed in the upstairs bedroom, as Sarah, pale and white, clutched her stomach and crumpled to the floor shaking and perspiring. The cook and Mrs. Moss flew into the room to 'help' and the three women together placed Sarah on the bed.

Mrs. Moss' control mode took over. She commanded Abigail not to leave Sarah's side. She instructed the cook to go find Dr. Lemerson. With prior arrangements between Mrs. Moss and the cook she lingered an hour before seeking Dr. Lemerson. The hemorrhaging increased within the hour as Abigail held Sarah's hand. Mrs. Moss calmly and efficiently changed towels. The doctor arrived too late. An hour and a half later the deed was done.

Edward was found and rushed to Sarah's bedside. Dr. Lemerson told Edward Sarah would pull through, but their baby girl was gone. Dr. Lemerson was caring and attentive and gave her a tonic to help build up her blood. Sarah, weak but conscious was being attended to by Abigail who never left her side. Edward returned to the bar so Sarah could rest.

Mrs. Moss walked in carrying a tray of hot soup. Abigail excused herself, saying, "I will feed Sarah the soup as soon as I return." Mrs. Moss' hands, folded quietly in front of her chose the opportunity to say, "Remember Sarah Ware, I control everything that happens in this house!"

Abigail returned to help feed Sarah and found her pale and upset. As Sarah finished her soup the cook came to the room to get the finished tray. "Good evening," said Mrs. Moss as she left the room behind the cook. "Well, our deed is done," said the cook. "Well done, I might add," said Mrs. Moss! The cook then replied, "Yes, it worked!" Mrs. Moss then handed the cook '*a ruby ring*' to accompany '*the ruby earrings*'!

As their footsteps faded down the stairs Sarah stifled her sobs with her hands. Abigail cradled Sarah in her arms as Sarah told her what Mrs. Moss had said. She quickly recuperated with the help of her husband Edward, who was attentive and Mrs. Moss was happier than ever! James and Fred Moss knew how much Sarah enjoyed roses and they brought Sarah a continuous stream of fresh flowers. Abigail nursed her to health but they never spoke of the 'incident' as long as Sarah recuperated in the Robinson House. They would talk later.

Sarah wrote the incident in her small secret diary, which she kept hidden in her trunk. Only Abigail knew of the diary. Sarah had time now to fill quite a few pages.

Having returned home after the horrendous injustice, Sarah and Edward were closer than ever. She never said a word to Edward, for she was frightened now. Who could she trust? Would Edward believe her?

Six months later Sarah was thrilled to discover again that she was pregnant, keeping it secret as long as possible! She gave birth to a beautiful son, whom she felt was the image of Edward, and she named him after his father. Baby Edward had delicate small round eyes that were a cornflower blue and he had a crop of thick dark hair, which accentuated his fair skin.

Two years later Edward and Sarah had a beautiful baby daughter, Mildred. Her looks resembled both parents and Sarah's sister Catherine. She had her father's blue eyes and her mother's chestnut brown hair, with her Aunt Catherine's bright smile.

Mr. Moss immediately loved these children as if they were his own grandchildren. He enjoyed playing the role of grandfather to Sarah's children since neither of his children had given him any grandchildren.

Mrs. Moss' dismay with James, playing the role of grandfather, was obvious to everyone. She would state, "James you don't need to be with Sarah's children so much! You buy them too many presents!" James Moss found ways to spend time with both of Sarah's children during his lifetime regardless of what his wife said. Mrs. Moss never found out how much time he spent with them for he and Sarah always took care sharing these special times together. James Moss was beginning to think they would be the only grandchildren he would ever have.

Fred and Isabelle still had no children as much as Fred would have liked to have a son, Isabelle was not about to bear him children! She did not want to lose her lovely figure! Nell also did not want children, however she was very kind to animals. She would never let a stray on her doorstep go away hungry.

Edward enjoyed being a father, but was quite busy earning enough to support his growing family. Sarah realized a short time after she was married, that Edward did not have the investments he had told her about. She realized he was deceitful. They were struggling and Sarah would have to pick up odd jobs as a domestic to supplement his salary.

As the Ware family grew Edward worked many late nights. He began spending less and less time at home with Sarah and their children. He began working late nights in the bar, which provided Edward with excuses to be away from his responsibilities. When cleaning the bar with the barmaid 'Bell', words would slide from Edward like warm whiskey, which she took in fully. Sitting at the table with the whiskey bottle half empty, they started a collaboration of drinking, lust and a sordid friendship. Bell was in her element; she was familiar with the ways of men. She had been 'charming men for years,' as a method of earning her living before she came to Bucksport.

Bell, tall and slender with a soft voice, wavy dark hair half way down her back and dark brown eyes with long lashes, slid comfortably into Edward's sorrowful pocket. Unknowingly to Edward, Bell relieved him of his money, along with his tensions every night. This became the pattern for these lovers.

Edward began realizing within a month that something was terribly wrong! He needed to see Dr. Lemerson! Dr. Lemerson did in fact diagnose and confirm his suspicions that he had a serious case of gonorrhea. He told Edward about a hospital in Boston where he could go and receive treatment. Apparently Bell got around, for Dr. Lemerson had been treating five other cases in town. Edward simply left town without a word, not even to Sarah.

Weeks, months had gone by, before she found out why he had suddenly just left. Sarah was hurt when her husband left, but the way she found out was more painful. She was thankful now that she and Edward had stopped having relations since the time after the birth of their daughter Mildred. She probably would have contracted this dreadful venereal disease from him if they had continued to have sex.

It was through several gossipy old biddies that she found out and she was just appalled. One of these biddies was Hiram Brook's wife, Ethel. Having been the sort of woman who wouldn't sell you her chicken eggs if you had not swapped a good piece of gossip, gathered her eggs in her gossip basket, and spread the news all over town.

Ethel's husband, Hiram, a local farmer, had come into town to see Mr. Elliott, an auctioneer, about selling a few cows at the upcoming auction. Innocently he asked Mr. Elliott if he knew where Sarah's husband had gone. He answered, "Oh yeah, he's in the big city in a hospital. I heard he was sent there by Doc for that same illness he treated Bell for."

"Say, Mr. Elliott, did you ever hear where Bell went?" asked Hiram. Mr. Elliott replied, "It seems she sort of vanished after one of the men's wives confronted her." With his business concluded, Hiram headed for home.

Within minutes after getting home Hiram couldn't wait to tell Ethel that Edward was in a Boston hospital with a sexually transmitted disease. Ethel answered, "Oh, I'm two steps ahead of you Hiram, that is old news to me!" Hiram stood and shook his head and said, "Poor Sarah." With this Ethel replied, "Sarah is lucky she didn't get gonorrhea!"

The Boston hospital was to be Edwards last home, for he died there. Sarah never chose to visit him while he was there, nor did she make the choice to divorce him. She decided to leave well enough alone and continue on with her life, working as a domestic for various families in Bucksport.

The only people who continued to be close friends during these troubled times were Mrs. Almira Files, Abigail and Mr. John Bolder. Fred Moss, and his father James Moss, continued to stay in contact with Sarah, though on a somewhat limited basis. Fred and Sarah were still friends, but not the way they had been in the past. It seemed that whenever she saw him it was either in one of the greenhouses or when cleaning Fred's house.

The three of them had an unspoken bond when it came to what was hidden in among the roses. Sarah felt that even if they were not family in blood, they were family in their feelings.

John Bolder's Residence

CHAPTER SIX

SECRETS

Life meant little to Sarah after Edward left. She began to enjoy the taste of liquor. What started out to be a way to ease her saddened heart, was becoming a habit. The men in town began to view Sarah as an easy woman. They did not verbalize this around town. It was only when they were at their gatherings that they discussed her.

Once Selectman Pall was heard to say, "Oh yes, I had Sarah two nights ago." He was just adding to the conversation out of jealousy for he knew she had refused his attentions in the past. The rumor mill about Sarah had gained momentum, speed and secrecy. Like burning grass it spread quickly, just like the secret pact of twelve prominent businessmen. These men had made this secret pact of illegal dealings years ago among themselves. The selling of 'White Lightning and drugs' brought large profits to those in high places.

It was said that these men made the pact with the underground men of Boston, who dealt in absinthe, ammunitions, opium and liquors. The boss man in Boston had been worried for several years, since he had in his employ a prominent shipping captain who lived in Bucksport. For several years government men had been inspecting Captain Nichol's ships while in Boston Harbor. These government men were also seen in Bucksport keeping an eye on the shipping harbor.

Sarah had her worries now, being the soul provider for her children. The year was 1885 with her children in grammar school. Selectman Pall was added to her list of clients for domestic service.

She had been cleaning his house for about six months. Of course, working for other prominent people, she had heard what sort of business he was in, other than his grain store on Main Street. The local citizens as well as government officials surmised just what he kept in the store besides regular grain, however nothing was ever found.

One evening, on his way home from the Robinson House, after drinks with his male friends, Selectman Pall stopped by Sarah's house on the pretense of picking up his laundry. He said, "Sarah, I am stopping to see if you have my laundry done." Selectman Pall appearing to be in a drunken stupor immediately made Sarah suspicious. She was leery that he had more than whiskey in his system. This stupor seemed more a combination of several drugs. She had witnessed these signs before while cleaning her client's homes. She had even seen the white powder being distributed to Mr. Tekworgy, though she was extremely careful not to be seen watching.

She answered Selectman Pall saying, "No I don't have your laundry done, I do it on Monday, you know that!" He ignored what she said, and again started to make advances. Sarah struggled to ward him off. The children who had been sleeping in their bedroom were awakened by the disturbance. Upon entering the kitchen, they witnessed their mother holding a frying pan in her hand about to hit Selectman Pall over the head! It's all right children I am just defending myself, now go back to bed!

Sarah was aware that the town had knowledge of the circumstances surrounding her husband's death. Providing for Edward and Mildred became increasingly harder. Sarah felt that she could not raise the children without the help of a husband. She considered the possibility of sending her children to live with her sister in Canada. Sarah recalled that she herself had gone away to live with another family in another country. She felt it would be advantageous for her children to go to Canada. Her mixed and confused mind was justified in thinking that it was normal and she was doing the right thing. Yes, this is the right thing to do, Sarah thought to herself.

Sarah felt sure that her sister Catherine would take Mildred and Edward in. It had always been that way in times of family crisis. This feeling of motherhood is something she would have to give up, feeling powerless to provide economically for her children. With leeriness of men instilled in her mind, it reinforced her way of thinking that she was doing the right thing. Family takes care of family! Mixed feelings and thoughts kept going through Sarah's head. She needed to provide for her children and was rapidly approaching a tragic economic situation.

Letters were exchanged between her and her sister Catherine. Sarah explained her dilemma and stated that she would stay in Bucksport and earn money. Sarah would send money to help Catherine and her husband with the burden of raising the children. Together, Catherine, her husband and Sarah came up with a plan they agreed upon. Catherine wrote to Sarah explaining that she and her husband had discussed the matter. The extra money would help their situation. Catherine, however, did not take into consideration that there would be an outstanding toll and cost for Sarah. Sarah was grateful to her sister because she could see and feel a lot of evil influences being filtered throughout her world.

Bucksport, a shipping town and a somewhat worldly port was moving faster and growing rapidly. There was trouble brewing; not only with the liquor agents but also with Sarah who had difficulty providing for herself and her family.

Sarah knew James Moss had other reasons for keeping a close eye on his greenhouses as he suspected trouble brewing with outside agents roaming the area. Bucksport, being a very oral community shared the rumored news that he kept white lighting among his roses. It was also rumored that James waited until the cover of darkness for the drugs to be unloaded on the schooners coming from Boston. These items were then distributed among the infamous prominent citizens.

Sarah had overheard conversations when cleaning certain houses. Why do they say things when I am around? I wish they would not talk about it when I am cleaning. One day Mr. Britewood told

Mr. Dorr that there was talk of government men in the town, even informants, but no one knew for sure who they might be.

It had been rumored through the county; Bucksport was the place to go to get liquor from small unlicensed people. If you wanted to get opium, you needed only to visit certain men and they could get it for you. It was known where to go and these people kept their mouths shut.

The small comforts Sarah once knew were disappearing. The town was becoming a cruel and harsh place and this gave Sarah a feeling of uneasiness. At least her son and daughter would be cushioned against all this; they would be in Canada away from this evil. Although Sarah had mixed feelings, she was happy that her children would be protected. She knew that it would be lonely for her, she would miss her son and daughter. Sarah with a strong sense of motherhood and determination told herself, I will give my children family and support, something I never had. It is a small sacrifice for me in order to give my children what they need. She felt strongly, they needed a sense of home! Perhaps they will not have feelings of displacement the way I had. I will give them a place of belonging, with people they belong to. I will invest in their future.

With these thoughts Sarah started to make plans for her children. Maybe John Bolder could help me get Edward and Mildred to Canada; he helped me come to Maine. John was her friend and Sarah had been doing domestic work for him for many years, since he had been widowed shortly after she came to Bucksport. He also was fond of Sarah's children, Edward and Mildred.

Sarah told John Bolder of her plan because Sarah felt that she could trust him to bring her children safely to Catherine and her husband. John agreed to do this for Sarah. He told Sarah that he also wanted what was best for the children. If she felt that this was best, of course he would help. Sarah told him that she would finalize her plan, then let him know. John said, "Sarah, I will make arrangements to be gone from the tannery for a few days."

Sarah explained to John that Edward and Mildred would go on ahead with him, while she would stay and work in Bucksport to earn her passage. When she would have enough money saved, she would visit her children. Sarah could not marry a well-to-do man and knew that in these times she would have to earn money anyway she could. She did not want her children to see how she would have to earn her keep.

She went to Mr. James Moss and asked for her children's fare, and explained she was sending the children to Canada. Sarah could not tell Mr. Moss why she feared that his wife might harm her children. Sarah knew Mrs. Moss had caused her to abort her first child. Sarah told him that she was doing what she considered best for her children. She had written to her sister Catherine, and she and her husband would take the children in. All the arrangements had been made.

Mr. Moss told Sarah that he would feel a deep loss with the children gone. Edward and Mildred were the grandchildren he never had. They had given him great pleasure in his life. He would be glad to help provide for Edward and Mildred's tickets. Should Mrs. Moss find out he paid for the tickets; he would suffer her wrath for some time to come. Sarah told him that only Edward and Mildred were leaving. She would visit them later when she had earned enough money.

Sarah explained to her children why she was doing this. Sarah and her children had many discussions about what she felt was best for them, always with the promise to write and keep in touch. She would visit them in Canada whenever she could. It was a sad day for all of them when the children and John Bolder left Bucksport two weeks later on a Saturday at 7 A. M. Sarah was grateful to James Moss for financially enabling her to send her children to Canada.

Later that day she decided to tell him that she knew about he and his son's illegal dealings with liquor. She had known the dealings had been going on in the rose conservatory for a long time. She knew how they had almost gotten caught once when the sheriff raided his place of business. She was in a position to hear these things. Sarah would be able to let Mr. Moss know when these raids were about to take place. Sarah had known it was the

Methodist Congregation who insisted the sheriff did the raids. Sarah also knew James Moss approached the Methodist Congregation about a new bell as a bribe. With this understanding between them their friendship took on a new meaning.

Mr. Moss did not tell Sarah all that he knew. He did not tell her about the other men who were involved in the secret pact and what the pact was about. It was better that she did not know. It might keep her safe not to know everything. James Moss did not tell Fred his son everything either, although Fred knew more than his father thought he did. When Fred made his trips to Boston, he would do his fellow businessmen favors by picking up shady packages for them.

When Sarah went to the Robinson House or the rose conservatories to see James or Fred Moss, their conversations would be quiet and serious. Each knew of the jealousy Mrs. Moss and Isabelle had over her, but would not speak of it. Because of the kindness these men showed Sarah, she was able to tolerate the insults of their wives. Sarah's silence protected Fred from Isabelle's jealousy and James from Mrs. Moss' wrath.

It was during one of Sarah's visits with James Moss at the greenhouse that he confided to her about his will, and why he felt he needed to make changes. James told Sarah that he felt he could protect her reputation in this way. Mrs. Moss had threatened to tell the town that he was the father of Sarah's miscarried baby. Mary Moss had assumed that this was so because of the evening her husband had leaned against Sarah's bedroom door, the night of his first heart attack. James then went to the desk drawer and pulled out a copy of his will for Sarah to read.

I, James Moss of Bucksport in the county of Hancock and State of Maine, do make and declare this to be my last will and testament which is to dispose of all my estate as follows:

First, I bequeath and devise all my estate real, personal and mixed, wherever situated or found unto my wife Mary Moss during her life, with full power to sell any or all the real estate if she so desires. If in her judgment the income derived from my estate is not sufficient for her needs she shall use so much from the principal as seems best to her. My intention hereby to give her absolute control of my estate during her life with right to use any or the entire principal if she needs it.

Second: At the decease of my said wife, I give, bequeath, and devise, what remains of my estate in equal shares unto my children Fred Moss and Nell Smith their heirs and assigns forever.

I hereby constitute my son-in-law, executor of this last will and testament, and request that he is allowed to serve without bond.

In witness where of, I have here unto set my hand this nineteenth day of October in the year of our Lord one thousand eight hundred and ninety six

James Moss.

When Sarah had finished reading it, she felt a deep sense of loss. Almost lifelessly she handed it back to James. "Sarah you do understand why I had to do it this way, don't you?" James asked. With crestfallen eyes, almost inaudibly she answered, "Yes, James, because of Mrs. Moss, your wife. Mrs. Moss never wanted me to have any part or share of the Robinson House." James said, "Sarah, take this $300. Do with it what you can to help your children, or yourself. I wish I could do more."

Did he feel guilty about the verbal agreement of adoption his wife Mary never let him follow through on? Sarah was more than surprised to learn that he had more than $8,000, almost $9,000 in his estate.

Sarah continued to write in her diary. She wrote of the goings on in the town, including the secrets of important people. She wrote why Bell the barmaid had gone away weeks after Edward had gone without a word to anyone. She had gonorrhea, which she had transmitted to Edward! Sarah knew that the society women went to Bell and quietly told her to leave town or they would expose her!

Sarah's mother had taken the time to write the family lineage in a Bible that she gave to Sarah, saying to her, "Continue writing all things of major importance about your life in your Bible; this way your children will know of their heritage." After the date of her birth, Sarah wrote her children's birth dates and the birth and death dates of her husband.

She had a brown trunk in which she kept her meager belongings, her Bible and her diary. She kept the trunk locked and the key on a small necklace, which she kept around her neck. She thought that the key would be safe and the trunk a secret hiding place, a place no one would look. She placed the Bible her mother gave her in the false bottom, hidden beneath articles of clothing. Sarah was a private person who kept her writings to herself, one day intending to give them to her daughter. Sarah wrote about her life as a child and as an adult in her diary. In it was when, why, and how Edward had gone away. She wrote about the death of Mr. Moss in February 1898, at the age of 76. She also wrote about the illegality of the 12 men.

Sarah's fearfulness of the prestigious people she knew had grown stronger since James had passed away. James Moss had defended her against these people more than once, when he was alive. Now even Mr. Tekworgy had given her reason to be distrustful of him. He had indicated on more than one occasion that Sarah knew about the illegal dealings in the town and that he could not trust her.

Sitting at her small brown desk looking at the words she had just entered in her diary, Sarah wondered, had it been five years since her husband Edwards's death? Sarah secretly wrote many entries in her diary while alone in her tiny room, for she knew if anyone saw what she had written her life would be in great danger. There were many secrets about the town and certain men that held high positions. She still kept her saddened heart for another man, saddened because he was a married man; a man she could never marry. She loved this man even though their social status was very different. I would like a man like Mr. Britewood to take care of me, but not as a mistress. It can't be helped, for Mr. Britewood is married.

Mr. Britewood's wife and Mrs. Moss socialized in the same circle. Sarah knew from the way these ladies treated her that she had been the topic of discussion between them on more than one occasion.

It was about a month ago Mrs. Britewood had been visiting Mrs. Moss. They had been having tea in Mrs. Moss' elegant parlor where Sarah had just finished dusting. As Sarah was picking up her cleaning supplies to enter another room she heard Mrs. Britewood tell Mrs. Moss, "I know my husband is having an affair with another woman!" Mrs. Britewood indicated to Mrs. Moss that she knew who the woman was. "I have great contempt for her and some day I shall confront this woman!" Knowing that Mrs. Britewood said this for Sarah's benefit, Sarah quickly left the room.

Once again life has led me down the path of disillusionment. Is there any light at the end of this tunnel! I'm getting older, I'm past my prime, I have had to give up what I know and yet what speaks to me from my heart, motherhood! I feel so depressed; I miss my children terribly!

I feel men only want to marry pristine virgins with dowries and they only use me to clean up their dirty laundry. All I do is work, work, work! There's always someone speaking a harsh word to me; you need to do this, this way! You need to do that, that way! The only time people speak to me is when they want something from me, especially the men. Well, at least I can get money from them when I need to!

My teeth have really been getting bad. I must keep my appointment with Dr. Lemerson next week. As usual I will clean his house first and then follow up with my appointment. It has been almost a week since I was to Dr. Lemerson and had several bad teeth removed. The medication he gave me is not relieving this pain. I have another appointment next week.

The letters from my sister Catherine, concerning Edward and Mildred are so few now. It seems that the news of what is happening in Canada is from John Bolder when he returns from visits. Then the news is not great! He tells me of what he has heard. My children are unclean and not fed well! I barely earn enough now to pay for living at Mrs. Files; there must be a way to earn more money to help support my children!

I know the men that play poker at Mrs. Files. They may think of themselves as upper crust elite citizens of this town, but I know the dual life they lead. I know they only want one thing from me. I'll take their money playing poker or any other way, if I have to.

Sarah then tucked the diary in the secret compartment at the bottom of her brown trunk, shut the lid and locked it. She put the key back on the chain around her neck.

With this thought Sarah could, and often would, sit in on the poker games and imbibe with the men on Saturday nights. These poker games usually consisted of Mr. Britewood; Mr. Pall; the Finn brothers; on occasion Captain Nichols; and Captain Calder.

Mr. Tekworgy would go to watch and have conversations with the men. He would check in and see when the next illegal shipment was coming up the river. Taking these shipments off the schooners under the shield of night was something he did well. Doing the dirty work for these men gave him a feeling that he was above reproach. Mr. Tekworgy thought these men in higher places, including Selectman Pall who had jurisdiction over the law officials, would protect him. They don't want me to go to jail, it would ruin everything for them!

Sarah also knew Walter, a drifter and Southern Confederate veteran, who helped Mr. Tekworgy unload the questionable shipments at night. With his home destroyed and his family dead, Walter kept drifting north until he ended up in Bucksport. He had been physically and mentally injured during the war and kept mostly to himself. He knew that the citizens of Bucksport considered him harmless and treated him like a neighborhood dog, giving him scraps, but not getting too close. Walter went through life talking to his imaginary friends. He knew that people considered him touched in the head and kept him on the fringes of society. It seemed that the only people Walter did interact with were the rougher dock-workers and Mrs. Files who would occasionally have him over for a meal.

He became friendly with Mr. Tekworgy, who worked on the docks when his shipments would arrive by schooner. Walter, the drifter and Will Tekworgy would occasionally drink and play cards together. They would unload the ships out in the deep dark harbor late at night and bring the shipments to the secret pact. He had learned from being a soldier to run with the pack and not to turn on them, because they will turn on you!

It seems that Sarah became an expert card player. She became adept at conversing with the men about the illegal dealings in town. Sarah began to gain the men's confidence. She kept a mental book on each man. On these Saturday night poker games at Mrs. Files home nothing escaped Sarah's eyes as she skillfully watched the men and listened to what they were up to. Walter would stop in and partake of the drinks. They were plentiful and free. He never stayed for long, a few hours or so, just long enough to hear things but knew enough to keep his mouth shut. Sarah was friendly to him only because he was there. All the men had an understanding; there was no need to verbalize any of the secrecy involved.

One night Sarah did not partake in a poker game. It was that night that Mr. Tekworgy accused Sarah of possibly being a government agent to several of the infamous twelve conspirators. The men had begun to enjoy drink, then the absinthe. It was while in this foggy state, another man kept the ball rolling and mentioned that Sarah seemed to act so pure, so innocent, maybe she was one of the people the government had hired. She did need the money. What if she knew too much; she knows some of what is going on by being at most of the card games. These men knew Will Tekworgy would do them any favor for a given amount of money. Secretly, as was their manner, they suggested Tekworgy find a way to keep Sarah quiet! Tekworgy's brilliant mind, which few knew about, immediately went into action! The seed having been planted became the focal point in Tekworgy's mind!

On Sarah's behalf Mr. Britewood said, "Yes it was true that she had heard them talking while cleaning their houses, but she would never say anything. Besides, I am sure she only knows part of what we are doing."

The following Sunday Mrs. Files invited Walter the drifter to dinner. It was also her custom to invite Mr. Tekworgy and his daughter almost every Sunday after church. Sarah always partook of these Sunday dinners as well. After everything was cleared it was Sarah's habit to go to her room.

Unknown to Sarah, William Tekworgy followed her quietly up the stairs. Sarah thought she had securely closed the door behind her as she entered her room, sat at her desk and carefully wrote in her diary. When she had finished writing in it, she put it in the large brown trunk at the foot of her bed. She did not see Mr. Tekworgy hiding and watching her from the hallway. He went into her room and said, "What were you putting in your trunk?" She did not want anyone to know what she had written, so she answered, "Nothing you would be interested in, Will. What are you doing up here anyhow?" He casually replied, "Just getting something from Mrs. File's spareroom."

A few days later when Sarah opened the trunk to retrieve her diary, she discovered both the diary and her Bible were missing! How long had they been gone, she wondered? Is that what William Tekworgy was up to when I asked him what he was doing upstairs? Did I forget to lock the trunk, she thought to herself? No I couldn't have, I always lock it! Did Mr. Tekworgy take my personal items? Did he see me put my diary in the secret compartment? Sarah began to speculate what if Will Tekworgy knew how to open the trunk without the key? His knowledge of locksmith works allows him to understand the mechanisms!

Sarah became deeply concerned and worried. She knew she had written secrets of great importance about certain people. If the information she had written got into the wrong hands it would certainly mean trouble for her! She had to get it back! Sarah knew that she could not trust William Tekworgy! They had their share of disagreements in the past.

Recently when she saw William Tekworgy and Joe Bogg Jr. on Main Street she thought that they had acted strangely, asking me all those queer questions. Why had they mentioned that the shipment of broadcloth had arrived at Mrs. Bogg's General Store? Why did they ask me if I was going to John Bolder's that night to clean his house? Also, why did they ask if I was stopping in to collect the material I had ordered? Sarah started to think that these men were too interested in what she was doing that evening. She had answered them by saying, "Yes, I am going to clean Mr. Bolder's house tonight and yes I am going to purchase my material. It seems you two men are very interested in what I am doing tonight!"

William Tekworgy continued with his questions by asking, "What time are you going to John Bolder's?" Sarah answered, "Why are you so curious as to what I am doing?" Mr. Tekworgy hedgingly said, "Well, there's a card game later tonight at Captain Calder's and one tomorrow night if you're interested."

Sarah answered him saying, "I might come, after I clean John Bolder's house, I'll see," She continued, "Oh William, after you have collected your vegetables from the garden at Mrs. Files later today, I want to have a few words with you!" She thought, if he did take the Bible and my writings I must get them back; I will confront him! Mr. Tekworgy not wanting a confrontation with Sarah made sure he collected his vegetables when Sarah was elsewhere.

Tannery and Tannery Bridge

CHAPTER SEVEN

THE POKER GAME

Early on Saturday morning, William Tekworgy had bragged to Selectman Pall when in his store, "You know what I have? I have something that belongs to Sarah; I have her Bible and writings! In her diary I found writings that she felt were important. It seems that Sarah knows about the secret pact of twelve influential men of this town."

With anxiety William Tekworgy continued, "Selectman Pall, maybe this information goes along with your informant theory! What if Sarah is an informant for these government men that we suspect have been in town. Maybe she knows who they are and can tell us. If true, Captain Nicholson and Colonel Barron, would like to know who they are. The government agents have inspected Captain Nicholson's ship more than once while it was in Boston Harbor. Knowing who these men are could be of interest to other parties.

I don't think Sarah knows I have her Bible and writings! Sarah also wrote another important fact in her diary, *that she suspected she could be pregnant.* There are some other things in here about other prominent men in town. I guess I am not the only one who knows about how rich men keep getting richer!"

Having overheard this conversation Mr. Britewood was appalled and said, "What are you doing with her Bible and writings, that is personal property? How did you get them? I know she would not just hand them over to you! You must be mad to have taken her things!"

Mr. Tekworgy said, "Well, I went in to Sarah's room one afternoon while I was over visiting Mrs. Files. I took it out of her locked trunk. I saw her put it in there. I suspected she wrote things in her diary that she did not want other people to see. I wanted to know what it was that she had written."

Also having heard this conversation one of the Finn brothers said, "Let me have that diary I want to see what she has written! I may be able to use some of the information for my newspaper." Mr. Britewood said to Mr. Tekworgy, "You have no right to show this to anybody! You should return her possessions!"

Ignoring what Mr. Britewood said, Mr. Tekworgy took other men into his confidence in the back room and they began to drink heavily. Mr. Tekworgy continued saying, "What if Sarah is called on to testify at the upcoming hearing in Ellsworth about the 'white lightning' that gets passed through Bucksport?

The government was trying to pass a law to make all retailers have licenses to sell liquor, of course not for 'white lighting.' Up until this time licenses were not required for legitimate retailers. At that time they were called liquor agents.

Will Tekworgy then left and started back to his mercantile establishment, feeling even more cocksure with himself. On his way he met his friend Joe Mank. Joe Mank had worked with him many times on the docks. He was an unsavory character. Charges against him had been of assault on the person of his half sister. The hearing had been before John Remmick, Esq., who after having heard the testimony found Mank guilty and had his bail fixed at $200 while awaiting his trial. William Tekworgy came to his rescue and paid the bail money.

One time when Joe Mank had been drinking heavily at Mrs. Willey's Tavern, he and another man got into a brawl. Joe had beaten the man quite severely. He was brought up on charges of assault and battery and found guilty and spent the night in jail. Will Tekworgy had known of Joe Mank's consistent trouble with the law, even as a young boy. Still he had invited Joe Mank to have drinks and perhaps some illegal drugs at Mrs. Willey's tavern on Main Street. They were there until late afternoon discussing Sarah Ware. Will Tekworgy then told Joe Mank in strict confidence that he had been given a great sum of money to shut Sarah up so that she would not be able to attend the liquor licensing hearing in Ellsworth. He then proceeded to lay out a devised plan with Joe Mank as to how they could accost her after a poker game with the intention of frightening her.

Sarah being down town knew it was getting late and she needed to take home the groceries for Sunday's dinner that she had bought for Mrs. Files. She could do her other errands later. She still did not have the opportunity to confront Mr. Tekworgy about her missing possessions.

While sitting at Mrs. File's kitchen table talking, Sarah noticed the time. She said, "Well, I had better get ready to clean Mr. Bolder's house, I told him I would be there in the early evening. She continued to tell Mrs. Files that, "John Bolder told me last week that a family member of his had passed away and he may have to hire his niece to do the domestic work. If I lose work with Mr. Bolder it will drain my financial situation. Even though my children are making preparations to be on their own and earning their own way, they still depend on me. Edward my son spends most of his time in Massachusetts with my brother who moved there several years ago. Mildred, my daughter, would sometimes stay summers in Massachusetts, going home to Canada to help her Aunt Catherine during the winter."

Sarah continued speaking to Mrs. Files, "I have a few errands to do. It is nearly six o'clock and I need to clean John Bolder's house. Also, Will Tekworgy told me earlier today that Joe Bogg is having a poker game tonight in his room at Captain Calder's. I still have to speak to Will Tekworgy about a personal matter! As soon as I finish cleaning Mr. Bolder's I am going to seek out Mr. Tekworgy about something he has that belongs to me! Joe Mank, Will Tekworgy, and Captain Calder are going to be at Joe Bogg's card game. First I am going to play for awhile at Joe Bogg's place and attempt to get back what belongs to me from Mr. Tekworgy, then maybe I will return to Mr. Bolder's poker game. I understand Mr. Bolder has a poker game at his house tonight with Mr. Britewood; Sheriff Genn; Wess Webber; Captain Nicholson; and the Finn brothers."

Mrs. Files said, "Sarah, what is going on? I know you need extra money and I know it is none of my business what you do, however, I feel that something is not right and you haven't been yourself lately. Sarah, you're going to attend two poker games, really now, tell me what is wrong! It is not like you to go to several games all in one night!"

Without answering her Sarah said, "The tea was nice. I am going to stop at Mr. William Bogg's General Store to make a purchase. Don't wait up for me." She gathered up her black handbag, her dark green waterproof and black hat. Sarah wore her black skirt and white blouse with a lace collar and she promptly left Mrs. Files.

Walking to John Bolder's Sarah saw several of her neighbors. She was the friendly type so she stopped and talked with the women folk. It was mostly small talk, but friendly enough. This was on Pond Street where Pine Street intersects.

Entering Mrs. Bogg's General Store, Mrs. Bogg greeted Sarah and said, "Are you going to John's Bolder's house this evening?"

"Yes," Sarah replied.

"What can I get for you tonight?" asked Mrs. Bogg?

"I'd like a cheroot." Sarah answered.

"Can't you sit awhile?" asked Mrs. Bogg.

"No, it's getting very dark and misty tonight, I must be going," said Sarah.

Sarah continued on to Mr. Bolder's home. As she was almost finished with the domestic work John's company began arriving. The men had asked Sarah to join their game of poker. She replied, "Not now, perhaps I will join you later this evening." With seventy-five cents in her pocket she left John Bolder's and walked along Main Street over to Pine Street to Joe Bogg's residence.

Mrs. Webber, an elderly woman living on the easterly side of Pine Street was looking out her window and saw Sarah walk past her house. She did not think anything about Sarah walking past her home in the late evening since she had seen her many times before.

Sarah knew that the men at the game would be rowdy and things would probably get out of hand, but she thought she knew how to hold her own against these men. She could drink and play cards with them. She could protect herself, or so she thought!

Sarah went to the side of the house that faced the stream. She proceeded into the carriage house but did not see Joe Mank's carriage. As usual Mr. Mank had left his carriage in Mr. Dorr's barn on Mill Street being friendly with him because he was a bootlegger as well as an agent. He had left it there many times before, whether or not Mr. Dorr was home. Taking the foot bridge to Joe Bogg's residence was shorter than going around to the top of Mill Street. Mr. Tekworgy had walked to Joe Bogg's from his home which was located further up on Pine Street. Sarah went up the stairs to Joe Bogg's room, where she knocked on the door. She thought she could win some money and leave shortly afterwards.

The men had already consumed several bottles of whiskey when Mr. Tekworgy answered the door. He greeted Sarah eagerly then invited her to join them. Of course, he had other plans for Sarah on his mind! The men invited Sarah to join the poker game. It lasted for about two hours. There was one problem, Sarah lost her money right away! At one point Will Tekworgy offered to let her stay in the game; all she had to do was put herself up for the stakes! He thought she would! They had already made jokes about it, with Sarah laughingly agreeing, but she had not taken them seriously!

As the situation deteriorated Sarah got agitated and upset with the men. She said, "You have cheated me out of my money, all of you are drunk, I think it is time I leave!" Foul talk was exchanged between Joe Mank and Will Tekworgy towards Sarah. Joe Mank called Sarah a bitch and a prostitute and Will Tekworgy made a proposition to Sarah saying, "You know how you can earn your money back, in fact you can double your money by taking both of us on!" Sarah replied, "Leave me alone you drunken slobs! You're not only thieves, you are cheats! I'm leaving!"

Captain Calder became suspicious of what Joe Mank and Will Tekworgy were up to because of their insinuations, things like Sarah can stay in the game in exchange for her services! The Captain tried to calm the situation.

Will Tekworgy shouted, "Be quiet Captain, mind your own damn business, this is between, Sarah, Joe Mank, and myself!" Will Tekworgy became furious when Sarah angrily began telling him, "No! I never said I would do you men! You only thought I would! Will Tekworgy, who do you think you are? I know of your dirty work in this town and the other men who are involved. Don't threaten me! I know all about your personal lives! How dare you insinuate I am a prostitute!" After vulgar words between them, Sarah said, "Will Tekworgy, just pay me the money you owe me and return my possessions, you thief! I want everything that you owe me right now! You know you stole my possessions, I won't leave until you return those things to me!"

Shouting and out of control with anger, Mr. Tekworgy said, "You slut! Shut up Sarah! I'm done playing for the night! Sarah, if you want your money I will give it to you tomorrow."

Sarah walked out blazing with anger and headed back to John Bolder's to join his poker game.

Sarah suspected someone was following her and she quickened her step. Suddenly, Joe Mank caught up with her and accompanied her to the top of Hincks Street when he surprised her by suddenly slapping his hand over her mouth. Sarah attempted to scream but only muffled sounds were heard like a blatting sheep! Will Tekwory was following Joe Mank and drinking from his bottle of liquor. He hit Sarah over the head with the bottle to quiet her. The dark brown glass went flying in every direction leaving Sarah in an unconscious state when she crumbled to the ground like a rag doll! Will Tekworgy laughed, "There, that will shut you up, you slut! They carried her back to Mr. Dorr's barn, where Joe Bogg was waiting for them.

Joe Bogg was horrified and confused and did not know what to do! Sarah always showed Joe kindness, he felt she was his friend. He was speechless at the horrible sight of his friend!

Tekworgy said to Joe Mank," Let's have some fun while she is dazed, in a half dead state and unable to fight back!" Joe Mank with his sick mind seemed to enjoy performing cruel sexual acts and proceeded to have his way with Sarah! Necrophilia was a sexual gratification for Joe Mank, and Will Tekworgy knew about it!

Mr. Tekworgy started to get in a frenzied state of mind. The liquor he had consumed put him in a confused fog of hatred. Joe Mank also knew that Will Tekworgy in a drunken state was not a man to deal with. Liquor made Will Tekworgy very mean!

After their sexual gratification Will Tekworgy suddenly picked up a board and hit Sarah on the head with such vehemence they all heard her skull crack! There was no reasoning with him. Now, these men were really in deep shit! Tears were slowly streaming down Joe Bogg's face. Will Tekworgy seeing tears on Joe's face said, "Buck up you stupid bastard!"

Will Tekworgy gave Sarah repeated kicks! Sarah nearly dead from her wounds was unable to defend the attack from Mr. Tekworgy that eventually ended her life. In a state of drunken delirium he continued beating and stomping on her head cracking the vertebrae in her neck. Bogg and Mank could not stop him, as much as they tried, he was a wild man!

Joe Mank, said, "Will Tekworgy get your wagon and you and Joe Bogg put her body in it! I refuse to touch her!" Will Tekworgy then realizing the seriousness of the matter; followed his directions automatically. He ran to his barn and retrieved his double axle wagon and hitched up his white horse.

Mr. Tekworgy needed to hide her body so he tossed a piece of canvas onto the wagon and he and Joe Bogg threw Sarah's body on top of the dirty greasy piece of canvas enfolding her within the remainder. Three men left with Sarah on the back of the wagon. They drove up Mill Street, across the Tannery Bridge, down Pine Street towards Main Street where Joe Mank jumped off to assure them that there were no people present. He then took a short cut through the woods while Will Tekworgy with Joe Bogg drove along Main Street then up Miles Lane to a deserted spot at which point Joe Mank joined them. Will Tekworgy, still angry with Sarah was saying things like, "You stupid prostitute, why did you make me kill you? I lined both our pockets from these rich men in town. You and I were the only ones that knew I set up arrangements between them and you for your favors. You were young and beautiful when it started. You could have still had your extra income from these prominent men!" Joe Bogg and Will Tekworgy lifted her off the wagon, threw her on the ground where Mr. Tekworgy stomped on her again and again and kept repeating, "I hate you, I hate you!"

"Stop it Will, stop," said Joe Bogg, but to no avail. "Oh, my God what have you done!" Joe Mank, trembling because he was already in trouble with the law, quickly made his way back into town making sure he spoke with several people.

Joe Bogg couldn't believe his friend was dead, he was overcome with remorse. The next day he went back to Sarah's body in the woods to make her comfortable. Crossing a stone wall Joe Bogg moved her body from the deep woods closer to the open field and placed her under a tall oak tree. He laid the waterproof under her head. He wanted to tell someone, but was too afraid of Will Tekworgy and what he would do to him. Will Tekworgy was a cruel and demented man.

Joe Bogg's Bible days came flooding back, *I am going to burn in hell.* Joe Mank was a brutal man and could care less, he was going to trial and knew he would probably go to jail for rape! Mr. Tekworgy still being in a rage showed little or no reaction. His primary concern was to dispose of her mutilated body!

Then Will Tekworgy having realized what he had done knew he had to cover up this horrible crime. Tekworgy was shocked and knew that if he got caught he'd be a dead man. Will Tekworgy went to his eleven compatriots to seek help from them to cover up his crime! He knew they would help him invent another story as to his whereabouts that night! Mr. Tekworgy checked on the body only one time and realized it had been moved from the original placement and the clothing was clean. He immediately suspected Joe Bogg of doing this because he knew of Joe's fondness for Sarah, however, he made no mention of this to Joe.

Nearly one week had gone by and not a word from Sarah. Concerned, Mrs. files sounded the alarm that consisted of asking friends and neighbors as to her whereabouts. She asked Will Tekworgy to go to Mr. Bolder's to find out if he knew where she was. Not hearing anything from Mr. Tekworgy she became alarmed.

Knowing that Sarah had gone to Joe Bogg's room in Captain Calder's home, she inquired of him if he knew where Sarah was. He did not know and it was fifteen days later search parties were hastily organized and sent on their way.

Is the story of Sarah leaving the Bogg's store and never being seen or heard from again a cover-up to what actually happened?

The town had it's own way of spreading the news about such things, things they did not vocalize in public, but in private; was it another matter?

Was Sarah dead at this time or in a semi-unconscious state or did she run off with one of her male friends?

* * * *

Obituary:

Sarah MacDonald Ware, 52, died on or about Sept. 17, 1898 of unnatural causes. Born Sarah McDonald at Rear Craig Nich, Cape Breton Island, Nova Scotia in 1846, daughter of Hugh McDonald she was of direct Scottish ancestry. Around 1878 she met and married Edward Ware of Bucksport. They were separated about or around 1888, and Edward died in 1893. Sarah bore three children; one a daughter died prematurely. She leaves a son living in Massachusetts and a daughter living in Kineo, Maine. At the time of her death, Sarah made her home with Mrs. Files of Bucksport.

* * *

Susan, a resident house keeper of Captain Calder whose bedroom overlooked the Carding Mill Stream which runs under the Tannery Bridge was awakened by a noise and was looking out the window when she saw the men load a limp and lifeless body onto the back of William Tekworgy's wagon. She had not known that the body was Sarah Ware. Susan went back to bed feeling unsure of what she had witnessed because she was mentally handicapped. It was when Sarah's body had been found that Susan realized the body in the back of the wagon was Sarah's. Susan was never questioned because of her handicap and the law had not realized that Susan was wakened by the noise on the Tannery Bridge and had been a silent witness.

* * *

When the news went through the town of Bucksport that Sarah had been found and thought to have been murdered Mrs. Britewood in her own way felt that it would possibly end her mischievous husband's affair. Thinking Sarah was her husband's mistress before Sarah was found murdered, she had even gone so far as to mentally devise a plan of her own to eliminate Sarah from her husband's bed. It was the day she had been in Bogg's General Store and overheard two women discussing how Mr. Britewood had again defended Sarah.

Remembering the day she left the store and had scurried home to confront her husband and shouting at him, "You must stop your affair with Sarah, or I will stop it myself!"

Mr. Britewood looked with dismay at his wife and thought, poor Sarah. Ten days later after Sarah's death the newspaper carried the obituary of Mr. Britewood, Mrs. Britewood was overcome with remorse.

Mr. Britewood died on September 27, 1898 at the age of 64. This was just 10 days after the death of Sarah Ware. His death was so near to Sarah's death and having been intimate friends; was he conveniently disposed of? Did these men or man that allegedly killed Sarah also kill Mr. Britewood because they thought Sarah had put her confidences in him? No one ever questioned his death. Presumably it was of natural causes.

Miles Lane

CHAPTER EIGHT

THE ARRESTS

Reading the morning newspaper article covering the death of Sarah Ware was as cold, dark and mysterious as the weather outside. The Bangor newspaper Wig and Courier on Tuesday October 4, 1898 published the following article;

BUCKSPORT MYSTERY DEEPENS:

In Bucksport on October 4th 1898 the mystery surrounding the disappearance of Mrs. Ware has only deepened by the discovery of her body in a thicket of alders about one-fourth of a mile from her abode, at the Files residence, which she left on Saturday evening, September 17th. The Files residence is located at the end of Pond Street in a lonely part of the town. The house is some distance from the road. It is nearly hidden by bushes and trees. Mrs. Ware left Mrs. File's house around 6 that evening to clean Mr. Bolder's home. There she stayed for about 30 minutes then she left, with the intention to go to another poker game, stopping at the Bogg's store on her way for a cheroot. If there had been no foul play, she probably would have reached Pond Street near her accustomed destination. When was she murdered? Was she murdered after she left Mr. Bolder's home or after she purchased her cheroot, or after another presumable card game? Was she then taken to this lonely spot further up on Miles Lane, where her body would not be found? Mrs. Files is an aged lady and lives alone. About a week passed before W. T. Tekworgy called at her house and heard of the woman's disappearance. Mrs. Files asked him to go to John Bolder's and make inquiries. He at once called on Mr. Bolder at the Tannery, but since Mr. Bolder reported her leaving his house in usual health, they decided that she was working somewhere in the vicinity. Nearly another week passed when Mr. Gogins called at the Files house and heard the story. He at once notified the Deputy Sheriff Genn, who organized search parties under the direction of Constable Robert Danvers. The woods and fields on Saturday in the vicinity were searched in vain. Sunday about noon Less Webster and Ike Richardson were searching through the bushes near the head of the lane when they detected a strong odor.

Following up the lane they discovered the body among the alders. The woods about the body were at once enclosed with a rope, and guards were stationed.

UGLY WOUNDS DISCOVERED—THE UPPER AND LOWER JAWS FRACTURED

The Coroner of Ellsworth was summoned and arrived at the Robinson House about 9 o'clock that evening. A large party accompanied the coroner to where the body was found. Dr. Lemerson, the undertaker George Ware, Selectmen Pall, and several others entered the area where the body was found to witness the doctor's examination. It was a weird scene. The night was dark and there was a heavy fog that shut out the surrounding world. The body was reclining on its back, with the right side of the head toward the south. The body was in an easy position with a waterproof cape that was doubled up and placed under the head. A pair of dark kid gloves encased the hands. The body was found badly decomposed, and the head presented little more than a bare skull.

STONE FOUND NEAR BODY—HER PURSE MISSING

Upon examination of the body, it was found that the right side of the upper jaw was broken and part of it missing. Near the corpse was found a large stone. The hat and bag containing the money was missing, but when the body had been turned over, the hat was found crushed underneath her. After looking at the body and the position as much as possible under the circumstances, Coroner Felds turned the body over to the undertaker and Selectman Pall. The search party went over the ground she had supposedly traversed. The next morning the coroner chose a panel of men for a jury. These men consisting of the Hon. Parker Koffard, Hon. F.F. Gilmore, S.E. Pall, M. Swazey, Bill Bezley and Guy Allister. A visit was made to the Files residence and to the place where the body was found. Everything was carefully looked over and a breast pin she wore was found near the place where the body was found. So far nothing could be found of the handbag or the money. With these missing and evidence that she met her death violently from the fact of a broken jaw, the case has an assumed ugly appearance.

At 1 p.m. this panel of men met at the office of Attorney Oscar.Bellows, where a large number of witnesses were questioned. The skull was brought in as evidence. That day Drs. Lemerson and Toole examined the body carefully. It was found that both the upper and lower jaws on the left side were badly fractured. On the body under the waist a dollar bill was found folded in an expensive woman's silk handkerchief. In a buttonhole of her open dress front was found the strings, which originally held the purse but no purse was found. It was known Mrs. Ware carried this small purse with her always. Also found around her neck was a chain with a Catholic medallion.

The death of Sarah Ware has caused the Bucksport citizens to become deeply enraged over the sluggish progress of the investigation. The following day October 5, 1898 the Bangor newspaper Wig and Courier continued to carry news of the events.

WAS IT MURDER IN BUCKSPORT?

The death of Mrs. Ware is still the principal topic of conversation in Bucksport. The finding of the Coroner's Jury held in Bucksport has not tended to decrease the interest. After working all day Monday and far into the night the jury announced a disagreement. It was commonly known that the five members found reason to believe that the woman came to her death by violent means. The three doctors, Dr. Toole, Dr. Lemerson, and Dr. Snow who testified before the jurors were unanimous in their opinion that no single blow could have fractured the jaw in the condition they found it at the examination. Two of them were of the opinion that violence must have pounded her face into a jelly. There was one member who did not find reason to believe that violence was used as reported accordingly, he had theories to support his position. If there was a murder what was the motive?

OPINION OF MANY THAT THE WOMAN WAS MURDERED FOR HER MONEY

Few who were familiar with the habits of Mrs. Ware were of the opinion that she did not carry very much money although stories were in circulation that she had $100 dollars about her person at the time of her death. It is probable that the money found in her handkerchief was all the money she carried. If murdered and carried into this lonely place it seemes but natural that the person taking her there would have taken some precaution to secret the body. Instead of the body being secreted it was in the open between the surrounding bushes instead of under them. Moreover, her clothes were not torn or in any manner disarranged, which indicated there could have been no struggle. Were her clothes rearranged or completely changed? Upon further investigation at the place where the body was found a mown path was discovered leading from the gateway ten to fifteen feet just below where the body was found. This was undoubtedly the path by which she entered or more likely was carried into the thicket. The idea that the grass was mown by some one to cover up blood stains was simply a fancy as the grass was cut some time in July by George Robbins who failed to gather this part of his hay crop. The chances of securing any light on the matter was very small, as the whole region of the scene of the crime had been trampled by hundreds of the curious and interested citizens of Bucksport. The discovery of the handbag might have lead to some developments, but in all probability that had been destroyed before the time of Mrs. Ware's death. A detective made an unofficial investigation of the place looking for clues. Undoubtedly the county officials will take some action in the matter. The citizens of the town are almost unanimous in their opinion that she was murdered for her money and they will be satisfied with nothing less than a thorough investigation.

DETECTIVE ODLAND CHOSEN

There were no special developments in the Ware murder case as yet. The county attorney of Bar Harbor had arrived. He had called a citizen's meeting at the office of the first selectman S. E. Pall. The town's officers and coroner's jury, a number of heavy taxpayers and representative men were also present. These men were called to decide what action they had to take. There was one distinct clue in the hands of the Deputy Sheriff and that after a consultation with the deputy, the county attorney had told the citizens he thought the case was strong enough to warrant the town officials in securing a first class detective to look after the matter. Some had been in favor of offering a reward. A vote demonstrated the fact that a majority had been in favor of every effort to apprehend the murderer. Detective Odland had been there within a short time to work with the town officers in unraveling the mystery. The case seemed that with the clues the authorities had, and the fact that the residents in the vicinity of the Files house probably had more information of Mrs. Ware's habits then what was discovered. With all the information given through the newspapers, the town's people were in an up roar and insisted something be done to solve the gruesome happening of Sarah Ware.

* * *

The newspapers had covered the murder of Sarah Ware quite closely at first. Who was giving them the information they sought to fill their pages? Was it the authorities? They undoubtedly knew better than the public. Day after day the papers carried articles concerning this grisly murder.

Theories had advanced the devious facts that were connected with the mysterious death of Mrs. Ware. It was popular for everyone to have had a theory as to the probable cause of the death of Mrs. Ware. There must have been a newspaper reporter that had been present at the midnight examination of Mrs. Ware's body by the Coroner and Dr. Lemerson that had noted with pencil some data as to the details of the position and surroundings of the body.

He obviously jotted down questions from his observation. Why, if Sarah Ware had been murdered and her body taken into the bushes and left as found, had that person or persons taken the pains *to* naturally arrange the arms and legs? Why place her waterproof under her head and arrange the clothes naturally? The body had been resting on the right side, as had been stated, and the hand near the face. The left arm, as had been reported, was lying diagonally across the body.

Few, who had seen the body, were of the opinion that there had been foul play. In fact the coroner himself had thought the case so clear that an investigation would be unnecessary. The only reason for suspecting foul play had been the fact that the upper jaw was partially missing and dislocated.

It seemed, at once, people had become suspicious, the story had circulated that she had a large sum of money that she carried with her. The front of her dress had been found to be unbuttoned, therefore it was thought she had been murdered for the money in a purse attached to a leather thong around her neck. Also, her handbag was missing.

Everyone knew that Sarah had renounced her allegiance to Catholicism and had become a Protestant when she married Edward Ware. Later when her husband died she felt she was a religious outcast and quietly had returned to the faith of her childhood. On the night in question a Catholic medallion had been found inside her dress. Sarah's Catholic faith was very strong. Somewhere between her death and her funeral it disappeared!

The question did arise however, about the fractured jaw. For some time Mrs. Ware had suffered intense pain from the fact that she had bad teeth. On September 15th only two days before she had disappeared she had gone to Dr. Lemerson's office and had them removed. She had been scared, but had consented to have five teeth removed.

These teeth had been one canine, the first and second bicuspid and the second and third molars. Her teeth had been removed from the fractured jaw less than 48 hours before her death. Sarah was to return on the following Monday to have all her lower teeth extracted.

The fact that she had been suffering extreme pain was all that could have driven her to Dr. Lemerson. This must have taken courage to brave the imaginary horrors of the dental chair without the use of anesthesia.

Naturally the diseased upper jaw had been very sore and painful by Saturday evening. This would tend to irritate the teeth of the lower jaw. It was theorized by some that, rather than going through the ordeal again, she decided to take her own life and had gone into that lonely place where by means of poison she had carried out her intentions.

The lacerated jaw, which was undoubtedly honeycombed with disease, was the first to attract flies and the elements. Once the flesh had been eaten away, there had not been enough to hold the jawbone together and for that reason a part of it had entirely disappeared. This was theorized by many of the citizens of the town.

Following the coroner's findings Selectman Pall had Sheriff Genn engage Detective Hacey from Bangor to start investigating the case. Through questioning various citizens Detective Hacey learned that Joe Mank and Will Tekworgy were overheard talking about Sarah in a negative manner in Mrs. Willey's Tavern. This led the detective to investigate the activities of Joe Mank on the night of September 17, 1898. It seemed that Joe Mank made a hasty departure after September 17th. The detective found out that Joe Mank had been in court on charges of assault and battery in a bar room brawl with another drunken patron. Joe Mank was nowhere to be found for he had gone on a coastal voyage as a seaman. Had he done this because he had wanted to avoid the law again?

The investigation into the alleged murder of Sarah Ware once again became the topic of interest for the town of Bucksport and the local newspapers. Was there a connection between Joe Mank and this murder? What information did Sheriff Genn have that led him to look into Joe Mank's possible involvement of Sarah Ware's death?

October 10,1898 headlines of the Wig and Courier newspaper came out concerning Sarah Ware's death. Much of the pertinent information had been omitted. The article read as follows;

DEVELOPMENTS IN BUCKSPORT MURDER CASE—
UNJUST AND INDISCRIMINATE SUSPICIONS:

The Ware murder case is still subject uppermost in the minds of Bucksport people. Never was public opinion so wrought up, and anyone who advances a theory contrary to that of out and out butchery is a fit person on which to fasten suspicion. Regardless of facts a half dozen names are connected with the murder in a way that must forever shadow them if the murderer is not apprehended. This indiscriminate accusation should be stopped, as the consequences of such a course may lead to something equal to the crime now being discussed.

EVIDENCE OF IMPORTANCE—LATEST PHASES

The information given about Sarah not following her usual route came to the authorities from Joe Mank while he was in jail. Doesn't it seem questionable how this information came to the officials when Joe Mank was in jail for the same past 24 hours on another charge of assault and battery? How did Joe Mank come to have this information? Is it possible he was also directly involved with the alleged murder of this woman?

The question of motive is one that has been most discussed and is undoubtedly the key to the crime. There is every reason to believe that Sarah Ware did not have more than one dollar and two cents when she left the Files residence. The two cents she spent at Bogg's Store and the one dollar was found on her person folded in a handkerchief. On the Thursday before her disappearance she paid the local dentist a small sum and had a very small balance remaining. Early the next week she was to call at the dentist's and have more work done which would require more money than she had on hand. Last April she received $65 from Charles Willham for which she gave a receipt. Later on in the summer Willham claims to have paid the balance of her wages, $13. The $65 she loaned to some party in Bucksport and at the time of her death had expended the $13 and was hard pressed for funds. This is proved by the fact that she placed a claim for the fee of $22 in the hands of a local attorney for collection of her loaned money. Was Tekworgy the party she loaned the money to? On the night of September 17th, it is believed she sought the party to whom she had loaned the $65 and if he could be located a flood of light might be shed on the mystery. The missing handbag may have contained a note, which she sought to collect with fatal results to herself. A threat was made on her life if this claim had been in the hands of her attorney. It may have provoked the unknown party to use violent means to silence his creditor. There is nothing to prove that the crime was committed in the vicinity where the body was found. A struggle in such a place and the necessary violence to cause her death must have left an unmistakable trace, and as these do not appear, it seems likely that she was murdered elsewhere and the body hurriedly disposed of in the alder thicket. This would account for lack of bloodstains or traces of a struggle. The only argument against this theory is the fact her hair switch was found some four or five feet away from the body, in the path where she must have been brought to enter the clump of alders. The switch was trampled into the grass, which would have been the case had the bushes through which she was carried pulled it off and her bearer tramped upon it. The hat, trimmed with red feathers was found directly underneath the body as if thrown down and the body placed upon it. The latest developments brought out by a thorough examination of the skull makes the suicide of death from exhaustion theory extremely improbable. The theory that the fracture of the bones could have been caused by cattle or wild animals seems improbable when it is known the field belonging to Captain Nichols was not used as a pasture and had not been so used for some time.

Anyone who has an idea that a fox might have been responsible for the broken bones should interview Alvin Dorr, as to the habits of that animal. Thus far Detective Odland has not secured sufficient evidence to warrant an arrest, but he is rapidly narrowing down the case and may soon be able to spot his man or be left without a clue upon which to base further action.

The reporter who wrote this article for the WIG AND COURRIER appears to have more vision into the actual crime that was committed. He realized the evidence would not have been from a natural death but rather from a crime. Where did this reporter get his information about certain facts such as: Who did she loan the $65 to; did she secure a lawyer because she needed her money; Was there a threat made against her life? Many citizens kept a close watch on the media as they came to Bucksport to gather any news on the Ware case. There were those with means of their own who made sure the media printed the stories that they wanted heard, read and seen. This news occurred in the Wig and Courier on October 12, 1898.

IMPORTANT DISCOVERY IN BUCKSPORT MURDER CASE—MONEY BELONGING TO MRS. WARE FOUND

The detective and Deputy Sheriff Genn in searching the room of Mrs. Ware at the home of Mrs. Files about 5 o'clock discovered nine $5 bills in the upper lid of Mrs. Ware's trunk. This lid had some of her wearing apparel in it and the bills were rolled closely together and tied with a hair string. Detective Hacey of Bangor and the Deputy Sheriff searched the trunk some days ago but found nothing. The officers thus far have run down one point in the case. The change purse and small handbag that are still missing. They apparently have some bearing on the case.

It was known several months before Mrs. Ware was paid $65 for work done. The finding of $45 with other amounts known to have been expended that about accounts for that sum and removes the idea that money was secured by the murderer if robbery was the object. She had little money with her on the night of her death. Some lean to the theory of accidental death since the discovery, while others are unshaken in their former conviction of murder alone.

How did this money suddenly appear when the trunk had been previously searched on October 4th? Unfortunately, at this point no one knows of, or has spoken of the missing diary and Bible. There were men that knew about these writings, but did not verbalize it.

On October 20, 1898 the Wig and Courier continues to delve on its own in hot pursuit of the Sarah Ware case:

TWO CLUES ON THE MURDER CASE IN BUCKSPORT

CLUE # 1 LADDER

Lewis Tepley, a friend of Sarah's and a postal worker, has for many years kept a short ladder that he discovered missing. Only a few steps from where Sarah Ware had been found was a short ladder. The ladder had always been at the front of the premises in a little alley between his house and the barn. He had been sure the ladder was in place on the afternoon of September 17, 1898. Monday, September 19, 1898 two days after the disappearance of Mrs. Ware, he started in as usual to trim his lawn when he was surprised to find this short ladder at the rear of the barn missing. Was this ladder which was short and light used as a structure to convey her body to the lonely spot where it was found? The ladder had several dark stains, which may have been caused by blood, oil or tar.

CLUE # 2 WHITE SHIRT

Two Bucksport men had made the other find, which may have proved to be of the most important. These two men had been out in a small fishing boat and were rowing against the tide close to the Verona Island shore, opposite old Fort Knox. One of the men thought that he had caught a large fish because his line had been pulling hard, or it was stuck on something. When the line had slipped he had noticed something floating near the end of his line, which was close to shore. The two men went ashore and were surprised to find in this lonely and seldom frequented spot, a businessman's white shirt, which had a laundry tag. This shirt had been soiled and wet from the rains and badly stained about the bosom and wrists with some substance which, the finders had thought to be blood.

* * *

How did this ladder which belonged to Lewis Tepley wind up next to Sarah Ware in the field where her body was found? Were the stains, which were found on the ladder her blood?

How did this shirt get in the water? Did a person or persons, in an attempt to clean the shirt row across the river in a small boat at night to the Chinese Laundry in Prospect? Perhaps, after cleaning, this shirt still had stains on it since blood is very difficult to remove. Seeing the stains were still on the shirt he decided to try and get rid of the shirt by tying twine around it with a rock for weight and then toss it in the river! What businessman always wore white shirts, which were laundered, at the Chinese Laundry?

The shirt then was brought to town by the two men and turned over to the authorities. This find caused suspicion but the people of Bucksport were anxious to know when and for what reason an individual chose this place to deposit a bloodied stained shirt. Unfortunately this evidence was destroyed and not revealed at a future date.

Was this shirt laundered at the Chinese laundry in Prospect? The laundry was within walking distance of the shore on a short wooded footpath right to the laundry; all one had to do was row a small boat across the Penobscot River to reach the Prospect shores since there was no bridge at that time. The Waldo Hancock Bridge was built in 1927.

Town citizens had begun to spread rumors as to what might have happened to Sarah. They spoke about the various poker games that night. One may have been at Mrs. File's home. Many people believed that there were a number of poker games going on the same night that Sarah disappeared. No one knew for sure! It had been said and was believed by many that she had witnessed two men fighting. Mr. Finn and Mr. Britewood as well as others, they all had been drinking quite heavily that night.

It had been rumored Mr. Finn called Sarah a prostitute and Mr. Britewood had been seen about to hit him over the head with a bottle when Sarah had stepped in. Had she stepped in? This reportedly had happened early in the evening. Did they hit Sarah by mistake? Did they think they had killed Sarah? They had not called a doctor in to examine her! Is this where Mr. Tepley's missing ladder comes into play?

Did the men panic and call Mr. Tekworgy and in turn Mr. Tekworgy called other shady characters to help him? If so, then which Joe? Was it Joe Mank or Joe Bogg or all three who disposed of Sarah's body around midnight?.

William T. Tekworgy

CHAPTER NINE

BUCKSPORT HEARING

Deputy Sheriff Genn and Selectman Pall were both out-of-town on the day that Sarah's body was found. They were expected to return later that night. Constable Danvers was left in charge of the investigation until assistance arrived.

The news spread fast, hundreds of morbidly curious people visited where she was found. The body of Sarah Ware lay covered from the eyes of the curious in the alders until Coroner Feld from Ellsworth arrived at 9 P. M. with Selectman Samuel Pall, Dr. Lemerson and George Ware the undertaker. Coroner Feld conducted a preliminary examination at the scene by lantern light and requested that the body be taken to the receiving tomb at the Silver Lake Cemetery.

A livery stable owner had been called to come with his light freight wagon, which contained a pauper's wooden coffin. A gruesome situation was made worse as Mr. Richards and Mr. George Ware were carefully removing the body to place in the wooden coffin at twelve o'clock that night.

Mr. Tekworgy came with a lantern of light and in an attempt to help when lifting Sarah's shoulders, ran into Mr. Richards, either by design or by accident. This was when her head fell from her body! The remainder of her corpse was then placed in the wooden coffin and her head in a separate box. Why was her head separated from her body? It was because her vertebrae had been cracked at the neck.

Sarah Ware's head was used as evidence in the murder trial. It remained until 1998 in a safe in the Hancock County Courthouse in Ellsworth. On the 100th anniversary of her death her head in the box was placed on top of the coffin, with the supposed rest of her remains, in the Oak Hill Cemetery in Bucksport. This was fair game for the news media that reiterated the entire murder!

Do the rest of her remains actually reside in the Oak Hill Cemetery or are they in the original paupers grave in Silver Lake? In the late 1800's all of the pauper's bodies were buried at the furthest and lowest part of the cemetery. They subsequently were removed and buried with their families. Silver Lake was then established as a major water supply for the paper mill, and the town of Bucksport.

The next week a coroner's inquest was held in Buckspsort and it was determined that a murder was committed. It then was decided to hold a Citizen's Hearing with a Circuit Judge. The jury was comprised of some prominent citizens of the town. Witnesses testifying were Mrs. Files; Dr. Lemerson; Dr. Toole; John Bolder; Mrs. William Bogg; William Tekworgy; Miss Abby Tekworgy; George Ware; plus those searchers who found Sarah's body.

Mrs. Files had testified that Sarah had left her home that evening at approximately 6:00 o'clock to go to Mr. John Bolders to clean his home before the poker game commenced. Mr. Joseph Bogg had testified that on September 17, 1898, Mr. Tekworgy had approached him and asked him to help him do a job. When Mr. Bogg was asked what that job was he answered, "Mr. Tekworgy wanted me to help him move a body up to Miles Lane." This caused a ghastly reaction from the spectators at the hearing! The rest of the testimonies were in regard to the finding of the body, the condition and the removal with lanterns late at night.

It was after 9 o'clock that night when the jury handed in their verdict, *death by means of violence by person or persons unknown.*

The verdict presented by the Circuit Judge was not unanimous, several jurors did not agree on the cause of death, however there were enough votes to request an investigation. The result of the inquest was filed in Ellsworth. The following Tuesday the County Attorney from Ellsworth came to Bucksport to mount a criminal investigation. Detective Hacey and Detective Odland from Bangor searched the crime scene and Mrs. Ware's room in Mrs. File's home. Little evidence was found.

Since the finding of the body there had been a continual search for new evidence but developments had been somewhat slow. Although Detective Hacey heard that Joe Bogg had helped Mr. Tekworgy the night of September 17, 1898, the testimony from Joe Bogg at the Citizen's hearing did not substantiate previous statements he had made to other people.

The following week Detective Hacey was in Bucksport investigating the crime when he noticed Joe Bogg and Mr. Tekworgy standing together in front of the Robinson House talking suspiciously. Detective Hacey, had asked the men about the last time they had seen Sarah and their answers put them under the detective's suspicion. Mr. Tekworgy's answer was that he had seen her get on the evening train to Bangor with Joe Bogg affirming this statement. Detective Hacey questioned the ticket agent at the train station and found their statements to be untrue!

This put Mr. Tekworgy high on the list of suspects! Furthermore Detective Hacey sought out Joe Bogg and grilled him extensively about statements he had made to other people concerning him helping Mr. Tekworgy move a body on the night of September 17, 1898.

There was an important article showing that Mr. Joe Mank was an unsavory character.

November 9, 1898 The Ellsworth American Newspaper carried the following:

Criminal Docket November 2, 1898

Joe Mank indicted for assault with intent to rape, pleaded guilty. Sentenced to two years in State Prison.

The newspaper reporters continued to write any information they could gather about the Sarah Ware case.

On November 9, 1898 The Ellsworth American Newspaper carried the following article;

NO ABANDENMENT IN THE WARE CASE:

It was at 10 o'clock in the morning that the old Bucksport Town Hall had been packed by representative citizens. They all had one purpose, to resolve the death of Sarah Ware. There had been apprehension and people had wanted punishment for the murderer or murderers of Sarah Ware. The meeting was amply attended and had been called to order by Mr. George M. Ware. He announced that the object of the meeting was to see if there was enough evidence for a Coroner's Jury and an investigation could be substantiated. He then called for a nomination to secure a permanent chairman. William. W. Smith Esq., was chosen chairman and J.P. Whitter a newspaper correspondent as secretary. Nearly a week had gone by when Detective Hacey from Bangor had announced that he would study the case and interview a large number of people. It had been claimed that Mrs. Files had given him important information that may have had some bearing on the case. Another important announcement was that the weapon believed to have been the one used by the murderer had been discovered near where the body was found. Evidently the town officials knew something new. They had sent word for Detective Odland to return. A large number of suspicious stories and theories had been afloat and hopes of further investigation would reveal some fact, yet unknown. One thing had been for sure, some parties had told detective Hacey an altogether different story than had been told to detective Odland. Some of these parties who had been under suspicion in that case were asked to explain.

With Detective Hacey and Detective Odland searching out further clues there may be more concrete discoveries rather than just speculation. In the following article the tremor of the story changes as Mr. Tekworgy becomes a strong suspect.

The following information came from the Bangor Daily Commercial on February 16, 1899. A man from Bucksport consented to an interview with this reporter. However this individual refused to make his identity known. Is Will Tekworgy the man accused of the murder of Sarah Ware on September 17, 1898, or the pawn of several other influential men who are now

straining every nerve to keep themselves out of sight in the case? This is an astounding proposition discovered by one newspaper reporter. The suggestion comes straight from a man who is known to every resident of Bucksport and who has had no active part in the case. He is a man who absolutely refused to give his name, and talked while a stenographer wrote his words. This gentleman said, "It's no use for you to interview me on this question. I don't want to talk with reporters. I have my ideas regarding the murder of Sarah Ware and you have yours. Everybody, I am sure has an opinion. Perhaps one opinion is about as good as another. What I would say to you would have no value in court. It wouldn't be testimony on either side. It is only my opinion, based on what I know of this community through a long residence and having an intimate acquaintance with some men whose names I shall not call." The reporter replied, "Sir, you have never held to the suicide theory?" The gentleman starts talking and explains his theory. "Of course not. There are perfectly good reasons why the suicide idea is not worth thinking about. One of them is that there are plenty of signs that the woman was murdered! Mr. Tekworgy, in my opinion, is not the man who killed Sarah Ware as some suspect. Whether he knew about it, I couldn't attempt to say, but that he committed the murder I do not believe to be reasonable. Where was his motive? He had no reason to quarrel with her. She was his friend. She would have given him money or assistance of other kinds had he needed it. In general she was generous to him in her personal favors. They knew one another a long time. There was not the slightest reason why Tekworgy should have either wanted to kill Sarah or have needed to do so. Perhaps the paper should be asking questions of where Mr. Finn and Dr. Lemerson was on the night in question since Mr. Britewood is dead. Perhaps Tekworgy is not the prominent citizen described so glibly in the Boston newspaper, but he has not been considered so dangerous as to be at large committing murder. He has his weaknesses and peculiarities like the rest of us. Some people may know things not complimentary to him, but Mr. Tekworgy is generally known as a man who will do any disagreeable work done for pay-cleaning up other people's messes. Now let us go back to the time before Sarah Ware's death. Everybody in Bucksport knew Sarah. A lot of men knew her. I am not casting aspersions on her character when I say these things. Her character told its own story long ago and people have their own opinions of it. Supposing she was a woman of rather liberal habits in the use of liquors—not regularly, but on occasion. I suppose Sarah was not of that strict make-up, that would cause her to refuse to meet men, who had been drinking. Well, one thing leads to another. Suppose several men go up to see Sarah in her room nights, to make a social call and have good times in a quiet sort of way. Before they know it they are brawling and somebody starts a row. Blows are struck. Someone is pushed down. There is a good deal of confusion, which, finally ends. When it does end Sarah Ware lies lifeless with a broken head. Nobody knows just how she got it. She may have fallen onto something. But life cannot be restored. Her wounds are fatal. Crazed for a moment they dump the body over a stone wall and fly home. The next day they begin to realize what the thing means. Here is Sarah's body lying in a field where someone is likely to run against it at any time. It lies, well ... too near a place they all remember. Days go by. Things are getting unbearable for these men. They can't sleep nights thinking of that body out there and knowing that its discovery is likely at any time. There is a consultation in an upstairs back room and they discuss plans for removing the remains. Nobody in the room dares touch the corpse. That isn't surprising, is it? All of them are friends of Mr. Tekworgy and when somebody mentions his name, more in desperation than anything else they jump at it. They think he will do it for a certain amount of money, and never open his lips. They know their man. Maybe Mr. Tekworgy is agreeable. The money is big to him and the men are his friends. He takes the night of September 22nd to do the work and gets a certain Joe to accompany him. You have been asking me why Mr. Tekworgy took anybody into his confidence when he moved the body. That is easy. It was because being innocent of the crime, he didn't think of the danger. It was no danger for him to hire another man, who doesn't know much anyhow, to help him that night. What would have been insanity, had he been guilty, wasn't so very foolish if he was innocent. So, Mr. Tekworgy and this certain person moved the body to the hilltop and did what they could to make things look like a struggle. Those may have been directions from headquarters. That was the end of it and after that the men concerned breathed easier. Mr. Tekworgy's coolness isn't supernatural. He is calm because he knows that when it becomes necessary he can tell a story that will let him out of the box. He won't tell till he has to do so because Mr. Tekworgy isn't going back on his friends." The newspaper reporter then asked, "What did Will Tekworgy tell a friend of his one day?" The gentleman answered the reporter's question saying, "Tekworgy said, I know all about the Ware case, but I'm not going back on my friends till I have to." Continuing in his own words without being asked he said, "No he isn't worried, of course he isn't, but there are some that well may be! I tell you Tekworgy and those who are behind him in his troubles know the whole truth. They know Mr. Tekworgy and that if he once opens his lips, the only thing he can tell will damn these men who are trembling in their shoes at present. I am certain that before long if the case against Mr. Tekworgy is pressed you will find out why he is so cool and why no defense has been made for him. Whatever theory may prove correct, the important fact remains that a decisive step has been taken to find the murderer."

Why did this man say anything to the reporter? What room was this person referring to, Sarah's room or one of the poker game rooms? What was it this man felt sure he knew? Was this another story told to the reporter to cast another shadow of doubt, or the real thing?

It was in the Bangor Commercial Newspaper on Saturday, March 11, 1899 that the headline of the Sarah Ware murder case read as follows:

TEKWORGY ARRESTED FOR MURDER OF MRS. WARE:

This quiet old town was thrown into a state of excitement on Thursday afternoon when Attorney General Brown of Waterville and Judge C. H. Chasson of the Western Hancock Municipal Court arrived on the scene. No one knew of their coming, not even the news gatherers. The one committee that did know was the Citizens Committee. Detective Hacey and this committee met them on their arrival. The attorney general and these men were in a meeting for a long time. There were little groups of gossip gatherers on the streets of Bucksport until nearly midnight Thursday and into Friday morning when it became evident a person was to be arrested. People came into town from miles around to see and hear anything that was going on in connection with the case. The Robinson House was to be the scene of a lot of hustle and bustle in the early morning. Judge Chasson had issued the warrant, and sworn to by Mr. Heyworth, who had been a member of the Citizen's Committee. A few minutes later Deputy Sheriff Genn, accompanied by Detective Hacey, had gone to Mr. Tekworgy's place of business to make the arrest. An anxious crowd watched the movements of these men. They had found Mr. Tekworgy in his store on Pine Street where he had cheerfully accompanied them to the hotel. On the way to the Robinson House Hotel, Mr. Tekworgy spoke to several citizens, and as he had passed one intimate friend, he slapped him on the back. He laughed as if the proceeding had been nothing out of the ordinary. The arrest of William Tekworgy had been in the parlor of Bucksport's famous old Hostelry, The Robinson House. He was charged with one of the most horrible crimes committed in this section of Maine. Arriving at the Robinson House Mr. Tekworgy had been taken to room number one, and once there was left in the charge of an officer. A few minutes later Mr. Tekworgy had sent for his counsel, Lawyer Bellows. He had been one of the best known lawyers in Hancock County. Mr. Tekworgy's daughter had been sent for and went to the room her father was in. It had been shortly before noon that it had been decided to hold a preliminary hearing at Emery Hall in Bucksport. Hundreds of people coming out from dinner were seen congregating on the streets waiting for word as to when they should start for the town hall. During Friday evening the excitement had grown in Bucksport. The next morning the citizens were astir, awaiting the developments of the day. The principal topic of discussion had been the totally unexpected testimony of Joseph Bogg Jr. in regard to his helping Mr. Tekworgy move Sarah's body. The prisoner was up early, after passing a quiet night. A reporter bolted into the Robinson House arriving on the train from Bangor and found Mr. Tekworgy pacing the floor in the hotel office. He was under guard but seemed in the best of spirits. Mr. Tekworgy had been granted an interview by one of the reporters. At 8:40 A.M. Mr. Tekworgy, the prisoner, had taken the chair assigned to him. Judge Chasson, and the attorneys with Counsel Bellows entering; the proceedings began at once. Detective Hacey was the first to take the stand, since his cross-examination by Counsel Bellows had not been completed on Friday night. Detective Hacey was questioned sharply by Counsel Bellows, in regard to the conversation he had had with Mr. Tekworgy at the time he had searched Mr. Tekworgy's premises. This conversation involved a razor and a hammer found in Mr. Tekworgy's barn. Detective Hacey testified that he had asked Mr. Tekworgy, "Where did you shave on the night of September 17th? Mr. Tekworgy said, "I cannot remember if I was shaved by a barber or not." Detective Hacey continued to say, "I asked Mr. Tekworgy if he was in his house at 9:30 that night," and he replied, "I could not say." Counsel Bellows asked detective Hacey, 'Did you ask Mr. Tekworgy what time he got up the next morning or what he used the canvas for?' In reply to this question Detective Hacey said," I did not ask him what time he got up the next morning or for what purpose he used the canvas that was found in Mr. Tekworgy's carriage. I did not tell him I cut a piece of the canvas and took it to professor Larvey at the University of Maine for determination as to what kind of stain was on it, nor did I tell him I took his hammer. I had a conversation with both Mr. Tekworgy and his daughter on the day I made my search." Attorney Bellows continued with, "Did you, Detective Hacey, examine Mrs. Files house or Mr. Tekworgy's house?" Detective Hacey replied, "No, I made no examination of the Files house or Mr. Tekworgy's house." When asked if Detective Hacey had given the Britewood house an examination his answer was, "Yes, I did give the Britewood house a thorough examination." Detective Hacey added, 'I did so because I heard there had been trouble there over a poker game. At the time it did not look as though anyone was living there!" The questions went on. Detective Hacey was asked if he had spoken with Walter and George Higgins. He replied, "Yes, and that they were willing to tell me where they were on that night." Detective Hacey was questioned about his conversation with Joe Bogg. Detective Hacey answered, "I spoke with Joe Bogg about the inconsistency of his stories and told him I had papers for his arrest." Joe Bogg said, "On the night I helped Mr. Tekworgy I saw a horse and jigger standing in front of Mr. Tekworgy's store, I also saw a canvas on the jigger." Detective Hacey continued, "I did not press him further. I saw Joe once afterward on Exchange Street in Bangor, when he came to divulge his secret. Mr. Heyworth and Mr. Tepley were there along with the Attorney General. We went into a room upstairs in a hotel, and he told the same story that he had relayed Friday; the one I just told you." Joe Bogg said, "I am afraid for my life; I don't dare go out at night and cannot sleep." Detective Hacey went on to say, "I made no promises to him in regard to his protection; Joe Bogg didn't say a word about being unfriendly to Mr. Tekworgy." I came down here to look into the case about November. It was on October 5th that I found a board and a sled runner in the pasture. I talked with Mr. Genn and Captain Nicholson. I did not come again until October 26th and stopped for two days simply looking into the case." Judge Chasson requested that a short break be taken. It was a little past one o'clock when Counsel Bellows announced he would be ready to resume by two thirty.

* * *

Many facts of this case, which were unknown, were brought out to the public concerning the death of Sarah Ware. These testimonies enlightened the public as well as the officials and questions were raised as to how Joe Bogg and Mr. Tekworgy were involved in the death of Sarah Ware.

It was in the afternoon that the small audience room again in Bucksport was crowded with the Town's citizens. The business of the hearing was conducted around a large table that had an official look about it.

Mr. Tekworgy, the respondent, sat tilted back in his chair with his hands crossed in front. He paid close attention to the proceedings. His daughter sat beside him, and his trained collie dog stayed near him most of the time. Mr Tekworgy pleaded not guilty to the murder of Sarah Ware of Bucksport on the night of September 17, 1898, which was the charge in the warrant.

"NOT GUILTY SIR!" SHOUTED TEKWORGY!

In the continuation of the first preliminary hearing other witnesses were questioned: George M. Ware, undertaker and brother-in-law of the murdered woman; Mrs. William Bogg at whose store she was seen on that fatal night; Louis Tepley whose ladder was involved; and Detective Hacey were questioned. Also, Joe Bogg was again interrogated. Mr. Ware testified as to the preparing of the body for burial. When Mrs. William Bogg testified she stated that Sarah had worn a light shawl over her shoulders the night she was in her store.

The great sensation of the day was when Joe Bogg repeated his testimony and stated that he went with Mr. Tekworgy to Miles Lane in the wagon. He claimed they hauled the body from a point at the side of Miles Lane to the pasture where it was found on October second. The testimony fell like a pall over the people present; it almost completely dazed them! Through all this terrible examination, Mr. Tekworgy never flinched under Joe Bogg's testimony. Joe testified that Mr. Tekworgy said, "You ever mention this and you will go the same way!" Mr. Tekworgy laughed a soft sinister laugh and gazed indifferently at the people next to him.

Detective Hacey, when questioned, testified again and was asked questions regarding the investigation of Mr. Tekworgy, which led to the arrest of the alleged murderer. He told of the visit he and another detective had made to Mr. Tekworgy's place of business. It was in the carriage house that they found pertinent evidence.

BANGOR, MAINE, THURSDAY

BOGG DECLARES HIS CONFESSION A FRAUD.

Scared Into It by Interested Parties. Says He Did Help Texworgy to Move a Dead Body.

MOTHER'S STORY BROKE HIM DOWN.

Newspaper Headline Bogg declares his confession fraud

CHAPTER TEN

HEARING CONTINUED

It was on March 15, 1899 four days after the TEKWORGY MURDER headline that a decisive step to unraveling the murder mystery was taken. William Tekworgy had been arrested for the death of Sarah Ware. Officers of the law had some tangible evidence against Mr. Tekworgy. This evidence had been made public at the preliminary hearing in Bucksport.

Ever since the murder, anger and suspicion had been pointed by many at Mr. Tekworgy. He was known to have been a frequent visitor at the File's house where Sarah Ware made her residence before her death. The chain of suspicious circumstances, which surrounded Mr. Tekworgy, became more evident and culminated in his arrest.

After his arrest, at the decision of the first Bucksport preliminary hearing, he was to appear before Judge Chasson of the Western Hancock Municipal Court in Ellsworth on a second preliminary hearing.

(In the 1800's, before the turn of the century, it was common to have several preliminary hearings.)

In Ellsworth a great amount of evidence was presented. The Attorney General and County Attorney had been present for the State. Mr. Bellows continued to represent Mr. Tekworgy in his defense.

The most sensational testimony was that of Joe Bogg Jr. in that he repeated what he had testified to at the Bucksport Citizen's Hearing where he confessed that he helped Mr. Tekworgy with the body of Mrs. Ware. He had stated that they had gone from Miles

Lane to the place where the body had been found. Joe Bogg had testified that Mr. Tekworgy threatened his life if he would say anything. Joe Bogg was also questioned about what Joe Mank had told Warden Smith while in prison for the rape of his half sister. Joe Mank said, "I knew about the murder before the body was found. It was told to me by Joe Bogg."

Joe Bogg had testified at the preliminary hearing in Bucksport that Mr. Tekworgy had confronted him in front of his store and asked if he would help him do a job. At this hearing in Ellsworth Joe Bogg added contradictory information. His testimony had gone on to say that they drove to the lane in Mr. Tekworgy's jigger. He continued to say, "Halfway up the lane Mr. Tekworgy had stopped the horse, taken a piece of canvas, and went over the stone wall at the left of Miles Lane. Mr Tekworgy returned carrying something in the canvas while I stood by the horse's head. Mr. Tekworgy returned with what looked like a body in the canvas. I helped lift the body onto the jigger even though I did not know what was in the canvass! We drove back in silence."

Was it at this point in time that Joe Bogg began to realize he was being framed and told a different version of the story?

That had been the substance of his revised testimony. On cross-examination Joe Bogg had admitted that he had not been on good terms with Mr. Tekworgy for about one year. Detective Hacey, who had worked up the case against Mr. Tekworgy, testified that he had found a large piece of canvas and a hammer stained with what looked like blood in Mr. Tekworgy's workshop. These items were found in Mr. Tekworgy's carriage.

Mr. Peters who was an employee of Mr. Tekworgy was called as a witness. He testified that he was an employee of Mr. Tekworgy at the time, caring for his horses at his stable. He said he had no idea of the wagon being out on the night in question. Mr. Tekworgy's horse, he said, would stand anywhere without being tied.

These were important points brought out at the hearing. There was also evidence tending to show that a handbag, which was found in the Files house, was the one carried by Mrs. Ware when she had left William Bogg's General Store the night of the supposed murder. (*How would this same handbag have gotten back into Mrs. File's house?)* The mackintosh coat found with the body had not been the one that was worn by Mrs. Ware. *(Who would have changed this?)* This was contrary to what Mrs. William Bogg had said. She said, "Sarah was wearing a shawl on the night she was last seen and carried a green waterproof on her arm." *(No where in the records does it show evidence of a shawl.)*

The theory generally thought by the news media was that Mrs. Ware after purchasing a cheroot had been attacked, either for purpose of robbery or assault while on her way home by a short cut across the fields after leaving the William Bogg's General Store. If the evidence regarding the purse and mackintosh could be established it would be of great importance. Mrs. Files had said, "These two items were not the same ones Mrs. Ware wore and she did not return home at all that night!"

At the second day of the hearing Mr. Tekworgy resumed the same pose as he had at the Bucksport hearing. He had his hands crossed in front of him as he continued paying close attention to the proceedings and again appeared relaxed. He wore a new pair of rubbers, striped trousers with a white shirt and had a long Ulster over a dark business suit. His daughter Abby sat beside him with his dog by his side. Mr. Tekworgy pleaded 'Not Guilty' to the charge that had been given in the warrant to the murder of Sarah Ware. Judge Chasson had read the charge. Mr. Tekworgy again responded in a clear voice, "**Not guilty, Sir!**" and he just glared at him and laughed. He looked indifferently at those who sat opposite him.

Mr. George Ware testified to what Sarah Ware had worn. He had testified as to the condition of the body on the night of finding Sarah's corpse. It had been the first time that there was mention of spectacles or glasses at the scene. *(As far as it is known, Sarah Ware never wore glasses.)* Mr. Ware told about three different visits he made to the site of the corpse and the times of his visits.

There had been a part in Mr. Ware's testimony when Mr. Tekworgy had winked at a friend across the room seated diagonally to his left where Sheriff Genn and the recorder sat.

Who was the person that he winked at?

Judge Chasson laid considerable stress upon this gesture made by Mr. Tekworgy when rendering his decision, but he plainly had been inclined to believe in Mr. Tekworgy's innocence however, the overwhelming evidence against him forced the Judge's hand. This had made it incumbent upon the judge to find probable cause to hold Mr. Tekworgy for the Grand Jury without bail. Joe Bogg's testimony went unchallenged by the defense.

William Tekworgy had been well known in Ellsworth. He had spent much of his early life in that town. He had been the son of the late Augustus Tekworgy of Surry, who had started a small store for himself on Water Street in Ellsworth. His father was known as an inoffensive quiet man, not particularly strong-minded. He had also preached and conducted prayer meetings in various small communities in the vicinity.

In Ellsworth where Mr. Tekworgy was well known, public sentiment had been almost unanimously on his side. The testimony Joe Bogg had given had been discussed and widely disbelieved. It was thought to have been absurd that a man guilty of murder would have taken into his confidence another, and especially one that William Tekworgy had not been on good terms with.

Mr. Tekworgy made arrangements for his absence from his business and had expressed with confidence that everything would come out all right and that he would be in Bucksport in April.

The Hancock County Court House lawn held several reporters standing around to gather any information of importance, which could be printed in the papers. One reporter overheard several spectators discussing a subject of interest. They were discussing Joe Bogg's story and why certain officials had gone to see Warden Smith at the state prison! It seemed they had gone to question Joe Mank who was serving his term at the time for rape on his half sister. Joe Mank had told these officials about the Ware case stating that Joe Bogg told him about the murder before the body was found. The spectators continued discussing, "Why did Warden Smith of Thomaston State Prison send back word to the detectives that Joe Mank made the following statement. 'Joe Bogg knew who killed Sarah Ware. Go ask Joe Bogg!'"

Was Joe Mank worried that the detectives were about to find out about his involvement in the case?

It was after Joe Mank's statement that Detective Odland had come to Bucksport in response to a summons. Several people had seen him and asked why he was in town and his reply to this was, "My visit has no connection with the murder case! I was merely waiting to take a train back to Bangor."

While Detective Odland had been there he had been seen making a few so-called social calls. One call had been made to the home of Joe Bogg Jr. He had also made a call at Charles Bosey's house, Joe's father-in-law. Mr. Bosey had not been at home, but Mrs. Bosey was. She gave him no information to his questioning. He then proceeded to see Selectman Pall about Joe Bogg's whereabouts. He told Selectman Pall that he had a warrant for Joe Bogg's arrest and needed to find him. Selectman Pall suggested that Detective Odland could go later that evening to see Joe Bogg at his father-in-laws home.

When they arrived at Mr. Bosey's home later that evening, they found that Joe Bogg was not there. They inquired as to his whereabouts. Selectman Pall then told Mr. Bosey to have Joe Bogg call at his office between 10 and 11 o'clock the following morning.

Joe Bogg and his wife did go to Selectman Pall's office as he requested. Selectman Pall asked them to come to his back room. Detective Odland was waiting in the back room. When Joe Bogg and his wife went into the back room Detective Odland proceeded to go over what Joe Bogg had said on the witness stand. Selectman Pall then produced a big book and had asked Joe if he knew the penalty for perjury? He had then proceeded to tell Joe the punishment for the crime of perjury, "It could be State Prison for you Joe! You had best tell the truth. You had better tell Detective Odland what you know!"

It was later in Selectman's Pall's office that Joe repeated the confession he had made to Detective Odland. Joe said, "I lied on the stand when I said that I did not know what was in the canvass that Mr. Tekworgy and I moved." Joe was in a state of shock when he was given the warrant for his arrest!

It was on Wednesday March 22, 1899 that The Bangor Daily Commercial announced that Mr. William Tekworgy was released on bail. As reported last week by the Bangor Daily Commercial, Joe Bogg Jr., on his former testimony, which indicted Mr. Tekworgy and was held for the Grand Jury and charged with the murder of Mrs. Ware, has now retracted his statements and admitted he had lied.

Consequently, Joe Bogg was arraigned before the recorder of the Western Hancock Municipal Court Wednesday afternoon, charged with perjury. He pleaded guilty. He made a statement to the effect that he had told the story at the instigation of Detective Hacey and others that had threatened him with arrest if he did not tell the truth.

This was an outrageous accusation, no wonder the bail was set so high.

The Ellsworth Judge then held Joe Bogg on bail for just under $5,000. He had been brought to the county jail in Ellsworth and was detained because no one put up his bail. With Joe Bogg recanting both his confessions claiming they were secured under duress, this allowed Attorney Bellows to take action for the release of William Tekworgy. Attorney Bellows took immediate steps to have him released from jail.

County Sheriff Cooper had returned from Bucksport to his office, which was in the jailhouse in Ellsworth, and met with Judge Walters. After the meeting the Judge released Mr. Tekworgy on $500 bail. Mr. Tekworgy then had been ordered to appear at the Superior Court on the second Tuesday of the April term. He had to await the action of the Grand Jury.

The Grand Jury at this time consisted of a Judge with twenty, State residents who were chosen for a term of one year. Only the State was permitted to present evidence.

The development of the case had been from the affidavits of Joe Bogg's parents. Their son had told them the Sunday before the body of Sarah Ware had been found and before any search had begun; he had helped Mr. Tekworgy move the body.

The Bucksport murder mystery became more complicated and it seemed that the authorities were no closer to a solution then when the body had been found. The arrest of Mr. Tekworgy had been on the testimony of Joe Bogg Jr., which had been retracted and Mr. Tekworgy had been released.

With such tangled evidence, then who could have said, what was true and what was false? But while the truth had been hidden, the public mind had also been busy with theories. They were not alone in believing there had been men in Bucksport, men that occupied places of trust in the community, that were involved in the murder mystery! The citizens believed that these men had knowledge of individuals who were involved in the death of Sarah Ware.

The citizens believed that officer's of the law; if they possibly could have hold of the loose end of the tangled skein; this would be the key to the whole scarf! If the loose end of the skein slipped away from their grasp again, would it be because there was a pull from a higher source?

It had been March of 1899 that Detective Hacey had made developments in the murder case. He had admitted that he had made recent discoveries, which had a bearing upon the murder of Mrs. Ware and that they would come out at the proper time.

The Grand Jury for the session in Hancock County convened until April 11th and the people would be obliged to wait for sensational developments until then. That had been at least as far as Detective Hacey was concerned, for he had a way of keeping to himself the evidence which would have perhaps defeated the ends of justice should they have been published before the proper time.

In reference to the vast amount of conversation that had been thrown at the public in this case, Detective Hacey had said, "let them talk." He also said, "They will only injure themselves, perhaps get into such contradictions and such hot water that ultimately the ends of justice may be rewarded." In reference to his trip to Surry on October 10, 1898, to confirm that Joe Mank had been there on the days concerning Sarah Ware's death, there wasn't a thing he would say about this investigation and its results. Detective Hacey's manner had indicated, however, that he had been entirely satisfied with this investigation and the results.

When Detective Hacey said "let them talk" did it mean that he had discovered new evidence which fit in with his previous discoveries? Detective Hacey obviously had discovered more information that he was not willing to disclose until the court hearing.

Saturday's retraction of Joe Bogg had proven to be what had been expected. Joe Bogg had rattled on in any old way without any idea of the meaning of what he was saying. He had not known that his retraction to Sheriff Cooper had been published in the newspapers and that was the reason he was in jail.

Joe's father and brother had visited him in jail and they talked over the case. Joe had told them that his original story of assisting to move the body with Mr. Tekworgy had been the truth. The visit of his father and brother had been to get the true story of his connection with the Ware murder case. Upon further discussion Joe again retracted his statement, leaving his father and brother totally bewildered.

The story Joe had told them had been substantially the same as the one he told on the witness stand in Bucksport—that he helped Tekworgy move a body! Then suddenly changed his statement entirely.

Joe had also given them a reason for telling the Bucksport newspaper correspondent, J. P. Whitter about the story of him being threatened to go to jail for Sarah's murder. Joe told his father that he had made his confession to Sheriff Cooper in confidence and later found out that it had been published. Joe told his father he felt frightened for his life when it became public knowledge. Without getting confirmed information from his son, that was his intent when visiting, Mr. William Bogg, Joe's father, and Joe's brother returned to Bucksport.

William Tekworgy had in the meantime, while out of jail, sent a half barrel of books, papers, cakes and apples etc. to 'the boys in jail,' who had for a short time been his companions in misery. Along with the items, he had sent a letter addressed to one of the inmates with directions to open the barrel and divide the contents among the boys indicating 'Joe Bogg' to be one of the recipients.

In the meantime Detective Hacey and Sheriff Cooper had been continuing the investigation. Several persons that Detective Hacey had spoken with thought that Joe Mank had been figuring quite extensively in the case. Interest in Bucksport in the murder mystery had shown no sign of abatement and active work had been carried on to find evidence in every corner of the town. The visit of Sheriff Cooper from the town of Ellsworth had added new fuel to the busy bystanders. Inquisitive neighbors had seen Sheriff Cooper entering the home of Mr. and Mrs. William Bogg and Joe Mank, who had served part of his time in prison and was released on good behavior.

Sheriff Cooper had spent Sunday and Monday morning calling on many that had been interested in the murder case along with Mr. and Mrs. William Bogg and Joe Mank, Mrs. Bogg's brother. As far as could be learned there had been nothing new in the case except that which had been furnished by the Bogg and Mank families. Everyone had been interested in hearing what the story would be after the joint session of the two families as well as Selectman Pall.

As a member of the Bucksport Citizen's Committee which was very influential in the judicial system at that time, Selectman Pall had been very active and confident with his own investigation. The members of the Citizen's Committee had claimed that they had evidence that would be forthcoming when the Grand Jury resumes. Their investigation had then turned on Joe Mank, being the first person having knowledge of the original Bogg story. They took Detective Hacey into their confidence with this information. Detective Hacey then went to Surry to verify Joe Mank's whereabouts at the time of Sarah Ware's murder!

Joe Mank told Detective Hacey that he had been in Bucksport Thursday and Friday, September 15th and 16th. He claimed that on Saturday the 17th the day of the infamous murder, he had worked for a man by the name of Fred Partridge of Orland, on a threshing machine which was verified. Later that same day, he had gone to Surry to work for a man by the name of Cluff, however Mr. Cluff had been away at the time and could not verify Joe Mank's presence. Joe claimed he had remained in Surry until September 20th when he went to the Blue Hill Fair and from there went to Orland, arriving home on the 23rd or 24th of September. He had remained at home until Friday October 7th when he went shipping to elude the justice system on charges of rape. Detective Hacey could not substantiate the whereabouts of Joe Mank on the evening of September 17, 1898!

Now, it had been claimed that Joe Mank had told of the murder in Surry just days after Sarah's murder and at the Blue Hill Fair on the 20th. If that were true, he either got his information from Joe Bogg, Jr. or had to have had first hand information himself! Could Joe Mank have been in Bucksport on the night of September 17th? Were he and Mr. Tekworgy together on the night of September 17th? What if the card game had not been at the Files house on the night in question but rather on Pine Street at another residence?

Mrs. Files made the statement that Sarah Ware had gone out that evening and that was the last time she saw Sarah so she could not have been at the house.

If Joe Mank had been in Surry as he claimed, where did he learn of the murder before she was found? Either Mank knew everything or he knew nothing. Where had Joe Mank been on the evening of September 17th?

Photo of Ellsworth
Main Street, Ellsworth, late 1800's

CHAPTER ELEVEN

ENTANGLEMENT IN SURRY

THE FOLLOWING ARE FORMAL STATEMENTS GIVEN BY JOE BOGG JR., AND LILLIAN BOGG HIS WIFE THAT WERE USED IN THE HEARING IN ELLSWORTH AND PRESENTED AS STATES EVIDENCE.

This occurred on March 14, 1899 in the home of Joe Bogg Jr. and his wife Lillian Bogg in Bucksport, Maine. Detective Odland was present at the time.

"I, Joe Bogg of my own free will in the presence of my wife and Detective Odland say: That the statement made by me in court last Friday, relative to Mr. Will Tekworgy in connection with moving a body, is false in all particulars! I was scared into telling the story by Detective Hacey and Mr. Heyworth, who told me they would send me to state Prison for life if I did not tell the truth. They said Joe Mank had told them that I knew all about it and that I knew Mr. Tekworgy and another man killed Sarah Ware and if I would tell all about it, he, Detective Hacey had $500.00 reward in his possession, and I should have $250.00 of it. The threats made by Detective Hacey and Mr. Heyworth caused me to tell this story and I am satisfied to abide the consequences and tell the truth and hope for mercy. Lew Tepley told me, every detail in the case pointed to me, and I must tell the story. So I told the story and then went into court and swore to it. I had a good mind to tell the truth and also what led up to me telling a lie instead."

Signed: Joe Bogg Jr.
Witness: Mrs. Lillian Bogg

"I, Lillian M. Bogg, wife of Joseph A. Bogg, of my own free will, and in the presence of my husband and Detective Odland do say: that on the 23rd day of February 1899 my husband Joe Bogg came home from down street. He told me a story of which the following is the sum and substance: 'Detective Hacey told me he had a warrant to arrest me if I did not get to telling the truth about the murder of Sarah Ware.' Detective Hacey said, 'I have a reward of $500.00 in my possession and you shall receive $250.00.' Mr Heyworth then said 'I believe it lies between Joe Mank and Mr. Tekworgy.'

"My husband told me he was scared and he acted so. I advised him to tell the truth about the card game. At court I had a good mind to tell the truth and tell the court all about the matter."

Signed: Mrs. Lillian M. Bogg.
Witnessed by: Joseph Bogg Jr.

What card game are you talking about Lillian and where was this card game? This statement tells absolutely nothing about what happened!

* * *

Because of the many and conflicting stories that had been told by Joe Bogg Jr. it would have been an impetuous man who ventured to say which of these stories were true. The Sheriff had read the affidavits of Joe's parents. Joe Bogg had testified that he had told the authorities what he said first was false. Then he had said that he did not remember what he had told them. Having thus committed himself, he then told the County Sheriff he had not moved the body with Mr. Tekworgy! Then he said, "I told my parents, Joe Mank and Mr. Tekworgy did it!"

Mr. William Bogg while visitng his son Joe in jail asked him, "Why did you tell Selectman Pall what you did?" Joe replied, "Selectman Pall knew I had been lying when I testified against Will Tekworgy; he could prove it! Selectman Pall read to me out of a book and said, 'If I told such a lie I would go to State Prison for life.' Joe continued, "I have been thinking of that ever since! I did not want to go to prison for the rest of my life, so I kept telling lies!" Mr. William Bogg bent over holding his forehead with his left hand pitifully saying, "Oh, my dear son, don't you know any better?"

The Ellsworth jail had never seemed to hold a more wretched prisoner than Joe Bogg. He was racked with fear and the possibility of being sent to prison for life as punishment for his part in the matter. He had stood between two fires hesitating which way to turn for safety. Pallid and unkempt, with the stare of insanity, a vacant look had entered into his eyes.

When a reporter interviewed Joe Bogg he told him that when he had testified on the stand at Mr. Tekworgy's hearing he had felt like taking it all back, but had thought the better of it. He had felt uneasy about it and had discussed it with his wife. He had told her he lied on the stand in his testimony, and she had advised him to tell the truth. He also told the reporter, "My wife, knowing my testimony to be false, had come very close to exposing the whole thing at the hearing, but had retained her impulse for fear that she would incriminate me." When Joe Bogg had been arrested, arraigned, and held for the Grand Jury with astonishing celebrity, he had been asked if he wanted counsel. He would be well defended by the State should he be put on trial for perjury. Joe Bogg did not accept the offer of counsel.

Meanwhile the citizens of Bucksport were more concerned about a conspiracy rather than Joe Bogg's conflicting stories. There had been talk of a conspiracy on foot, between prominent citizens of Bucksport to shield the murderer. A statement made by Mr. Tepley indicated he also felt certain of a conspiracy. He had been a United States mail clerk and a member of the Citizens Committee. As a citizen of Bucksport he had taken a deep interest in the murderer of Sarah Ware. Detective Hacey had said sometime before, that much credit had been due to Mr. Tepley and Mr. Heyworth for their aid in the work. They had been very active and zealous in their endeavor to find the murderer.

Mr. Tepley had stated that the Citizen's Committee had been in possession of important evidence, which would be presented at the proper time. This had been in corroboration with Detective Hacey, which was after his return trip from Surry.

Furthermore, Mr. Tepley had boldly stated that he felt, "Detective Odland, Deputy Sheriff Genn and other prominent men had been in the conspiracy mentioned and that before the investigation of the famous case had been ended the guilty parties would emerge!" Had Mr. Tepley information to back up his statements?

Was Selectman Pall also involved in the $ 500.00 conspiracy? Was this even a fact? Was this a reason why Detective Odland at one time quit the case? Why would these men jeopardize their careers?

Selectmen Pall had stated that "something would drop within 48 hours," which had not materialized as far as anyone had known. Deputy Sheriff Genn and Attorney Bellows for Mr. Tekworgy, had been keeping there own counsel and stated that they had been satisfied with the course of events.

These three men had professed confidence in the ability to bring the murderer to justice and if they could do that they would have the support of the people, for that is what had been desired and demanded. The people had been united in their demand for atonement. There were no sides, except for right and justice. The Bucksport murder case was still the principal topic for discussion and the theories appeared to be exhaustless.

Mr. Tepley, and the Citizens Committee had said they were in possession of important evidence in the form of signed statements from Mr. and Mrs. Joe Bogg, which had an important bearing on the case. In less than two weeks the accusers of Mr. Tekworgy would have a chance to tell their story before the Grand Jury. Joe Mank would also have a chance to reveal his involvement.

It had been alleged that on April 8, 1899, Detective Odland had been sent for by a telegram. He was to go to Bucksport, but it was also alleged no one knew who sent it. Events that followed Detective Odland's visit to Bucksport had been the retraction of Joe Bogg's statement at Tekworgy's hearing, which resulted in the charge of his perjury at that time. Detective Odland wanted to further investigate Joe Bogg to find out the whole secret of his connection with the case. New interest had been aroused again in the Bucksport murder case by the appearance of Sheriff Cooper of Ellsworth.

Rumors had been floating around concerning why he was in Bucksport. Was that because, perhaps a portion of his mission was to have a talk with Selectmen Pall? Was it about the celebrated retraction of Joe Bogg's statement saying that his testimony against Mr. Tekworgy was false? Perhaps it had been in relation to the methods, which were allegedly employed by Detective Hacey and others. Joe Bogg claimed that he had been influenced and intimidated to retract his testimony, which he gave at Mr. Tekworgy's hearing. The officials had not apparently devoted much time or labor to discovering what caused Joe Bogg's 'retraction'!

Mr. Tekworgy himself had stated that if he were indicted he would let out some things that would astonish the people of Bucksport. It had created a good deal of interest and discussion in a case in which it had been supposed that absolutely nothing new would be divulged until the case came to a hearing in the Supreme Court. It appeared that the general impression was that the mystery could be cleared up if a trial were held. It had been stated that the people making the allegation believed it to be the truth that Detective Odland had been sent for, at the time Joe Bogg made his 'retraction'. Detective Odland, when questioned, had told a reporter at the time, he had gone to Bucksport out of curiosity about Joe Bogg's retraction and to see Deputy Sheriff Genn. It was around the same time that Sheriff Cooper and Mr. Owen Tripp had gone to Bucksport to make some further investigations and inquiries concerning the Ware murder case. Sheriff Cooper of Ellsworth had interviewed Mr. Heyworth of the Citizen's Committee, as well as Selectman S. E. Pall, Deputy Sheriff Genn, Attorney Bellows and several other parties.

From the very start of the Sarah Ware case, it had been easier for parties at some distance to solve the whole matter, than for those who had been on the spot and knew the details and facts in the case.

On many occasions officials had started for Bucksport with an apparent belief that the case would be easy to solve, but facts had been stubborn and a fine theory had been spoiled. Those who had studied the case professed to have known the least about it.

Everyone had anxiously waited for the Grand Jury to resume when it would consider the evidence in a hearing. If Mr. Tekworgy were to be tried, it seems likely that a hundred or more citizens would have a chance to visit Ellsworth for a few days. Before the Grand Jury reconvened, Tekwory who was out on bail and Bogg who was in jail on perjury had to go before the Judge who would either indict them or not.

Consequently **Bad Feelings** had been one main heading on April 17, 1899 in a local newspaper. The failure to indict either man by the Judge had caused bad feelings among citizens in Bucksport. The people had wished to get the true story of the murderer of Sarah Ware without further necessary delays.

Bucksport people had not taken kindly to the action of the preliminary decision at the Ellsworth Court. The judge had failed to indict William Tekworgy and Joe Bogg. It had been a surprise to everyone and had been the subject of much discussion. People of the town of Ellsworth had also closely followed the famous Bucksport murder case.

Detective Hacey had not given the case up by any means and continued his diligent work extending his investigations and feeling confident that he would discover something, which would absolutely clinch matters. He had stated that he had evidence, which could be presented, but had not yet been made public. Detective Hacey had written to the State Attorney twice and told him that he had important evidence, more important than that of Joe Bogg. He had stated that he had wished to present that evidence to a Grand Jury for their consideration, but that he had received no answer to either of those letters. Detective Hacey had furnished Sheriff Cooper of Ellsworth with a list of people who could give important testimony before the Grand Jury.

The preliminary action in the cases of W. T. Tekworgy and Joe Bogg Jr, had not received a great deal of favor. The case had been left in a very doubtful state and a bad feeling of personal hatred had been brewing for some time. The majority of the citizens had been in favor of a hearing where Mr. Tekworgy would have a chance to tell what he knew of the murder of Sarah Ware. Those who were best informed were of the opinion that knowledge was limited, but all or nearly all, were anxious to hear the story.

It was early April and Joseph Bogg Jr., of Bucksport had been released from custody. It had been assumed that he would probably go home with his wife. Joe Bogg had stated that Sheriff Cooper had treated him in a very gentlemanly manner and that he had been perfectly satisfied with his treatment. Joe had had enough of the law and would keep his mouth shut in the future! If he kept this resolution there would be no more commotion by any of Joe Bogg's retractions. He surely must have been amongst the biggest fools in the world!

Bucksport Fire House late 1800's

CHAPTER TWELVE

STRANGE HAPPENINGS

With the firm belief that both Mr. Tekworgy and Joe Bogg knew things about the mystery, the people had turned confidently to the Grand Jury. They had expected the Grand Jury to discover the truth and set in motion the machinery of the law that would eventually bring the murderer to justice. The failure of the Grand Jury to take any action had been a surprise, as well as a disappointment. The Grand Jury had come under fire, people had felt they were hasty and they had been criticized. Citizens had followed the Ware case closely from the discovery of the body in the unfrequented pasture through all the devious windings, to the arrest of Mr. Tekworgy and the appearance on the scene of the impenetrable Joe Bogg.

When the Grand Jury had resumed, Judge Lemery presided. He clearly and in strict conformity with the law explained to the twenty persons selected for one year of duty that only the State could be represented. They were here to judge and carefully weigh evidence presented to them, beyond that, their duty did not extend any further.

There was one question on the minds of many, why was Joe Bogg not summoned before the Grand Jury? Some believed this a simple answer. Joe Bogg had not been able to testify without incriminating himself and everyone else.

The County Attorney and the Attorney General of the State had stated that they felt there had not have sufficient evidence for a conviction. Therefore, they had not felt warranted to summon witnesses before the Grand Jury, many of whom could only testify to hearsay evidence. The failure of the Grand Jury to indict, to so many, had seemed a tragedy.

Did the people of Hancock County think otherwise? Did they believe the Attorney General and County Attorney were actuated by the lack of evidence to pursue this case?

If William Tekworgy did know something about the murder and many people believed him to be guilty, then instead of extracting from him his story, they had put him under the protection of the law and placed his story out of reach. The same was true of Joe Bogg, with his false testimonies they could indict him at a later date. The State felt Mr. Tekworgy and Mr. Bogg would be more valuable in the future with such knowledge, as they seemed to have possessed of the murder. The State felt they needed more supporting evidence. Detective Hacey had stayed on the scene while others had abandoned. Mr. Tekworgy had made a remark in the presence of Constable Danvers, which Detective Hacey had considered highly significant. Mr. Tekworgy had said, "If ever this murder is hunted out, there will be more men go to Thomaston than you've got fingers and toes. They'll be the white shirt men, too! If the officials will give me $250 or put the money in my bank account, I will deliver the murderer of Sarah into the hands of the law."

Though this remark had not been incriminating so far as Mr. Tekworgy was concerned, it was presumed that he knew something, which he had not revealed. It was also known that Mr. Tekworgy had been indebted to Sarah and that he had been in desperate need of money. He had been heard to make the remark that gossip from William Bogg and his General Store had all but ruined him in his business. Detective Hacey had then turned his attention to William Bogg who had made the statements against Mr. Tekworgy.

The theory had advanced that Mrs. Ware's murderer had been connected with some of the best families in Bucksport. Incidents and circumstances were pointed out by people who had held to the theory men of influence were shielding Mr. Tekworgy. The residents of Bucksport were soon divided and everyone was stirred up. The card game had been a subject in question by many. What if there had been two card games and one was a cover up, or even three card games?

Many ugly rumors had been afloat as to the doings at the File's house. The character and integrity of private citizens, town and county officials had been attacked and openly charged by those who presumed to have the cover up theory. It was theorized that men who had pretended to be active in trying to solve the mystery had been using their influence to get the management of the investigations into their own hands by leading the detectives astray. There had been ugly hints of bribery and intimidation.

It was rumored that the men involved in the murder of Sarah had made an agreement, which had been, never to reveal the secret no matter what the cost! These white shirt men had known it would ruin their families for generations to come if the true identity of the murderer was revealed!

Several days after the trial, Mr. Tekworgy's daughter Abby had gone to visit with friends in Danvers, Massachusetts. She stayed there for two or three weeks. When she returned from her visit it was discovered that she had engaged Detective Haskell for her father.

The public interest concerning the Bucksport murder case had been considerably piqued again when Mrs. Files, the woman with whom Mrs. Ware had lived, had returned home to pass the summer. Mrs. Files had left after making statements at the Citizen's Hearing and the preliminary hearing. There had been speculation as to why she had left so suddenly after the Grand Jury hearing. All sorts of stories had immediately started as to why Mrs. Files suddenly disappeared. It had been strenuously claimed that the woman had probably known all about the disappearance of Sarah Ware and that is why she went away! It had even been rumored that she had been paid a great sum to go away. It was presumed that if she could be made to talk, the whole story of the famous case would be brought out. If the authorities intended to solve Mrs. Ware's murder this was the time when an opportunity presented itself in securing a possible clue in the voice of Mrs. Files.

Many citizens in Bucksport feared that she had gone on her contemplated trip to Oregon and could not be reached in case she was wanted as a witness. Those people who had been sure she would never be seen in Bucksport again were astounded when she later returned.

Authorities also knew of a certain young laundry girl who lived and worked for Captain and Mrs. Calder. Their home was on the corner of Pine Street near Mr. Tekworgy's business. She had been willing to swear that on the night when the body had been moved, she had seen Joe Bogg drive away from the Tekworgy store. She had seen Mr. Tekworgy, the white horse and his jigger, as had been stated by Joe Bogg Jr.

The town authorities said they had not bothered to speak with this young girl due to her mental handicap. However, they had stated they were still at work on the case, but had not seemed hopeful of success. To all appearances nothing had been discovered that seemed likely to lead to the discovery of the murderer of Sarah Ware. Many statements and pet theories had been proven to be untrue and nothing of a positive nature had been revealed.

* * *

Among the many happenings there were several strange incidents in Bucksport that happened in conjunction with the finding of the Grand Jury. It was believed by many that a huge mysterious fire occurred at the beginning of April. The fire spread rapidly from the fourth floor to the roof of the building. A large part of the damage was from water. The loss to Mrs. Willey of the Summer and Winter Hotel was estimated at $600 or $700. The stock in W.B. Remmick's Upholstery and Wallpaper Store and Dinsmor's Boot and Shoe Store on the first floor were all severely damaged. The Page Drug Store, under the hall, escaped with but slight damage. It had been rumored through the town that the fire had been started deliberately to avert attention. Had there been illegal drugs and booze stored in the cellar? The result meant the loss of evidence for the Government investigation.

The other incident occurred on April 28th in a dwelling, which was at the rear of Bradley's Harness Shop on Main Street. There had been the closing of another life's tragedy. Did Mr. Dorr succumb to death by means of liquor or other means? Mr. Door had been visiting Walter Emerson the Civil War veteran who occupied this dwelling. Both Mr. Emerson and Mr. Dorr had been drinking excessively for the past couple weeks. Could this have had anything to do with the trial of Mr. Tekworgy since Mr. Dorr was in this secret pact?

It was said two fishermen had joined in the carousal, but no one seemed to know who they were, or where they went. Mr. Dorr had been seated at a table and as the bottle was passed around he had failed to respond. It had been rumored that his companions, thinking that Mr. Dorr had been under the influence of liquor, had carried him to bed. When they discovered that he was dead, they then gave the alarm. Selectman Pall was notified by one of the fishermen at the scene. They then took off! Selectman Pall appeared at the house quickly. When later questioned as to why he was there Selectman Pall said, "I was called to the house by an unidentifiable party and found the dead body. A coroner's inquest had been considered unnecessary because not a mark of violence was found on his body."

Who were the two fishermen in Mr. Dorr's room that no one seemed to know? Were these men perhaps in some way responsible for the death of Mr. Dorr, and if so were they paid? If not, then perhaps these fishermen were a figment of Selectman Pall's imagination.

In 1851, Mr. Dorr had begun a livery and trucking business in Bucksport and had been considered an honored member of the community. Was his death accidental? It seemed that his appetite for liquor had grown more and more. He neglected his business and seemed not to care that others were doing a flourishing rum business, which he contributed to. Nothing was done to stop this business that had been a menace to every individual in Bucksport and was probably responsible for the death of Sarah Ware. Had Mr. Dorr's death been another coincidence related to the death of Sarah Ware or not?

Walter Emerson, Selectman Pall and Mr. Dorr were usually poker players Saturday evenings at Mrs. File's house along with Mr. Tekworgy and Sarah Ware. The night of the murder Mr. Tekworgy, Joe Bogg, Joe Mank and Sarah were supposedly playing cards at another location, being Captain Calder's residence on Pine Street.

Certain churches of Bucksport had taken some decisive moves to regulate the rum traffic! In one of the saloons a gambling machine had been introduced. People said, certain citizens were looking for notoriety. It was time action should be taken to regulate the liquor business.

Main Street, Bucksport in the 1890's

CHAPTER THIRTEEN

ALMENA'S ENCOUNTER

The year was 1902 a beautiful warm spring day. The warming sun came through Almena's bedroom window waking her early Saturday morning. She and her parents were going into Bucksport, which was seven miles away. Almena looked at the small round alarm clock on her nightstand and saw it was 5:30. Choosing the right dress to wear would require selecting the correct accessories, what few she owned. Almena could purchase one of her favorite large round colorful lollipops at Mrs. William Bogg's General Store in town.

Her father needed grain and feed for the animals. He wanted to have enough for the coming winter. The signs of nature had been telling the farmers it was to be hard this year. The cows supplied the milk with which her mother made butter and cottage cheese. The hens supplied eggs, which would be needed for a variety of cooking. The pigs and several young bulls, that her father kept, supplied most of the meat for the long cold winter months. Three older bulls were to be sold at auction in late September.

Almena's father, Austin, had relied on the signs of Mother Earth. These signs had not failed him in the thirteen years he'd been farming. The apples in the orchard were small this year. He knew the apple barrels in the dirt cellar would not be full. There had not been much rain; the blueberries had not been plentiful either.

"Hurry up Almena," she heard her Father say, as she was putting on her blue cotton bonnet matching her darker blue dress. Hurrying down the hard dirt walkway as fast as her ten year old legs would carry her she noticed how nice her Mother looked sitting there in the carriage wearing her brown dress, with her lighter brown hair neatly tucked under the beige colored linen hat. "Coming father," she answered softly, to the tall stocky built man standing next to the open black family riding carriage.

She knew her father's first visit would be to the local barbershop, which Mr. MacInnis owned. Almena would wait patiently on the wide wooden bench in front of the Barber's Shop. Her father was usually in there for quite some time catching up on the town gossip.

She would be by herself; watch the activity of other people and not have to talk to anyone. Her mother would be off shopping and visiting with her friends who lived in town. Living seven miles out in the country did not allow her much of a social life.

Almena liked being by herself. She knew that people thought she was a little strange because she preferred her own company, it didn't bother her. She was used to being alone. While sitting quietly outside the Barber's Shop she could hear the men discussing the alleged murder of a woman named Sarah Ware. They were talking as though she was not there.

Almena heard one man say to another man, "Well you know, I heard that Joe Bogg and Mr. Tekworgy did it together and perhaps with the involvement of Joe Mank." The gentleman answered saying, "They couldn't keep their stories straight when questioned back in 1898 when this whole thing happened, what makes you think they can keep it straight now?" Mr. Rubert added to the conversation by saying, "Well, you know, enough money will buy anything." Another man asked, "Wonder how Mr. Tekworgy will make out at the trial? There certainly are plenty of holes in his story; even though it seems as though there is enough evidence stacked against him!" "Yea, but incriminating records have a way of disappearing when people smell trouble," the barber said. Almena's father added to the conversation by asking," Why would Detective Hacey seem so sure that Bogg and Tekworgy killed Sarah if the detective didn't have enough proof to produce a warrant for their arrest? First Mr. Tekworgy was accused, then put in jail, then released on bail till Spring term! With Mr. Tekworgy released they jailed Joe Bogg for perjury. Then both men go free! Things sure have been busy around here getting nowhere!"

The barber asked, "Are you going to the trial next week, Austin? I hear there are witnesses that could do damage to Mr Tekworgy's defense. It seems Mrs. Files has now gone to Boston after she came back from her first trip to Oregon, now the State of Maine is anxious to get her back here again. She went to Boston a couple of days after that deceptive Massachusetts Detective Haskell interviewed her. It seemed he had been on the verge of getting some information from her before she left but had been interrupted by a certain prominent citizen of this town. Austin, what do you think about the rumor of Sarah being killed at Mrs. Files house?"

Almena's father answered, "Not much, you know how certain men of this town cover for other people, it isn't public knowledge but people know it just the same." The barber asked, "Do you think that there was a brawl at the poker game and she witnessed something she shouldn't have?" "Could be! I hear the game might have been at another house, on another night, not at Mrs. Files, and those men who played poker that night are all covering for one another," answered Austin. "Maybe that is why Mr. Tekworgy doesn't seem so worried, because maybe he knows these men will cover for him," another man replied.

One thing all the men in Mr. McInnis' Barbershop agreed on that day was that Detective Hacey had been persistent with his investigation. He had pursued it through the winter of 1899 into the spring of 1902. One could be heard to say it had been his diligent work that led to Mr. Tekworgy's arrest again. Mr. Tekworgy was the man suspected all along.

The men discussed the evidence and how Mr. Tekworgy maintained a vegetable garden at Mrs. Files and how he was a frequent visitor. They talked about how he had been on what some called intimate terms with Sarah and how he was indebted to her. People knew she carried a promissory note with his name on it in a purse laced to her bosom. One man had been bold enough to say that he thought Mr. Tekworgy could have been secretly in love with her and that maybe that was why she loaned him the money.

Was it robbery and assault that had led to her death? Maybe it was a heated argument that had turned to anger, then an uncontrollable rage over this money. Everyone was waiting to see if he would be indicted by the Grand Jury.

Almena, sat quietly, almost motionless, as she listened intently to the conversations around her. Things that had been said were of importance. Suddenly, she could not believe what she was seeing or hearing. She had turned her head, cautiously, to see if anyone else could see or hear what was happening. She then realized that she was the only one who could hear or see the woman wearing a white dress standing next to her. She had brown hair with streaks of gray and brown eyes. The woman and Almena started talking to each other without an audible word spoken between them.

The woman dressed in white had asked, "Do you know who the men are, or the dead woman your father and the others are talking about?" "No," replied Almena.

"Do you know who I am, asked the lady in white?" Again Almena answered, "No."

"Have you ever heard the term ghosts," asked the woman? "I heard my mother say once to one of her friends, 'they are like spirits still searching'" Almena answered.

The woman in white talking to Almena said, "I see your father is on his way out of the barbershop and he has bought the local paper." "He usually reads the paper in the evening when it is quiet," said Almena.

The woman in white continued to say, "Tonight his reading of the paper will prove to be very interesting, there have been people convinced that the murder trial in 1899 was not all fair and just. I have heard the Judge and other prominent individuals will pay a great sum of money to try and get Mr. Tekworgy off again. It is even believed that high law officials are involved. There were interested parties from Boston who do not want to see Mr. Tekworgy get convicted of this crime, for if he did, many other secrets of the town and people in it may come out. With new and interesting developments there will be another arrest of Mr. Tekworgy. New developments, and other aspects will be revealed as well."

With this, the lady in the white dress faded away saying, "Perhaps in another time, another place, ages of society can remember the seriousness of abuses whether emotional, physical or psycological. They need to be recognized many times over, through many generations. **Echoes From the Past** need to be heard time and time again."

Almena's father came out of the barbershop saying, "Let's go and find your mother. There are still things that I need to get done while we are in town." Almena, taking her father's hand, was tempted to tell her father about the lady in white but thought it better to keep it to herself.

Seven o'clock that night, Austin sat in his overstuffed easy chair to read the paper. Almena had gone upstairs to her room one half-hour prior to do her schoolwork. He could not believe all that he was reading. Almena's mother, Vesta, had joined her husband in the sitting room. She had brought a hot cup of tea with her. She took out her knitting needles as Austin opened the paper and started to read the news. Astonished by what he saw in large bold dark type, he anxiously said to his wife, "Listen to this Vesta! It seems the State plans to reopen the Sarah Ware murder case. They have some stories in here never told to anyone before."

Interesting statements for the first time were published in The Bangor Daily Commercial Newspaper in July 1902.

TRIAL IN FAMOUS WARE CASE:

"No murder trial since that of Cain and Cornwall murders of several people in northern Maine, in 1893 has attracted so much attention in the State as that of William Tekworgy, for the murder of Sarah Ware, which will begin in Ellsworth next Tuesday morning. From the day that the disappearance of Mrs. Ware was announced up to the present time the case had held almost constant attention of the people of Maine and at frequent intervals of the entire New England States. It had been plagued with peculiar and blinding incidents, which have puzzled the minds of some of the best authorities on crime, for they were entirely unexplainable and it had been impossible to understand why they were allowed to come into the case. There had been charges and counter charges, arrests, but no prosecutions. There had been theories upon theories. Move after move, but never anything tangible until the reporting of the indictment, under which Mr.Tekworgy now awaits trial by the Hancock Grand Jury. What the outcome of the trial could be at best was one of speculation, for no man acquainted with the evidence possessed by both the State and the Defense can possibly make a prediction with any degree of certainty. There was deep-rooted belief in Bucksport and Hancock County that this was to be the final move in the case. In conclusion, the guilt or innocence of the accused would be established, or the matter may be classified among the list of unfathomable murders in Maine."

After having read the articles in the paper Austin and his wife discussed the incident and reviewed what happened. Austin said to his wife Vesta, "You know there are many stories as to where Sarah Ware went and what she did after she left the Bogg General Store. It was unfortunate that at the time of her husband's death, she had to support herself by doing housework and odd jobs for Bucksport people making her home with Mrs. Files, an elderly widow. Also, it is speculated that she took up prostitution and poker playing to support herself. While living with Mrs. Files she ran many errands for her, including the night of her murder.

It is said that Sarah first left the Files house for the purpose of making purchases for Sunday dinner. She went to the store of Finson and Brown on Main Street, returning home somewhere between 6:30 and 7 o'clock. She left immediately saying; 'I need to keep my cleaning appointment at Mr. Bolder's.' I understand Mrs. Files urged her not to go, but Sarah insisted that she must, telling the elderly woman that she would not be gone long.

Sarah then proceeded to the Bolder house and thence to the Bogg General Store where she made a few purchases and bought a cheroot leaving sometime after 8:30 o'clock at which point all direct evidence concerning her movement ends, at least so far as the public knows. Up to this time Mrs. Files was never questioned as to the knowledge of Sarah's whereabouts. An alarm was not given, nor was any stir made. The next trace of her was when her body was found. Word was sent at once to the proper authorities and the Coroner's Jury who investigated the case and returned a verdict that the woman came to her death by violent means at the hands of some person or persons to them unknown."

Vesta added to the conversation by saying, "The authorities had started another investigation. Detectives from Bangor worked on the case as well as local officials. At the end of the first week the murder was no closer to being solved then when the investigation began. Next, came the employment of Detective Odland of Bangor by Bucksport's Selectmen. He worked on the case for several weeks with no apparent results. He felt certain he knew the identity of the murderer, but that it was not possible to procure the evidence to secure a conviction and therefore he did not feel warranted in making the arrest."

Vesta looked at her husband with a puzzled expression saying, "At first, it was said the assault was thought to be one of robbery. Sarah's effects, having been searched on October 12, 1898 by Detective Odland, discovered some money was missing and could not be found. He said he later found the missing money in the dead woman's room, which was a falsehood." Vesta questioned, "Austin why was the story changed? Detective Odland and Sheriff Genn had previously searched the trunk. None of them had been able to find the money. The finding of the money had always been one of the peculiar incidents of the crime, one that caused so many tongues to wag."

"Then came the withdrawal of Detective Odland from the case," said Austin. "The efforts of the authorities to solve the mystery, at that time, practically came to an end. Was that a coincidence? The agitation of the case was so great among the citizens that a mass meeting was held and the town of Bucksport raised $500 as a reward to the one whom could secure the conviction of the murderer. This reward attracted Detective Hacey of Bangor and he went to work on the case.

Soon after this a suspicious board was discovered in the field near where the body of Mrs. Ware was found which was not found earlier.

This discovery created a new interest in the case, but there were no new developments until the tenth day of March 1899. Detective Hacey and Deputy Sheriff Genn made a complaint to Sewell Heyworth of the Citizen's Committee requesting that a warrant be issued to arrest Mr. Tekworgy." "That is right," said Vesta adding, "They must have made some startling discoveries to have made an arrest!"

Austin replied, "For weeks the State authorities had been investigating quietly. Thursday night brought the train from Bangor to Bucksport carrying the Judge of the Western Hancock Municipality. The train also brought the Attorney General of Waterville and Detective Hacey. All of these men as well as the Hancock County Sheriff had been called into conference at the Robinson House. It was surmised that an arrest was to be made. The identity of the person was not positively known until Mr. Tekworgy's arrest. Vesta, I have to wonder why it was kept such a secret that these law officials all had to be present at the arrest of Mr. Tekworgy."

Vesta continued, "It is well known that Sarah Ware worked at Mr. Tekworgy's house, perhaps they had evidence unknown to the public. Mr. Tekworgy was a widower. His first wife died after having given birth to their second daughter, both of whom are now grown. His second wife left him a very long time ago. She moved to Massachusetts. When his first wife was ill Sarah Ware had taken care of her. They had known each other very well. Mr. Tekworgy at times would board at Mrs. File's house and when he did he occupied the room adjoining the one where Mrs. Ware boarded. He even continued to board frequently at this place long after Sarah's body had been found. He always stayed in the room adjacent to Sarah's room. If so, he would have had an opportunity to search Sarah's room for any incriminating evidence or to plant something in the room! Austin, you know Mr. Tekworgy had been arrested for the second time in April of 1902."

Austin replied, "Wouldn't you think with all this information that there was some hanky panky going on between Mr. Tekworgy and Joe Bogg?" "It certainly looks that way," answered Vesta.

Jurymen in the Tekworgy trial

CHAPTER FOURTEEN

SUPERIOR COURT

After much awaited anxiety the day finally arrived when the Grand jury would listen to the States evidence and make a decision. This process involved questioning each witness chosen for the State. During this trial only the State was represented. Twenty jurors were chosen for a one-year term.

The speculated rumors started when a newspaper reporter printed what he overheard Mr. Tekworgy say to local Constable Danvers back in 1899. This pertained to the statement about the white shirt men. Many citizens were beginning rapidly to believe that the murderer of Sarah Ware would never be truly discovered. There were people who laughed and said that Sarah Ware's murderer would never be revealed and another trial would be had. Who else were they referring to as suspects in the murder case?

These speculators were wrong for the Attorney General Seiders and County Attorney of Hancock County, together with Mr. Tepley of Bucksport had worked the case up. They were bound that the murderer should be found and the case settled once and for all!

After an examination of several days in April of 1902 the Grand Jury reported an indictment charging Mr. Tekworgy with the murder of Sarah Ware. He was again arrested, put in jail to await the date of the Superior Court Trial which was set for early July 1902.

The Superior Court Trial began with the selection of the jury, next came the opening statements of the State and Defense. The jury consisting of twelve men had been secured on July 18, 1902. One individual was refused when he said, "I have some opinions in this case." The deputies of the Sheriff's staff closely guarded the twelve men, they were farmers; merchants; shopkeepers; sailors; and came from various surrounding towns such as: Stonington; Deer Isle; Bar Harbor; Sedgewick; and Castine. They were good hard working men with common sense. Both the counsels for the State and the Defense were satisfied with the selection.

Mr. Tekworgy had been ushered in thirty minutes before the opening by two deputies and seated by his Attorney Bellows of Bucksport and his junior counsel Hitchins from Verona Island. Mr. Tekworgy had been dressed in a black suit and pants with a black string tie. His shoes had been polished and his hair neatly combed and he had been cleanly shaven. With this neat appearance Mr. Tekworgy had appeared to look far from a criminal. Upon the opening statement of the State Attorney he twisted in his chair while twirling his handkerchief in between his fingers.

With confidence, the State prosecutor, in his opening statements of the trial had made many various postulations. This confidence undoubtedly had come from his witnesses. The State was sure of a conviction of the man that may have allegedly murdered Sarah Ware. The first fifteen minutes of the trial the public had not been allowed in, after that the room was filled to capacity.

THE OPENING STATEMENT AT THE SUPERIOR COURT TRIAL STARTED WITH THE PROSECUTION, STATE ATTORNEY GENERAL SEIDERS:

"The State will have no problem in showing that Mr. Tekworgy, the respondent, is the man responsible for Mrs. Ware's death. The State will present witnesses testifying to unknown sounds at the time her death occurred. The matter of identification of Mrs. Ware was not difficult with evidence made by means of rings and clothing, as well as by the examinations made at the time by doctors.

I will present the skull as exhibit number four showing several depressions on the skull and distortion on the bottom jaw. It will be shown that blows to the skull must have caused a concussion and had been inflicted by the respondent. The motive will be shown it was a fact of their intimate relations and that she loaned him money, which caused a violent disagreement.

It will be shown to the jury that Mr. Tekworgy was in the neighborhood of Mrs. File's house on the night of the murder. In testimony, it will be shown that he was a constant visitor at the File's house and did go to her residence the day after Mrs. Ware disappeared. Mrs. Files told Mr. Tekworgy several days later that Sarah had not come home and asked him to go to Mr. Bolder's house to see if Sarah was there. It will be shown that he did not do so until after it was generally known that she was missing approximately a week later. Search parties had been formed to look for her and they found Sarah Ware after several days of searching. A medical examination was performed whereupon she was taken to the tomb.

Extremely important evidence will show that William Tekworgy moved the body on a Thursday night. Joe Bogg, who had gone up Miles Lane with Mr. Tekworgy at his request, will put this into evidence. Particularly Mr. Spaulding's testimony and other evidence will further substantiate what Mr. Joe Bogg testifies to.

Mr. Tekworgy in his effort to clear himself has made some damaging statements against himself. He had endeavored to put the guilt on another person. Mr. Tekworgy had been heard to say that, 'I could stand in my back door and almost throw a rock into the yard of the murderer of Sarah Ware.' Also he said that, 'I could stand on the Tannery Bridge and do the same thing.' Mr. Tekworgy also said, 'There must have been a drunken carousal that occurred on Miles Lane that night.'

The respondent's mysterious actions, in not reporting Sarah Ware's disappearance and not participating in the search made him even more suspect. In March of 1899 at the preliminary hearing in Bucksport tangible evidence had been developing against Mr. Tekworgy by detectives investigating the case.

The State feels this man has had full opportunity to divulge to the Grand Jury the great secrets, which he claimed. Instead of divulging those supposed secrets, it led to his arrest. William

Tekworgy stands at the hands of justice to be tried in open court. The State will show that Sarah Ware came to her death by violence and at the hands of this man charged in the indictment, William Tekworgy!

The State will give a background of the night of September 17, 1898, that it was dark and misty the night of Sarah Ware's disappearance. Sarah had made her residence at the File's house, which was located on the outskirts of town. It was the same night she went to the house of Mr. John Bolder. From there, she supposedly went to the Bogg General store, where she had purchased a cheroot. From there she had been seen passing the Cosby house on School Street, apparently on her way home. At this point on Middle Street, adjoining Pond Street, a distance of two hundred rods from the File's house she seemed to have disappeared. Sarah was never more to be seen alive or known of by friends or townspeople again.

In evidence is a large map of the village of Bucksport on the courtroom wall, it shows where Sarah was found. While the features of the dead woman were unrecognizable when the body was found, her clothing and form were sufficient to establish the identification of the remains as being those of Mrs. Sarah Ware.

The State will put witnesses on the stand that can testify that on the same night shrieks were heard by residents of the neighborhood and those shrieks came from the direction of Miles Lane. That the shrieks had been those of a woman and they had sounded as if one had been in mortal terror or great pain.

The State will show how well Mr. Tekworgy knew Mrs. Ware! Mr. Tekworgy was in the habit of visiting Mrs. File's house on Sundays after Church and taking dinner with Mrs. Files and Mrs. Ware. He also knew Mrs. Ware's habits and which room was hers and had spoken with her in her room at various times! It will be shown that Mr. Tekworgy went to Mrs. Files the day after Mrs. Ware disappeared. He was told of it and was asked to go to a Mr. Bolder's house to see if Sarah was there. It will be shown that he did not do so until it was generally known that she was missing. The motive will be shown in the fact of their intimate relations and that she loaned him money. In conclusion, the State will show the many opportunities Mr. Tekworgy had to perpetrate Mrs. Ware's murder!"

When the State had finished with it's opening statement it was then Defense Attorney Bellows turn to make his opening statements. It was 3:30 in the afternoon when Attorney Bellows and his assistant Attorney Hitchins were in the courtroom.

OPENING STATEMENT OF THE DEFENSE BY ATTORNEY HITCHINS, ASSISTANT TO ATTORNEY BELLOWS:

"Mr. Tekworgy is a man 40 odd years old. A hard working man, a good citizen and we will show that up to the time of Sarah Ware's murder no charges had ever been brought against him. We shall show Mr. Tekworgy's relationship with Sarah Ware began when he had employed her. Their relationship was always friendly, although not intimate. The State has implied that Mr. Tekworgy owed her money. We will show you that there was never any business relationship between them since she left his house years before. We shall convince you, by the testimony of many witnesses that there could have been no motive for this deed, no jealousy, no hatred in his heart.

This Government has based this case upon the story of Joe Bogg's testimony, and all other testimonies, of witnesses which it has produced that cluster around Joe's story. The defense will prove to you beyond a doubt, that Joe Bogg's story is a falsehood; he is a liar and an acknowledged perjurer. The recorder, of the Western Hancock County court will tell you on the stand that Mr. Bogg came to him voluntarily and said that the story of moving a body was a lie, and that Mr. Joe Bogg pleaded guilty to lying in a lesser court in 1898. We shall show that he confessed to many people, at many times, that the story was a lie. We shall show that the story, as originally told, differs in many features from the story he has told this week.

We shall further show by reputable citizens of Bucksport that the situation in the pasture where the body was discovered was such that it would have been impossible to drive a team in and out, which Mr. Bogg says Mr. Tekworgy did with his jigger. The first time Joe Bogg told his story he said it was on Tuesday night that he helped move the body, and that he was very certain it was Tuesday. Now, he says it was Thursday night. We shall show you that on Tuesday and Wednesday night Mr. Tekworgy was miles away in Orland. He will go on the stand himself and tell you, as near as he can remember, just where he was and what he did on Thursday night.

There is another man in Bucksport, whom I think you say should rather fall under suspicion, other than Mr. Tekworgy. We will show that this man, Mr. Viles, was in the vicinity of Miles lane with a team of horses on the night of the alleged crime. That Mr. Viles had fashioned a club of wood weighted with lead the day before the crime and that same night a team of horses was heard to come from the direction of Miles Lane, driving furiously. He is now nowhere to be found. Mr. Viles left on a shipping vessel shortly after Mrs. Ware was missing. It was learned Mr. Viles had threatened Sarah Ware at some date before her demise. Mr. Viles also, according to Mrs. Files' testimony threatened Mrs. Files."

With the ending of the statement of the Defense the trial proceeded with the State calling its first witness.

THE FIRST WITNESS FOR THE STATE WAS KATE DEEHAN:

STATE: Would you please state your name for the court?
WITNESS: My name is Kate Deehan.
STATE: Do you reside in Bucksport, Mrs. Deehan?
WITNESS: I reside in Bucksport on the West Side of Bridge Street and I lived there as well in 1898.
STATE: Did you know Sarah Ware?
WITNESS: I knew her well. Mrs. Ware visited my house from time to time and purchased butter and milk. I last saw her on September 17, 1898 walking along Pond Street. I passed her on the street at six o'clock, as she

was going downtown. She wore a dark suit and short shoulder cape.

STATE: What did you see later that night?

WITNESS: That night I saw a man about my house when I went to close the gate of my hen yard. I had stepped from the stable door, when a man jumped out from the left side. The light from the lamp had been glaring in my eyes so I shaded them with my right hand. From where I was standing I saw a man by the lamppost. He could have looked right through my kitchen window from where he was standing. To the best of my knowledge the man that came from the stable door was tall and looked to be dark. He ran straight down through the apple orchards and disappeared. This was about 9:00 or 9:30 in the evening.

STATE: Did you mention this to anyone?

WITNESS: Yes, afterwards I mentioned the matter to Mr. Tekworgy. It was on Monday night after the body of Sarah Ware was found. He visited my house. It came about when we were talking about the case. I told him of the occurrence on the night of her disappearance and he asked me if I recognized the man. I told him, "No, it was too dark."

STATE: Did Mr. Tekworgy have anything else to say about that night?

WITNESS: He only said, "Yes, it was dark that night."

STATE: You had cows pastured in 1898, is that correct?

WITNESS: Yes.

STATE: Where did you pasture your cows at that time?

WITNESS: My cows were pastured on Miles Lane and were driven by a small boy. He drove the cows back and forth every day.

STATE: Mrs. Deehan, do you know of a small handbag that Mrs. Ware carried?

WITNESS: Yes, I saw her carry a small black handbag. She used to carry it with her all the time inside a larger one. It contained some letters.

STATE: And how do you know this?
WITNESS: I know because I saw them. I also saw a post office key and a handkerchief. She had newspapers in her handbag too. One time my children, while playing with Mrs. Ware's handbag, dropped it and letters fell out. I picked them up, passed them to her and she put them back inside her bag. The small bag was quite worn out and could not be securely fastened.
STATE: When was the last time you saw Mrs. Ware?
WITNESS: The last time I saw Mrs. Ware was two weeks prior to her death. Previously she'd come every other day. July and August of that year she had come every day when she purchased butter and milk. Usually she came at night, sometimes she came around 7:30, sometimes around 8:00.

DEFENSE ATTORNEY BELLOWS CROSS-EXAMINES MRS. DEEHAN:

DEFENSE: Did you testify at the preliminary hearing in Bucksport, March 1899?
WITNESS: Yes.
DEFENSE: Did you swear under oath that it was Mr. Tekworgy you saw on the night of September 17, 1898?
WITNESS: Well, what I said was, "I thought it was Mr. Tekworgy. I did not say it was Mr. Tekworgy, sir! It became dark at 7:30 and it was quite foggy. I do not remember how dark it had gotten before 7 o'clock, and it surely was very dark at 9 o'clock.
DEFENSE: You say you know what the man wore and looked like that jumped from behind your stable door, and yet it was very dark. Are you sure you saw a man at all or could it possibly have been Mr. Viles?
WITNESS: I know what he looked like and that man was tall and appeared to be dressed in dark clothes. I could see his shadow even though it was a very dark night. I was standing at my stable doors when he jumped out.

DEFENSE: Did you know Mrs. Ware?
WITNESS: I knew Mrs. Ware well and that Mrs. Ware once had a husband. I am not sure when he died. I know that Mrs. Ware had a son and a daughter and that they had not lived with her for 10 years prior to her death.
DEFENSE: Are you familiar with the area where Mrs. Ware was found?
WITNESS: Yes. I was at Miles Lane once prior to finding the body.
DEFENSE: Do you know how many years Mrs. Ware lived at Mrs. Files home?
WITNESS: I cannot remember how long Mrs. Ware had lived with Mrs. Files, but it had been a number of years.
DEFENSE: Did you see Mrs. Ware the night of the murder?
WITNESS: Yes, I remember seeing a man and Mrs. Ware walking down Pond Street being the same date of the disappearance of Mrs. Ware.
DEFENSE: Did you recognize the man?
WITNESS: No, I did not.

THE NEXT WITNESS FOR THE STATE WAS CAROLYN BROWN:

STATE: State your name for the court please.
WITNESS: Mrs. Carolyn Brown.
STATE: Where did you live in September of 1898?
WITNESS: I lived with Mrs. Barr and Vivian Innis on the south side of Pond Street.
STATE: Can you tell us what you heard on the night of September 17, 1898?
WITNESS: On September 17, 1898 I heard a sound like that of a sheep crying. I was coming from the outhouse at about 9:30. I heard the cry three times. It appeared to come from across the Swazey field in the direction of the barns on Miles Lane. Sheep were not kept pastured in the field at that time. The last sound did not appear

to be so long as the others. The last cry was like that of a human person who was being prevented from calling out. That is all I can tell you of that night.

JUDGE LEMERY: Cross?
DEFENSE BELLOWS: Not at the present.

ANOTHER WITNESS FOR THE STATE WAS MRS. BALLINGER:

STATE: Would you please state your name for the court.
WITNESS: My name is Mrs. Ballinger.
STATE: Where did you live in 1898?
WITNESS: On the south side of Pond Street just below Hincks Street in Bucksport.
STATE: Did you know Mrs. Sarah Ware?
WITNESS: Yes, I knew Mrs. Sarah Ware.
STATE: When did you last see her?
WITNESS: I saw her last on the night of September 17, 1898. I heard a strange sound that night. It came from the direction of Swazey's field off Miles Lane. It sounded like sheep at first, but later took on the form of a human voice. There were three cries and gurgling noises also. This was about 9:30 P.M., I then retired about 10 o'clock.
STATE: Were you at Mrs. File's house before the finding of Mrs. Ware?
WITNESS: I had been at Mrs. File's house just before her body was found, I think it was Friday or Saturday. While I was there I viewed Mrs. Ware's room. I saw underclothes on the bed. They were clean and appeared to be spread out. The bed was made up, and I saw her trunk, it was open and set back against the wall.
STATE: Did you and Mrs. Files discuss anything else during your visit?
WITNESS: Yes, Mrs. Files mentioned an unusual fire she had seen in the Swazey field; she recalled it being the night of

September 22, 1898. Mrs. Files said that all the migrant workers had left town at the beginning of September and there should not have been any fires in the field at that time.

STATE: Mrs. Ballinger, did Mrs. Files state what her concern was about the fire?

WITNESS: Mrs. Files told me that the blouse Sarah wore when she left her house was never found and that she was attired in different clothing when she was found in the lane. She strongly suspected that the fire was to dispose of unwanted evidence such as the blouse she originally wore.

STATE: Do you know Mr. Tekworgy?

WITNESS: Yes I do. He is a prominent businessman in Bucksport.

STATE: Did you see Mr. Tekworgy around the time of Sarah's death?

WITNESS: I saw Mr. Tekworgy pass my house going toward Mrs. File's house, after Sarah Ware was missing. I don't remember the day or the time. He used to go by quite often as he had a garden up that way. Mr. Tekworgy never made any inquiry of me about Mrs. Ware being missing. I first heard of her disappearance when she had been gone a week or more.

STATE: Did you tell anyone of the noises you heard?

WITNESS: Yes, I told Mrs. Files about the noise after I heard of Mrs. Ware's disappearance.

DEFENSE ATTORNEY BELLOWS CROSS-EXAMINES MRS. BALLINGER:

DEFENSE: Mrs. Ballinger, I understand that you have trouble hearing!

WITNESS: I am not deaf! You don't need to shout at me!

DEFENSE: Have you ever seen Mr. Tekworgy?

WITNESS: Yes. I have seen Mr. Tekworgy frequently.

DEFENSE: Have you ever seen his horse and jigger?

WITNESS: Yes, he drove a white horse and a blue jigger with sideboards. Several of my near neighbors kept teams at the time.
DEFENSE: When did you hear of Mrs. Ware being missed?
WITNESS: It was about a week after hearing the same strange sounds my sister Mrs. Brown testified to hearing.
DEFENSE: Did you report the noises?
WITNESS: I did not report the noises that I heard, I only discussed it with my sister Mrs. Brown.

WITNESS FOR THE STATE MARION WEBBER:

STATE: State your name please.
WITNESS: Mrs. Marion Webber.
STATE: Mrs. Webber where do you reside?
WITNESS: I live in Bucksport on the West Side of School Street and I also lived there in 1898.
STATE: Did you know Sarah Ware?
WITNESS: Yes, I did.
STATE: Tell us what you know concerning the night of September 17, 1898.
WITNESS: I saw Mrs. Ware last on September 17, 1898 in front of Pond and School Streets. It was between 6:00 and 6:30. She had been wearing dark clothes. I did not notice what she had over her shoulders.
STATE: Do you know Mrs. Files?
WITNESS: Yes, I do.
STATE: Did you visit Mr. Files concerning Mrs. Ware?
WITNESS: Yes, I visited Mrs. File's house on the day the body was found. I went with Mrs. Amos Cosby, and Mrs. Robinson. Mrs. Files and Mrs. George Sawyer were there too. We were all upset over the horrific event that had taken place.
STATE: Did any one else visit while you were there?
WITNESS: Mr. Tekworgy and George Abbott came soon after I arrived. Mrs. Files told me she wanted to have Mrs.

Ware's body brought home for burial and that her body had been badly decomposed. I told her it was too bad her body was not found sooner. If she had been a rich woman no stone would have been unturned!

Mr. Tekworgy visibly twisted in his seat at this time and looked very uncomfortable.

STATE: Mrs. Webber can you tell us more about Mr. Tekworgy's reactions.

WITNESS: Yes, Mrs. Files said to Mr. Tekworgy, 'You know that you were here several days after Sarah was reported missing and I told you about it, and asked you to seek her!' It was then that his daughter Mrs. Abbott said, 'Yes, father that is right, Mrs. Files did ask you to go see Mr. Bolder.' He answered her saying, 'I know she did. I went to John's house and no one was there, I was very busy and could do no more.'

STATE: Mrs. Webber, tell the court what you saw on the night of September 17, 1898.

WITNESS: I saw some men in front of Mr. Allan Dorr's house near the Tannery Bridge about 9 or 9:30 that night.

STATE: And who were these men?

WITNESS: Herbert Badger, Fred Britwood, Walter Badger and a man I did not know, standing by a lamp-post. I am not sure what he looked like. I am not sure what the stranger was wearing; I do know he had on dark clothes and the man was of medium size. It was very dark that night. I could see the man by the gas light while passing Mr. Dorr's house when I was coming from Mrs. Robinson's house. I don't know how long they remained there.

STATE: Did you see anyone on the Tannery Bridge after 10:00 that night?

WITNESS: No, I did not.

STATE: Did you have a conversation with Mrs. Files about Mrs. Ware being missing?
WITNESS: Yes, I did, but I did not testify about a conversation with Mrs. Files at the preliminary hearing in Bucksport. I was not asked about it.

Attorney Bellows chose not to cross-examine the witness at this time. With the completion of this testimony the court had convened for one hour for lunch, it had already been a long and hot summer day. Court resumed with the afternoon session calling Mr. Bolder as the next witness.

STATE: Tell the court your name.
WITNESS: John Bolder.
STATE: Mr. Bolder where did you reside on September 17, 1898?
WITNESS: School Street in Bucksport.
STATE: Did you know Mrs. Sarah Ware?
WITNESS: I knew Mrs. Ware well for about thirty or thirty-five years.
STATE: When did you see Mrs. Ware last?
WITNESS: I saw her last on the night of September 17, 1898. She was at my house about 7:00 or 7:30. Sarah mentioned she was going to Bogg's General Store and then perhaps to another card game.
STATE: Did you notice what she was wearing on the night in question?
WITNESS: She wore a black dress, with big ruffles and dark brown waist gloves. I did not notice that she had a hat on. I did not notice what she had on her shoulders. I don't know if she had a shawl on or not. Sarah told me, she felt someone was following her. She did not want anyone to see her leave. I watched her from the door until she passed the corner of my house. From there I don't know which way she went.
STATE: Did she indicate she felt it was Mr. Tekworgy?

WITNESS: She did not tell me who she thought the person was.
STATE: Is there a triangle of grass and woods a short distance from your house?
WITNESS: Yes, there is a triangle of grass and another dirt road about fifty or sixty feet from my house.
STATE: Is there a lamp at this intersection?
WITNESS: There is no lamppost at that corner.
STATE: Could a person stand there and not be seen in your opinion?
WITNESS: Yes, I suppose one could. There are bushes.
STATE: How did you learn of Sarah Ware being missing?
WITNESS: I first heard of her absence about two weeks after her visit. Captain Calder told me of it. I met Mr. Tekworgy later that same day at about 1:30 in the afternoon and asked him about Sarah Ware being missed. He said, 'Oh I forgot, Mrs. Files wanted me to ask you about her but you was not home.' Then I told Mr. Tekworgy I just heard she was missing, and he said, 'Yes, since September 17th.' He then abruptly walked away.
STATE: So you did not know that Mr. Tekworgy came by your house the night Mrs. Files asked him to in 1898?
WITNESS: No, I only know what he told me several weeks after I knew she was missing. Mr. Tekworgy said at that time, 'I came to your house to tell you Sarah was missing.'
STATE: Was there a poker game at your house on the night of September 17, 1898?
WITNESS: Yes, I had a few friends over for a short while.
STATE: Did any detectives ask you questions about the card game at your house?
WITNESS: Yes, after the body was found Detectives Hacey and Odland came to my house. They came around noon. They asked me a question and I answered it. After I had gone away they came and searched my house. They had no right to do this. They had no warrant!

Why didn't the State further investigate the question Mr. Bolder was asked and what his answer was? Also, when Mr. Bolder's house was searched why wasn't any information revealed as to what they were searching for?

DEFENSE ATTORNEY BELLOWS CROSS-EXAMINES MR. JOHN BOLDER:

DEFENSE: How many times was Mrs. Ware at your house?

WITNESS: After the demise of my wife, she had been to my house a great number of times. She would always come once or twice a week to clean and after she was done cleaning Mrs. Ware would visit with me. When she was very busy working, she would not come to clean at all. Sarah usually did come to visit on Saturday evenings. I was living alone and she would stay an hour or so during these visits. On the night of her disappearance she visited with me about half an hour, or a little longer.

DEFENSE: Did you visit Mrs. Files when you learned of Sarah's disappearance?

WITNESS: I did not go immediately to Mrs. File's house after I heard of Sarah's absence. The following Sunday I went since I had to work Friday and Saturday.

DEFENSE: How long did you know Mrs. Ware?

WITNESS: Ever since I accompanied her here from Canada when she was a young woman. I went home to Canada with Sarah once, about five years ago to visit her children.

DEFENSE: Do you know Mr. Odland?

WITNESS: Yes, I have met him on the street a number of times, only to pass the time of day. I know he is a detective.

DEFENSE: Why do you think Mr. Tekworgy did not get in touch with you after Mrs. File's request?

WITNESS: I honestly do not know, he probably just forgot!

DEFENSE: Thank you, you are excused.

THE NEXT WITNESS FOR THE STATE WAS
RUSSELL LEACH:

STATE: Please, tell the Court your name sir.
WITNESS: Russell Leach.
STATE: Where did you reside in 1898?
WITNESS: I live in Bucksport now and lived there at the time of Mrs. Ware's disappearance.
STATE: Where were you employed at that time?
WITNESS: I was employed at the store of Finson and Brown as a clerk. The store is on Main Street near the foot of Central Street. I knew Sarah Ware, because she traded there considerably.
STATE: When was the last time you saw Mrs. Ware?
WITNESS: I saw her on September 17, 1898. She was there about 6:30 and procured merchandise for herself and Mrs. Files. She paid for them with separate bundles of money.
STATE: Thank you Mr. Leach, that will be all, you may step down.

Again, the Defense declined cross-examination of this witness.

At this point the Judge closed session for the day as it was getting late. He announced the trial would continue on Monday morning at 8:00 A.M.

Horse and Jigger

CHAPTER FIFTEEN

TRIAL CONTINUED

It was a Monday in July 1902 and another day of the trial had begun. Detective Hacey received many compliments of the day for the clever work he maintained in the case. He also met with a considerable amount of opposition from different sources, but he had persevered since last fall and had reason to feel most proud of his work.

The prisoner Mr. Tekworgy had been turned over to the Hancock County Sheriff in Ellsworth to spend the night in jail. He had gone to sleep at 11:30 that night sleeping soundly and evidently had not worried about the coming events of the day which will be long remembered as one of the most interesting because Joe Bogg was to testify on the stand against Mr. Tekworgy.

Mr. Tekworgy was brought into the Superior Court Room unknowing that Mr. Bogg was to appear on the witness stand. Mr. Tekworgy with a smug expression wore a black cutaway, black striped trousers, with a white standing collar and a black tie made up in the four-in hand style. His shoes were neatly polished rather than the usual glistening bright shine. His face was once again clean-shaven and his dark hair cropped and combed. The upper lip held the same dark moustache.

The people he knew seemed to embrace the room, some even within his range of vision. He greeted them with a kindly nod and smiled and when at recess during the day friends came to shake his hand and wish him a speedy acquittal. He then responded pleasantly to their words. All in all he was receptive, however his dark eyes and demeanor showed contempt.

The people had been in hopes of finding the source to the smoke that had been building and that it would turn to fire. It had not been easy to get into the courtroom. The witnesses had filled most of the seats on the floor. The spacious gallery above had become quickly filled. The space within the bar had been filled with some of the prominent members of the Hancock County legal representatives.

Joe Bogg was the witness that the people had been waiting to hear again. When he was called to testify a sudden hush fell over the courtroom. There were those people craning their necks to see the man who had been discussed over and over in the stores, homes and shops of Hancock County for the past three years.

Joe Bogg reappeared with an uneasy expression on his face and walked with hesitation in his gate. Joe told his story in a matter-of-fact way. He did not waver from a straight line; he gave the same details that he had testified to previously. It resembled a rehearsed scene.

JOE BOGG JR. BEGAN THE TRIAL AS THE STATE'S FIRST WITNESS:

STATE: State your name for the court please.
WITNESS: My name is Joe Bogg.
STATE: Where do you live?
WITNESS: Presently I live in Bucksport with my in-laws.
STATE: For the court records Mr. Bogg tell us about yourself and how old you are.
WITNESS: I am 29 years old. I can only write my name, but not spell it. I have not had much schooling.
STATE: Mr. Bogg, tell us your occupation, and what you did prior to September 17, 1898.
WITNESS: I work on sailing vessels. On September 15, 1898 I shipped with Captain Stubbs to Rockport. We got there about noon and stayed until Monday unloading merchandise. I then left the vessel and went to Rockland, then to Thomaston until Tuesday morning

STATE: when I returned home. Being separated from my wife at that time in 1898, I lived on the easterly side of Pine Street at Captain Calder's's house.

STATE: What did you do when you returned to Captain Calder's?

WITNESS: On Wednesday, I worked for Mr. Swazey. On Thursday I was resting in my room at Captain Calder's. My wife was staying with her parents. On the way home I had passed Mr. Tekworgy's Department Store. When I got home I washed, I then ate supper, then I went into town to Captain Nicholson's store for about an hour or hour and a half. I passed Laurel Spaulding's house on my way home. We talked for about 30 minutes. There had been an elm tree with lots of bees in a crack in front of his house. I suggested that we cut the tree down. His reply was, 'No'. We looked at the tree, crossed the street to the sidewalk and stood near Mr. Tekworgy's store.

STATE: Did you see Mr. Tekworgy on the night of September 17, 1898?

WITNESS: Yes, Mr. Tekworgy came along with a jigger and his white horse and asked me to help him do a job and I jumped on the jigger.

STATE: What did you do after you got on the jigger?

WITNESS: We went up Pine Street to the head of Miles Lane without any conversation during the drive. Up Miles Lane, about half way we stopped. It had been about 9:30 or 10:00 o'clock and it was very dark. There were some alders on the left side of the lane. It had been at this point we stopped in the lane and Mr. Tekworgy had said, 'I've got a body to move and if you mention it you'll go the same way. You remember that!' Mr. Tekworgy did not tell me before what we were to do.

STATE: What happened then?

WITNESS: Mr. Tekworgy then took a canvas off the jigger and crossed a stone wall where he met Joe Mank. I knew it

was stone because I heard the stones rattling but I could not hear any conversation.
STATE: Did you at any time actually see Joe Mank?
WITNESS: No, I didn't but I knew he was there!
STATE: What makes you think it was Joe Mank?
WITNESS: I just know it!
STATE: Why did he cross the stone wall with the canvass?
WITNESS: He and Joe Mank then moved the body on to the other side of the stone wall and brought the canvass back to the wagon. I think her bloody clothing was in the canvass. He then went back with the canvass to the stone wall.
STATE: Why do you think Tekworgy did this?
WITNESS: I think they just wrapped her up in the canvass and brought her to the wagon.
STATE: What did you do next?
WITNESS: We went up the lane just above the Dodgett Field, which is located beside the Swazey Field and drove right into the pasture. No fence bars had been taken down. We went in about 2 or 3 rods where there was a clearing and then there were alder bushes with a small opening of about fifteen feet in width. Mr. Tekworgy took the canvas and what was in it from the right side of his jigger and placed it on the ground.
STATE: Are you sure it was the right side of the jigger?
WITNESS: Yes. Then we turned the jigger around.
STATE: Did Joe Mank get on the wagon at this point?
WITNESS: No, I don't know where he went.
STATE: All right, Joe, go on.
WITNESS: The horse had been made to walk along. Mr. Tekworgy went around on the left side laid the body on the ground, drew the canvas out and placed the canvas in the wagon. The wagon struck a large tree in the lane, I think it was a maple tree, might have been beech. The ground and pasture was rough, but we drove down the lane. We went down Miles Lane and over to the

	corner of Pine and Pond Streets, where I got off the jigger.
STATE:	Did Mr. Tekworgy say anything to you at this point?
WITNESS:	As we left Mr. Tekworgy said, 'Now you remember, if you say a word about this you will go the same way!' I made no answer. I do not know what time I got home. I believe it must have been late at night for it was very dark and foggy.
STATE:	Did you visit the place where Sarah Ware was found?
WITNESS:	Yes, I visited the place where the body had been taken after she was found. I went there with William Bogg, Detective Dennis Hacey, and again with several others at a later date.
STATE:	Where were you when Sarah's body was found?
WITNESS:	I was in Bucksport when Mrs. Ware's body was found on Sunday. I was at the corner of Pine and Oak Streets. I ran across several vacant lots to the place where I knew the body was, but at the time I had not heard where the body had been found, but I knew where, because I helped Mr. Tekworgy move Sarah's body.
STATE:	Mr. Bogg, why did you go to where you thought the body was?
WITNESS:	I went across the lots because it was the quickest way to reach the spot where I thought the body had been. I did not see Mr. Tekworgy there. I stayed until 3:00 o'clock in the afternoon waiting for him to show. I did not get to where the body was found because the authorities would not let me. Constable Davis stayed with the body and asked me to get his revolver and bring him a lunch.

Wasn't this a ludicrous thing for Constable Davis to ask of Mr. Bogg? However, this does exist in the testimony.

Mr. Tekworgy leaned well back with his arms folded and eyes fixed intently upon Joe Bogg who was telling the story which meant so much to the case against himself. Still at no time had the prisoner indicated unusual interest, except on one or two occasions, when he leaned forward so he could hear more distinctly what Joe Bogg had to say.

STATE: Have you worked for Mr. Tekworgy?
WITNESS: Yes, I worked for Mr. Tekworgy on and off. I worked on Mr. Tekworgy's jiggers. He has two jiggers, one lighter than the other. There are moveable sideboards for the lighter jigger; it is a dropped axle jigger. His horse would have been white had it been clean.
STATE: When did you see Mr. Tekworgy again?
WITNESS: I saw Mr. Tekworgy some months later after the body was found. My Grandfather, Jerri Mank and I went to Mr. Tekworgy and spoke with him. I went there for a purpose which grandfather did not know about. I told Mr. Tekworgy the authorities were after me for moving that body. Mr. Tekworgy then threatened me saying, 'Keep your mouth shut, they can't prove we moved it! If you talk it will ruin everything!' He accompanied his remark with a violent gesture!
STATE: How long was Mr. Tekworgy gone when he got off his jigger?
WITNESS: Not more than fifteen minutes when he moved the body.
STATE: Did you hear any noise as though someone jumped a fence?
WITNESS: I did not hear any sound as though a person had climbed or jumped over a fence.

The Defense Attorney Bellows then cross-examined Joe Bogg, a questionable witness at best! Attorney Bellows went after him heavily. There were many questions that Mr. Bellows vigorously asked, and could not get sworn answers to from the preliminary hearing.

ATTORNEY BELLOWS CROSS-EXAMINES MR. JOE BOGG:

DEFENSE: Mr. Bogg, are you sure you did not see anyone other than Mr. Tekworgy at the scene of the crime?
WITNESS: I told you, I did not see anyone else there.
DEFENSE: Didn't you hear another person jump the fence?

WITNESS: No one else was there just Mr. Tekworgy.
DEFENSE: Mr. Bogg, at the preliminary hearing did you swear you did not see Mr. Tekworgy on the Saturday in question when you screened coal?
WITNESS: No, I did not swear to it.
DEFENSE: Mr. Bogg, can you now swear that it was starlight that night and not dark?
WITNESS: No.
DEFENSE: Can you swear Mr. Tekworgy's horse was in front of his store when you first saw him?
WITNESS: No.
DEFENSE: Can you swear it was 10:00 o'clock when you got home?
WITNESS: No.
DEFENSE: What about telling your wife's sister, you would lie if you had to?
WITNESS: No, I never told her I would lie.
DEFENSE: Did you talk with Joe Mank, your Uncle, at the Orland fair about Mr. Tekworgy being the reason Sarah was missing?
WITNESS: Yes, I told him Mr. Tekworgy was suspected for the reason that Sarah Ware could not be found. I never liked Mr. Tekworgy, but I worked for him because I needed money for my family. I felt a good deal better after I told the detectives my story.
DEFENSE: Didn't you tell Joe Mank it was you they suspected and not Mr. Tekworgy?
WITNESS: NO!
DEFENSE: Where were you born?
WITNESS: I was born in Orland, my father's name is Joseph Mank.
DEFENSE: What is your mother's name?
WITNESS: My mother is Avellia Bogg. Her maiden name was Mank.
DEFENSE: Does your mother have a brother named Joseph Mank?
WITNESS: Yes, her brother is Joseph Mank.

THE STATE THEN ASKED FOR
A RE-DIRECT OF JOE BOGG:

STATE: Mr. Bogg what was your conversation about when you spoke with your Uncle, Joe Mank at the Orland fair?

First, Joe Mank is his father then he is his Uncle. What a twirled up mind this young man had! He can't tell the difference between seeing and hearing!

WITNESS: I told my Uncle, Joe Mank about the Ware case. I told him people knew Sarah Ware was missing, and that Will Tekworgy was the suspected man. On or around September 28th, my Uncle, Joe Mank spoke with the detectives and then the detectives asked me if I told my Uncle about the murder. I told my uncle I knew it was him and Will Tekworgy that were trying to make me look like the guilty party.

Why did Joe Bogg believe his father to be Joe Mank when he was not? Did stress bring on his psychotic insecurities again about his father? Why didn't the State question this statement? Did the State suspect that people already knew about Joe's mental disability? It had been at that point that Joe Bogg had been allowed to step down and another witness, Mr. Willham, had been called to the stand as a State's witness.

Mr. WILLHAM'S TESTIMONY WAS BRIEF
AND TO THE POINT:

STATE: Mr. Willham, when did Sarah Ware work for you and what did she do for work?

WITNESS: Sarah Ware worked for me cleaning my house for a number of months. She had worked for me in the summer of 1898. I paid Sarah $65.00 earlier that year. I gave the money to her in $5 bills.

At that point the Defense did not question Mr. Willham.

THE STATE CALLED MILDRED WARE, SARAH'S DAUGHTER:

STATE: Tell us your name please and how your are related to Sarah Ware.
WITNESS: My name is Mildred Ware. I am the daughter of the deceased Sarah Ware.
STATE: Where are you presently living?
WITNESS: In Massachusetts with my Uncle, my mother's brother. Edward, my brother, lives there too.
STATE: Do you recognize these rings, exhibit H and this handbag, exhibit C?
WITNESS: Yes, they belonged to my mother. I don't know why anyone would want to kill my mother!
STATE: Are you currently staying with Mrs. Files?
WITNESS: No, I am not.
STATE: Where are you staying?
WITNESS: I am staying in my deceased Uncle Ware's home.
STATE: When did your Uncle Ware pass away?
WITNESS: About one year ago.
STATE: Thank you, Miss Ware.

The Defense declined cross-examination of Mildred Ware.
Being almost noon the Judge called an adjournment until 2:00 o'clock.

Mildred Ware slowly walked toward the large oak doors at the back of the courtroom where the spectators had begun to filter out. The doors led down the wide winding wooden staircase to the lower floor of the courthouse. She felt stifled, almost to the point of suffocating. She needed to reach the double glass doors that opened on to the large wide cement steps outside. *I need to breathe the fresh air,* she thought.

Finally, after what seemed an eternity she was outside. She could see the tall oak tree at the far right corner of the spacious green lawn where it had stood tall and proud for many years. A wooden bench was in the shade that the oak leaves provided. Hurrying to be alone with her private thoughts of her mother, she still felt as if she was on display in the courtroom during her testimony. She could still feel many eyes watching her every move.

Sitting on the bench she privately kept asking herself, why would anyone want to murder my mother, why? She may not have walked among the elite citizens of Bucksport, but she was a kind person. She meant no harm to anyone! She had to do what she had to do in order to support my brother Edward and me.

Mother, I remember once in one of your letters you told me about a black servant, Jacob, who wanted to learn how to read and write. He worked and also lived at Captain Spurling's residence on Main Street. The Captain demeaned him constantly. I remember how you met Jacob; it was in the Finson and Brown Grocery. You had gone there for Mrs. Files to purchase some needed supplies. He was having difficulty reading the labels on the merchandise and you offered to help him.

Jacob and you had developed a friendship. Discreet as it was, it was a friendship neither of you could share openly. Jacob was a poor black servant and mother, you were thought of as poor white trash. Mother, I have respect and love for you, for you did what a friend would do; you taught Jacob to read and write!

Mrs. Files

CHAPTER SIXTEEN

STATE CONTINUES

At the afternoon session, the question of taking the jury to Bucksport to view the premises that the Attorney General had requested was argued and the presiding Justice A. Lemery decided that for the present the trip was not to be made. The Bucksport City Engineer being on the stand for some time explained the trip was necessary to show the territory on the map, which he had made and was displayed in the courtroom. However, the trip did not come to pass.

THE STATE THEN PROCEEDED TO CALL DETECTIVE HACEY AS A WITNESS:

The following shows information from Detective Hacey that he had withheld until the trial.

STATE: You are the detective that worked up this case, are you not?
WITNESS: Yes, I am.
STATE: Tell the court what you have learned.
WITNESS: I have spent considerable time working on the Ware Case. I talked with Mr. Tekworgy on November 7, 1898. I met him on the street in Bucksport. He asked me, 'Don't you think that the remarks made at the Citizens Meeting were personal and pointing?' I replied, "I do not wish to make any comments at this time." He continued to ask me about the reward. I

told him that money was a bad thing, and he said, 'Yes, murder is sometimes committed for it!'

STATE: Did you speak with Mr. Tekworgy again after that?

WITNESS: Yes, on December 12th, I talked with him when Sheriff Genn and I searched Mr. Tekworgy's premises. In his carriage house we found a claw hammer under the cushion in the carriage. I had it examined by Professor Hinkley in Orono and it was inconclusive.

STATE: Did you ask Mr. Tekworgy about Mrs. Ware's missing Bible and diary?

WITNESS: Yes, Mr. Tekworgy first stated he did have a Bible and a diary that belonged to Sarah Ware, and later he refuted his statement saying he did not.

STATE: What else can you tell us about your investigation when questioning Mr. Tekworgy?

WITNESS: He told me, 'I was at the File's house on the evening of September 17, 1898. I was hauling vegetables from my garden between 4:00 and 5:00 that afternoon.' He also said he took the book without any reason, he just wanted it. He said, 'Sarah and I had talked about my having her Bible and diary and that she wanted them returned. I told her that I would return them the next day.' However, we still have not located the missing diary and Bible therefore Mr. Tekworgy must know where they are! I said to Mr. Tekworgy, "Wasn't Sarah angry about you having her personal property?" 'Oh no,' replied Mr. Tekworgy. I questioned him about what time he went to bed on the night of September 17, 1898 and he said, 'I don't remember.'

The Defense listened intensely to the testimony given by Detective Hacey.

DEFENSE ATTORNEY BELLOWS THEN GAVE DETECTIVE HACEY A GRUELING CROSS-EXAMINATION:

DEFENSE: Detective Hacey, where was Mr. Tekworgy when you made a visit to his carriage house?

WITNESS: Mr. Tekworgy was standing at his workbench in his barn when I went to see him. He is a tin worker as well as a department store owner. He made no objections to me searching his premises. He readily took off his work jacket and remained in the barn.
DEFENSE: What did you discover?
WITNESS: Detective Odland, who was also with me, dug around in a little shed next to the stables. Mr. Tekworgy didn't ask any questions as to what we were doing. In the carriage we found a medium sized claw hammer under the cushion that was examined and found inconclusive. The window curtains of his carriage were removed and lay over a piece of canvas.
DEFENSE: Did you examine the canvas?
WITNESS: Yes, the canvas had bloodstains on it.
DEFENSE: Wasn't the blood pig blood?
WITNESS: We had the canvas examined and it could not be determined whether it was human or pig blood.
DEFENSE: Have you spoken with Joe Bogg about this case?
WITNESS: Yes, I have spoken with Joe Bogg many times.
DEFENSE: Wasn't it Joe Bogg who stated to you that Sarah Ware was wrapped in a canvas?
WITNESS: Yes, he told me this.
DEFENSE: Did you ask Joe Bogg how he had knowledge of the canvas being in Mr. Tekworgy's carriage?
WITNESS: No, I did not.
DEFENSE: Couldn't Mr. Bogg have put the soiled canvas in the carriage himself?
WITNESS: Not according to Mr. Bogg's statement.

When the Defense Attorney was finished questioning this witness he was asked to step down.

The next witness called for the State again was **Mrs. Files** with whom Mrs. Ware resided prior to her disappearance. Mrs. Files is a kindly faced elderly woman with a pleasant voice and cheerful manner, unless she is provoked. She sat in the courtroom since the beginning of the trial. Her smile was warm and her determined gait indicated one of great interest in the proceedings. When she took her place upon the *stand she was clothed completely in black. She wore a bonnet and long black veil in mourning for her friend Sarah.*

STATE: Please, tell the court your name.
WITNESS: Mrs. Alvira Files.
STATE: Mrs. Files, would Sarah, while working out, sometimes stay at her employer's residence?
WITNESS: Yes, Sarah frequently, when working, stayed for days and even weeks without letting me know with whom she lived or where she was. Sarah received no wages for her labor at my house. She just received board.
STATE: Can you tell the court if she said anything to you about a relationship with Mr. Tekworgy?
WITNESS: She and William Tekworgy always appeared to be good friends. Although shortly before her disappearance she mentioned she was somewhat nervous about him. She told me she had something of an important nature to discuss with him, but she did not tell me what it was.
STATE: Please, tell us in your own words about the events just before you realized she was missing.
WITNESS: The first time I became worried about Sarah's absence was on Thursday of the second week of her absence.
STATE: At what point did you realize Sarah was not working, but was missing?
WITNESS: I found out she was missing when Captain John Calder told me. He said, 'Sarah Ware started from Mr. Bolder's house to go home and that she went across the pasture.'
STATE: Did he tell you how he knew this?
WITNESS: I did not ask him how he knew this.
STATE: Can you tell us what you know happened after that?
WITNESS: I asked Mr. Tekworgy to go to Mr. Bolder's house to see about Sarah. She sometimes would live in the home of families where she worked. She had stayed at Fred Moss' when cleaning his house.
STATE: Where was Mrs. Ware's room in your house?
WITNESS: Mrs. Sarah Ware had a room upstairs on the north

	side of my house. Mr. Tekworgy had a vegetable garden also on the north side of my house and he occasionally did some work for me.
STATE:	When did you last see Sarah Ware?
WITNESS:	The last time I saw Sarah Ware was on September 17, 1898. She left the house at 6:00 P.M. to go shopping for Sunday dinner. When she came back Mrs. Ware went directly to her room. When she came down we had a bite to eat, talked and then she went out the back door.
STATE:	When she left what was she wearing?
WITNESS:	She took a large cape that hung in the shed and put it over one arm. She always carried a small handbag that was faded black in color. I don't know if she had it that night.
STATE:	Mrs. Files, these are exhibits J-1 and J-2, the handbag and the cape. I ask you is this the handbag, and the cape that Sarah took that night?
WITNESS:	Yes, it is the cape. The handbag is not the one Mrs. Ware had, it was blacker than that one. *Then she proceeded to lay it aside abruptly!*
STATE:	Can you tell us more about that night Mrs. Files?
WITNESS:	When Mrs. Ware returned she gave me my change. This was the change from the dollar bill I gave her to get Sunday dinner. She told me where she was going when she left. She said, 'I am going to Mr. Bolder's.'
STATE:	Can you describe what the weather was like when she left?
WITNESS:	It was a dark night. I could scarcely see my hand before my face. The weather had changed and Sarah put a green waterproof over her arm. About 10:00 o'clock that night I lay down on the couch anticipating Sarah would return shortly.
STATE:	Did you tell anyone during the week that Sarah was absent?
WITNESS:	Yes, I told several people that Sarah was absent and that I did not know of her whereabouts.

STATE: Can you tell us anything more about Mr. Tekworgy's Sunday dinners?

WITNESS: Mr. Tekworgy came to my house usually on Sundays after church and stopped for dinner. His daughter most always accompanied him. He was at my house Sunday, September 18, 1898, but he was not at my house on Saturday, September 17, 1898 and he was there the following Sunday.

STATE: Was there a card game at your house on September 17, 1898?

WITNESS: No, there wasn't a poker game at my house on Saturday, September 17, 1898!

STATE: Did you see Mr. Tekworgy after Mrs. Ware's body was found?

WITNESS: Mr. Tekworgy came to my house the day Sarah's body was found in October. He did not stop for long. I am not sure if he came the day after that.

STATE: When was the next time he came to visit?

WITNESS: He and his daughter came the following week on a Wednesday and stayed for four days. He slept in the room next to that of Mrs. Ware

STATE: Did Mr. Tekworgy have access to Mrs. Ware's room in any way?

WITNESS: There was a door between the two rooms.

STATE: Could Mr. Tekworgy enter Sarah Ware's room?

WITNESS: Yes, Mr. Tekworgy could have gone into Sarah's room without me noticing. The door was not locked from Sarah's side. I slept downstairs as well as his daughter.

STATE: Did any detectives come to your house?

WITNESS: I couldn't say if there was a detective at my house or not. I wouldn't know one if I saw one! Oh Yes! A man by the name of Mr. Henderson came and said he was a detective! He came on Saturday before Sarah's body was found. He was there about an hour asking me questions and he told me he was going to Mr. Bolder's. I went upstairs to see which way he was going and watched him go up Miles Lane. I saw him until he nearly got to Mr. Nickerson's pasture. He jumped over the fence and came back again in about three or four minutes and then he crossed the Swazey field. I thought this was odd! I did not trust him!

STATE: I understand that William Bogg and Mr. Bolder went upstairs in your home on October 2nd and according to Detective Hacey they took something from Sarah's room. Did these men do this?

WITNESS: No! Mr. William Bogg and Mr. Bolder did not go upstairs in my home on Sunday October 2$^{nd.}$ I do know, that is what these two men told Detective Hacey! Why they said this I don't know!

STATE: Could they have entered your house without you knowing it?

WITNESS: Possibly, because after dinner Mr. Tekworgy offered a ride in his carriage to his daughter and myself which was unusual!

STATE: Do you have any idea what these two men could have done in Sarah's room?

WITNESS: No, I do not know! I was not there!

DEFENSE ATTORNY BELLOWS CROSS-EXAMINES MRS. FILES:

DEFENSE: Mrs. Files, did you, or did you not ask Mr. Tekworgy to go to Mr. Bolder's house when you became concerned about Sarah's disappearance?

WITNESS: Yes! I did ask Mr. Tekworgy to go to Mr. Boulder's to see if Sarah Ware was there.

DEFENSE: Didn't you ask him to go to Captain Calder's house instead of Mr. Bolder's house?

WITNESS: No, I did not tell him to go see Captain Calder! I went to see Mrs. Calder and the Captain!

DEFENSE: Isn't it true that Mr. Tekworgy went to Mr. Bolder's house and he found no one at home?

WITNESS: Well, that is what he said, but he did not tell me this directly!

DEFENSE: Do you know if Captain Calder had a poker game at his house the night in question?

WITNESS: I know that Sarah told me she was going to Captain Calder's house for a poker game that night in Joe Bogg's room. She also mentioned there was a poker game at Mr. Bolder's house that same night.

DEFENSE: Weren't you worried for Sarah going to Joe Bogg's poker game because of the rowdy behavior of the players?

WITNESS: Not really, I felt Sarah could handle herself.

DEFENSE: When did you go to see Mrs. Calder?

WITNESS: On the Thursday of the second week after Sarah went away, I went to Mrs. Calder's to speak to the Captain. I asked him to go in the Tannery and tell Mr. Bolder, please tell Sarah to come home and get her clothes because I was angry with her at repeatedly staying away without telling me.

DEFENSE: Do you know of any animosity between Sarah and Captain Calder?

WITNESS: No, I never discovered any coolness between the Captain and Sarah before Sarah disappeared.

DEFENSE: Didn't you in fact check Miles Lane for Sarah knowing that it was her usual route to take on her way home?

WITNESS: It is Mr. Swazey's Lane you are referring to and I have not been up there. Miles Lane is south of Pond Street from my house!

DEFENSE: You knew that Sarah had money that night didn't you?

WITNESS: Yes, I knew she carried a sum of money with her the night in question. She had given me my change earlier; then she went upstairs to get money from her room before leaving that night. All I know of her having money, is the money Mr. Willham paid her for cleaning.

DEFENSE: Didn't you go into Mrs. Ware's room to see if she took the sixty-five dollars Mr. Willham paid her?

WITNESS: No, I first entered Sarah's room to see if I could discover any reason for her being missing. Mrs. Ballinger, a friend was with me. I think, the next time I went into her room was with Sarah's daughter Mildred after the body was found. However, I believe I went in with Sheriff Genn when he searched the house.
DEFENSE: No more questions at this time your Honor.

When court was dismissed for the day Mrs. Files and Mr. Bolder were met and interviewed by a reporter from one of the local papers;

The Ellsworth Eagle. The title of the story was as follows:

AN UNPUBLISHED STORY

Statements of Mrs. Files and Mr. Bolder, but never before printed.

Mrs. Files stated that when Mrs. Ware went out she had said, "Don't worry as I am only going out to a friend and will not be gone long." When ten o'clock came and Sarah did not return I became worried and I did not retire but sat and watched for the absent one; though I dozed on occasion. The next day Mr. Tekworgy and his daughter came to my house to have tea. I told Mr. Tekworgy about Sarah's going away and requested that he go over to John Bolder's and see if she was there, which he promised me he would do.

I did not see Mr. Tekworgy again for a day or two. When he called next I asked if he had been to Mr. Bolder's and he said yes, but the doors were locked and the curtains down and he supposed that Sarah had returned home, but that he would go again and see.

Mr. Tekworgy called again in a few days and told me he visited John's and that Mr. Bolder told him that Sarah had not been there, except for a few moments on Saturday evening. I became worried, but gave no alarm as I supposed that Mr. Tekworgy was endeavoring to learn what had become of her."

FEARED TEKWORGY

Mrs. Files said, "Mr. Tekworgy and his daughter stayed with me a few nights after finding the body of Sarah so that I should not be alone." Mrs. Files further added, "In substance he acted queer, he appeared to have an aversion to remaining longer in the house than was absolutely necessary. He would come late at night and left as early as possible in the morning."

When asked what the relations between Mrs. Ware and Mr. Tekworgy were, she replied, "I don't think that they were any great friends, for Sarah had an aversion to being alone with him and had often told me that she was afraid of him."

Did she ever say why she was afraid of him? "No, not that I recollect of."

MRS. FILES ANGRY

Mrs. Files is the elderly lady with whom Sarah Ware lived with for a number of years prior to her death and from whose house she went forth on the fatal night in September nearly four years ago. Mrs. Files is angry at what she terms the abuse that has been heaped upon her by the people of Bucksport.

Mrs. Files is 81 years old though she would tell you she was 70 or even 65. When angry she does not raise her voice to an extraordinary pitch nor forget to be extremely polite. When talking to her, her temper is unruffled, constantly uses the expression, 'Dearie' and rubs her hands together. When the least bit angry she forgets both of these.

'They've abused me shamefully sir,' she said the other day in talking to a visitor who hadn't mentioned the Ware case at all, 'Shamefully, and I never did none of them any harm. How could I, an old woman of 81 years of age? I never did anything that was wrong in all my life!'

Continuing on Mrs. Files said, 'I'll make 'em suffer for the way they've treated me. I'll send em behind bars for talking of me as they have. I've got the money to do it with, too, plenty of it and

I'm going to! I tell you sir, I never gave them any reason to talk about me as they have. I'm going to punish them for it too for they have no right to do so. Do you blame me sir? Where do you come from sir, from Bangor? Well, I threw a Bangor man right out this door once, it was that skunk Detective Hacey. He had the effrontery to accuse me of having men room here. I told him that I'd give him $50.00 if he could find a man that ever came here and he said, he didn't know them, but it was so. He reached for a revolver and I got up and ordered him out of the house and he went, I tell you.

Mr. Bunker, who was County Attorney then, was with poor Mr. Genn who is dead now. At that time Mr. Bunker got up and took hold of Sheriff Genn's hand and said, 'Mrs. Files, if the whole world should tell me you are guilty of running a house of ill repute, I wouldn't believe it!'

TORE UP THE DOOR STEP

'Yes, sir, they've abused me fearfully and shamefully and I never gave them cause! Why, one day a man asked me where did I keep my money, and I told him under the doorstep. I always did do that if any men came to get it they wouldn't have to come into the house! No men ever come into my house. What do you think? Within a few days when I got up one morning, someone had torn up this very step to get that money!'

RAT HOLES MEASURED

'They dragged me over to Ellsworth twice and are going to do it again and what for I don't know. What did ever a poor old woman like me do? They harassed me, terrible. They measured every room in the house. Even to my chamber, and the only things they haven't measured are the two rat holes in one of the rooms. If they want to measure them I wish they would come and do it and leave me alone. But I'll punish those who have abused me; I will!'

WHEN COURT WAS RESUMED THE FOLLOWING DAY THE STATE BROUGHT FORTH ITS NEXT WITNESS EX-CONSTABE DANIEL DANVERS:

STATE: Tell the court your name please.
WITNESS: My name is Daniel Danvers.
STATE: Were you the Constable of Bucksport at the time of Sarah Ware's murder?
WITNESS: Yes, I was.
STATE: Did you know the victim Sarah Ware?
WITNESS: Yes, I knew Sarah Ware very well.
STATE: How well did you know her?
WITNESS: Well, she had worked at my house cleaning on a regular basis after my first wife died. Occasionally Sarah would visit with my present wife and me while not cleaning, we always enjoyed her company.
STATE: When did you last see Mrs. Ware?
WITNESS: I saw her last on September 15th or 16th of 1898. I first heard of her disappearance on the 29th. I told my wife of this.
STATE: When Mrs. Ware would work at your house, did she have any visitors?
WITNESS: Yes, Mr. Tekworgy would visit a number of times to see Sarah while cleaning. It was annoying. She had asked him several times not to visit her while she was working.
STATE: Did you or your wife do anything when you heard of Mrs. Ware's disappearance?
WITNESS: Yes. After I told my wife, I went to Mrs. Files to see if she knew that Sarah was missing. She said, 'Yes.' The next morning I went to Sheriff Genn's office to tell him. The office workers told me they already knew about it and that Sheriff Genn and Selectman Pall had gone to see Mrs. Files.
STATE: Did Sheriff Genn ask you to help look for Mrs. Ware?
WITNESS: Yes, Sheriff Genn and Selectman Pall told me to go

and look for Mrs. Ware. I went to the places I knew she worked, to see if she was there. I did not find her at any of the places I called on. Not finding her, I organized a search party to look for her. It was on Saturday while searching near Nicholson pasture, near Miles Lane, that I saw wheel marks going in. I did not go into the pasture until the next day. That was when I saw hay had been cut, and that the hay looked to be spread over the ground, covering the wheel tracks I had seen the day before. I continued into the pasture and saw where alder bushes had been bent down.

STATE: Did you see anything where the alder bushes were bent?

WITNESS: Yes, when I saw a body, I was convinced it was that of Sarah Ware. The alders had been bent and leaning toward the body. I saw an old waterproof that looked like the one Sarah had worn many times which lay on a bush next to her head.

STATE: Did you see anything else?

WITNESS: Yes, her hair switch was about fifty or sixty feet away.

STATE: Mr. Danvers, I show you this waterproof, is this the one you saw?

WITNESS: Yes, it appears to be the same one.

STATE: Tell us more of your observation at the scene, Mr. Danvers.

WITNESS: Well, when I looked at the body I saw that the right side of her face, at the jaw line, had been crushed in and the other side of her head had been crushed as well. There was a bump with a bruise the size of a large hen's egg accompanied with deep dark, discolored marks.

STATE: Mr. Danvers is this the same skull you just described to the court?

WITNESS: Yes, it appears to be the same crushed, deteriorated skull I saw.

STATE: Mr. Danvers when you found Mrs. Ware was Mr. Tekworgy with you?

WITNESS: No one was with me, I was alone.
STATE: Did Mr. Tekworgy and you ever have a talk about him accompanying you in the search?
WITNESS: Yes however, he refused to accompany me in searching for Sarah Ware.

DEFENSE ATTORNY BELLOWS CROSS-EXAMINES DANIEL DANVERS:

DEFENSE: Did Mr. Tekworgy and you ever have a conversation about who organized the search party for Mrs. Ware?
WITNESS: It was a long time later. I remember it was on April 11, of 1900.
DEFENSE: What did you and he discuss?
WITNESS: Mr. Tekworgy came to my house and we had a conversation regarding the organization of the search party. During our conversation I remember telling Mr. Tekworgy, "I thought that in some way Selectman Pall knew something about the murder of Sarah Ware." Mr. Tekworgy replied to me emphatically, 'I don't think he does, I know he does!' Then he said to me, 'If ever this murderer is found out, there will be more men go to Thomaston State Prison than you've got fingers and toes, Dan Danvers, and they will be the white shirt men, too!'
DEFENSE: So in your opinion Mr. Danvers, do you feel Mr. Tekworgy was saying he suspected Selectman Pall?
WITNESS: Yes, I think that was what he was implying.

It was at this point that Defense Attorney Bellows spoke to the Judge at the bench.

DEFENSE: Your Honor, there may be some things of an offensive nature to the ladies and they may want to leave the courtroom.
JUDGE LEMERY: They will just have to abide by it, this is a trial.

After the Judge's statement court continued:

DEFENSE: Mr. Danvers, when did Sarah Ware first start working for you cleaning your house?
WITNESS: It was after my first wife passed away six years ago.
DEFENSE: Were you and Sarah intimate before your second marriage?
WITNESS: No. Not at all!
DEFENSE: Your job was Constable at the time of Sarah Ware's death, is that right?
WITNESS: Yes, that's right, and I worked on the case. I was working under Sheriff Genn's instructions, so I made all my reports to him and he in turn reported to Selectman Pall. He requested at the time, I engage another person to accompany me in the search for Sarah Ware.
DEFENSE: Were you present when Mrs. Ware's body was buried?
WITNESS: Yes, I was there when the body was buried in the pauper lot at the Silver Lake Cemetery. I don't think a funeral was ever held.
DEFENSE: Was anyone in attendance at the burial?
WITNESS: Yes, Mrs. Files was, and a few officials.

Detective Hacey

CHAPTER SEVENTEEN

CRUCIAL TESTIMONIES

The next day, Tuesday, July of 1902, pertained again to the murder of Sarah Ware against William Tekworgy. The confidence of the Detectives led to feeling there was enough evidence to convict Mr. Tekworgy of this grisly murder!

Mr. Tekworgy had once again been brought into the courtroom. He maintained, with no exception, the same self-possessed demeanor as before and showed neither by look nor action that he was the most popular person in the room, or unpopular as the case may be!

This day, during the trial, Mr. Tekworgy was dressed fashionably and as before, was clean shaved with his dark hair neatly combed. It seemed people Tekworgy knew were scattered throughout the courtroom, some within his range of vision. Mr. Tekworgy greeted them with a kindly nod and smiled.

One time, when a witness was being examined, Mr. Tekworgy leaned forward slightly, opened his mouth as if to say something and with a hint of nervousness apparently changed his mind. There had been no change of color in his face from the attack of various witnesses. It was only for an instant that his color changed; it was the State's witness, Coroner Fields who spoke about Sarah's crushed head as it was shown in evidence. He then went back to his impenetrable self. Mr. Tekworgy would occasionally turn toward his Attorney Mr. Bellows, at the same time showing signs of distress on his face.

WITNESS FOR THE STATE, WILLIAM BOGG:

STATE: Sir, state your name for the court.
WITNESS: William Bogg, Joe Bogg's father.
STATE: Where do you live, and what is your occupation?
WITNESS: I have been a resident of Bucksport for ten years. I am familiar with the law. I was a policeman in another state before living in Bucksport. I keep a store in Bucksport, on the corner of Central Street.
STATE: Did you see Sarah Ware on September 17, 1898?
WITNESS: I did not see Mrs. Ware on the night of the 17th. My wife saw her in the store that night. I was in the kitchen of the house adjoining the store when Sarah Ware came in. I heard her talking and I recognized her voice. It was probably about 8 o'clock.
STATE: How were you involved with the search party?
WITNESS: When I heard that Sarah Ware was missing I went with Mr. Bolder and joined the search party. First we went to Mrs. File's house and found Mrs. Files was the only one at home. We looked all through the house then left through the front room on the south side. Mrs. Files then led us to the west side of her house to visibly see the view of Miles Lane. We looked up the Lane, then went to get others to help with the search. Groups took different parts of the lane. Within a short time others came and went up the lane to a maple tree. An easterly direction was then taken that led into the pasture.
STATE: After the body was found, did you ever return to the scene of the crime?
WITNESS: Yes, and I saw alders broken down as though a team had passed over them.

DEFENSE ATTORNEY BELLOWS CROSS-EXAMINES WILLIAM BOGG:

DEFENSE: Mr. Bogg, did you examine the garment Sarah Ware wore?

WITNESS: No, I did not, but there was a waterproof I saw when the body was found. The garment exhibited is not the same waterproof. I am positive of it. It is not the same one I saw in the pasture with my son Joe Bogg. We saw it in the interim between the body having been found and the removal that night. Joe showed me how the waterproof had been placed. It was in the same manner as he saw it with the head of Mrs. Ware on a portion of it.
DEFENSE: How do you know about the stone wall?
WITNESS: My son pointed the stone wall out to me.
DEFENSE: When did you go to the stone wall?
WITNESS: My son and I went to the wall after Sarah's body had been removed and Joe was released from the Ellsworth City Jail. We went alone and stayed about an hour. Joe and I felt heartsick over what had happened to Mrs. Ware.
DEFENSE: Did you and your son speak about Joe Mank?
WITNESS: No, we did not.

After a brief recess, Mr. Bogg was recalled and again questioned about the waterproof. He said that since his direct examination for the State about the question of the waterproof, he then was convinced it was the one Mrs. Ware wore.

THE NEXT WITNESS FOR THE STATE WAS IVAN RICHARDSON:

STATE: Where did you live in 1898?
WITNESS: I lived in Bucksport in 1898.
STATE: Did you know Mrs. Sarah Ware?
WITNESS: Yes, I knew her.
STATE: Were you with the men in the searching party that found Mrs. Ware?
WITNESS: Yes, I was. The body was near the head of Captain Nicholson's pasture.
STATE: Tell the court how you found Mrs. Ware's body.

WITNESS: As we proceeded up this path we could smell the odor of a severe stench, so we followed it, and we came to the body of a dead woman.
STATE: Describe to us what the body looked like.
WITNESS: The dress was up to the knees, and her hands were crossed on her chest. Her waist shirt and corset were open. I saw a garment on some bushes. These bushes were about four feet in height. The jaw of the head was shattered. I recognized the body as that of Mrs. Ware. I felt sure there had been foul play so I notified the authorities right away.

This testimony is entirely different than any preceding information. The clothing is described differently.

STATE: Do you recognize this mackintosh?
WITNESS: Yes, it is the garment I saw on the bushes, near the body.

Why would this garment be on the bushes, when it has consistently been found under her head?

STATE: Were you present Sunday October 2nd when Mrs. Ware's body was placed in a box on a wagon bed?
WITNESS: Yes, I helped put the body in the box.
STATE: Tell us what happened at that time.
WITNESS: Mr. Tekworgy was there and as I went to lift the body by the shoulders with another person at the foot end, Mr. Tekworgy ran to me and grabbed my shoulders to stop me. It was at that point Mrs. Ware's head rolled away from her body and had to be put in separately.

According to the testimony of Ivan Richardson Mr. Tekworgy attempted to grab his shoulders to stop him from moving Mrs. Ware. Why would Mr. Tekworgy do this?

ATTORNEY BELLOWS CROSS-EXAMINES MR. RICHARDSON:

DEFENSE: Don't you think Mr. Tekworgy was trying to be helpful?
WITNESS: Well, maybe he was.
DEFENSE: And what time was the body placed in the box?
WITNESS: It was probably around midnight that we placed the body in the box.
DEFENSE: Who else was there when this was done?
WITNESS: Besides the undertaker, Mr. Ware; I think there was Mr. Googons who went in with his team; Dr. Lemerson, William Bogg, Mr. Tekworgy and myself."

At that point, he looked at the Doctor and said, "am I right Dr. Lemerson"? The Doctor didn't answer the question!

DEFENSE: Did you see her hair switch and hat?
WITNESS: Yes, It was trodden down so much that it took considerable strength to get it removed from the ground. Her hat was found under her right hip. It was so badly damaged and crushed that I can't really describe it.
DEFENSE: Her neck at that time was in what position?
WITNESS: Her neck was bent down to her corset. I don't remember if the scalp was intact, but the flesh was very much decomposed.
DEFENSE: Who took charge of the body?
WITNESS: Mr. Ware, the undertaker, who was Mrs. Ware's brother-in-law, took charge of the body.
DEFENSE: Are you sure Mr. Tekworgy was there with you and the others, when the body was put in the pauper's box?
WITNESS: Yes, he was there that night and carried a lantern and also a number of times during the day.
DEFENSE: Did you see a rock near the body?

WITNESS: Yes, I saw a sizeable one near the body.
DEFENSE: Did you know Mrs. Ware well?
WITNESS: Yes, I knew her quite well.
DEFENSE: Was she heavy?
WITNESS: She was not overly heavy. When we put her in the box Mr. Tekworgy said to me, he thought several men could carry her up the lane.
DEFENSE: Now that you have identified her, how much would you say she weighed?
WITNESS: Well I don't know! I have never weighed many women and it would have to be guesswork!
DEFENSE: Just take a guess then!
WITNESS: Oh probably about 150 pounds!
DEFENSE: As to the clothing, are you sure you described them correctly?
WITNESS: How would I know, I never bought women's dresses, but those were badly stained!
DEFENSE: Aren't you mistaken about her weight according to what Mr. Tekworgy said to you?
WITNESS: No, I am not. I said to Mr. Tekwowrgy, "I don't believe she could have been brought up here alone and that a team must have been used, she was too heavy." Mr. Tekworgy had said, 'Oh I don't know, she's not so heavy, I guess several men could have carried her.'

THIS WITNESS WAS THEN EXCUSED AND THE NEXT WITNESS FOR THE STATE WAS THE HANCOCK CORONER MR. L. D. FIELDS:

STATE: Tell us your name and what your occupation was in 1898.
WITNESS: My name is Lyle D. Fields and I reside in Ellsworth. In 1898 I had been the Hancock County Coroner. I was called to Bucksport the night of October 2, 1898. I viewed Mrs. Ware at the site, then ordered the body removed to the Silver Lake Cemetery. George Ware

was the undertaker at that time and he removed her body to his funeral parlor located on Elm Street.

STATE: When did you see the body again?

WITNESS: I saw the body again during the inquest.

STATE: Did you see any depressions on the skull at that time?

WITNESS: I can't say if I did or did not. I did see the broken jaw bone.

STATE: Going back to October 4th, in 1898, were you in Bucksport?

WITNESS: Yes I was. County Attorney Bunker accompanied me. We got there about 9: 00 o'clock that day and visited a number of places in town returning to Ellsworth that night.

STATE: Did you go to Mrs. File's house?

WITNESS: I visited the File's house with Mr. Bunker. Mr. Tekworgy and others were there. Attorney Bunker and I searched Mrs. Ware's room. We searched two trunks, looking for her bankbook, handbag and money. We took each article out and shook it to see if anything was concealed. We made a thorough search. We also carefully examined the trays of the trunks. The second trunk did not contain so much stuff, so we did not remove those trays. (*When a search is being conducted, everything is searched!*) We did not find any of the articles we were trying to locate. One dollar was found under corsets. We moved furniture in order to get behind the commode. When we searched Mrs. Ware's room we found 10 cents in a pocketbook under some clothes in a drawer.

STATE: When did you see the skull again?

WITNESS: On October 3, 1898 after having made an examination of the body at the Silver Lake Cemetery tomb. After the inquest, I gave the skull to Mr. Ware. Mr. George Ware is dead now.

STATE: You were shown a rock at the inquest, was anything on it?

WITNESS: Yes, I was shown a rock at the inquest and examined it.

No blood, hair or flesh was on the rock. The rock, personal effects and Sarah's head were turned over to Sheriff Genn at that time whereupon he brought them to the tomb.

DEFENSE ATTORNEY BELLOWS CROSS-EXAMINATION OF CORONER FIELDS:

DEFENSE: Coroner Fields, did you move the body when you saw it in the woods?
WITNESS: No, I did not move the body when it was in the woods. I ordered the body to be removed. I saw a hat under the body with a mackintosh near it.
DEFENSE: Did you make a careful examination of the body when you saw it that night?
WITNESS: From what I saw that night, I didn't think it was necessary for an examination at that point. The next morning with all the talk, it was evident an inquest had become necessary.
DEFENSE: Did anyone accompany you to where the body was in the woods at a later date?
WITNESS: Yes, Selectman Pall and I went. Then later we went to Mrs. File's house.
DEFENSE: Was anything found in the waterproof?
WITNESS: Yes, a cheroot was found in a pocket.
DEFENSE: Where did the inquest take place?
WITNESS: The inquest was held in your office and I went to the tomb to get the skull to bring to your office. Part of the jaw-bone was missing.
DEFENSE: Did you make a search at that time for any blood on Mrs. Ware's clothing?
WITNESS: I did not make a search for blood on her clothes. Everything looked clean.

STATE RE-DIRECTS THE WITNESS, CORONER FIELDS:

STATE: Who informed you as to when and where the inquest was to be held?

WITNESS: Selectman Pall had told me about it the following Sunday. He also told me of the cheroot at the coroner's inquest. The body was in such a condition that it could not be handled.
STATE: Do you recognize this as the skull of Mrs. Sarah Ware?
WITNESS: Lifting the skull out of the black box he said, "Yes, it is the skull I examined at the funeral parlor of Mr. George Ware. As you can see, it is in a severely damaged condition!"
STATE: Is this the trunk you examined? (**A trunk was shown as State Exhibit # 3. When it was shown to the witness, he replied:**)
WITNESS: I cannot swear it is the same trunk that I examined in Mrs. Ware's room. There are things in it that I have never seen.
JUDGE: Cross?
DEFENSE: No, not at this time your Honor.

NEXT WITNESS FOR THE STATE WAS U. S. MAIL CLERK, LEW TEPLEY:

STATE: State your name sir and where you lived in 1898.
WITNESS: My name is Lew Tepley. At that time I lived in Bucksport.
STATE: What was your occupation at that time?
WITNESS: I worked with the U.S. Mail Department at the Bucksport Post Office in 1898.
STATE: Did you visit the place where Sarah Ware's body was found?
WITNESS: I visited the spot where the remains were found a few days later at about 2:30 in the afternoon. I met Mr. Tekworgy coming down Miles Lane with another man and they were having a conversation. I didn't know the other man. I heard Mr. Tekworgy say, "I am willing to be questioned by anybody at any time." Mr. Tekworgy was wearing a coat on that day even though it had been very warm. The coat was buttoned around him tightly.

STATE: Why did you go to Silver Lake Cemetery with Mr. Heyworth and Mr. Ware?
WITNESS: Being a member of the Citizen's Committee I was requested to go to Silver Lake Cemetery with Mr. Heyworth, and Mr. Ware.
STATE: What did you do there?
WITNESS: We removed the casket lid to acquire access to her personal belongings. We removed the body out of the pauper's box. We proceeded to attempt to take off the gloves, however the fingers remained in the gloves. A ring fell out of the glove from the left hand. We then cut away the rest of her clothing. We took the waterproof but did not take her hair switch, as it was very filthy!

It is inconceivable to me that this entire preceding paragraph was enacted as described!

STATE: I ask you to examine these State exhibits and tell me if they are the waterproof and rings you took from the box.
WITNESS: Yes, they look like the same ones.
STATE: Did you take charge of the cape?
WITNESS: No, Mr. Heyworth did and Mr. Ware took charge of the rings. We then put the rest of her clothes in the box and covered it up. Her body was headless. Her head was in a pail of solution. Two weeks later after preservation of the skull I examined it again. It was in Mr. Ware's funeral home where Mr. Ware lifted the head out of the solution and I examined it. I saw it several times after that. A week later Mr. Wood, who was in charge of Mr. Ware's funeral parlor at the time, turned over the skull to me in a locked wooden box. I opened the box to make sure it was in there. I sealed the box with wax and placed it in the Bucksport National Bank vault. I turned the key over to Detective

Hacey. Detective Hacey then took the skull out of the vault in October to place it in a vault in the basement of the Ellsworth Court House.

STATE: Mr. Tepley, I show you States exhibit number 4, the skull. Is this the same one given to you by Mr. Wood?
WITNESS: Yes, it is the same one.

The witness was then turned over to Defense Attorney Bellows for cross-examination.

Defense Attorney Bellows, known for his persistence, had given Lew Tepley grueling questions on the stand. He had been determined to show that the witness had taken quite an interest in the Ware case.

CROSS-EXAMINATION OF LEW TEPLEY BY THE DEFENSE:

DEFENSE: Mr. Tepley, in 1898 you say you drove up through the path to where the body was found and out Miles Lane by the maple tree and yet you did not get out of your buggy. Why was that?
WITNESS: I just didn't!
DEFENSE: Did you and Dr. Lemerson make a wager on the outcome of the trial?
WITNESS: No, I never made a wager! I had offered to bet a 'long-necker' with Dr. Lemerson on the case. I made the statement that no one would go to prison over the Ware case.

The Attorney General for the State thought the testimony should not go in and objected, but Attorney Bellows had wished to show the interests of the witness and it was allowed.

DEFENSE: What is a long-necker?
WITNESS: You can use your own opinion.
JUDGE LEMERY: Mr. Tepley, answer the question please!
WITNESS: It is a term used in horse racing. I did say to Dr. Lemerson, that I'd bet a long-necker that someone

would not go to jail. I also called him a liar when he said, 'someone would go to jail.'
DEFENSE: Mr. Tepley, how far were the bushes into the field?
WITNESS: Don't know.
STATE: Didn't you look? You said you were there.
WITNESS: I wasn't there to look at the bushes, I was there to look at the stone wall!
DEFENSE: Answer my questions please!
WITNESS: I have, I tell you I was looking for a stone wall, and not for alder bushes, so I didn't bother to examine them. I only know I brushed the bushes aside to get to the stone wall.
DEFENSE: You said, you did not know the man with Mr. Tekworgy, are you sure you don't remember who it was?
WITNESS: I remember now, George Braham was with Mr. Tekworgy when I met him on Miles Lane. It was he, pointing in Mr. Braham's direction. I heard George inquire of Mr. Tekworgy, 'Why didn't you go to Mr. Bolder's as Mrs. Files asked you to?' Mr. Tekworgy answered, 'I did.'

The witness, Mr. Tepley, was questioned at length by Attorney Bellows as to the incidents leading up to the first arrest of Mr. Tekworgy, being interrupted several times by the State's Attorney General, Judge Lemery said, "these questions have no bearing on the case."

JUDGE: Mr. Tepley in future questioning, answer all questions directly.
WITNESS: I am willing to answer all questions by Attorney Bellows, your Honor.
ATTORNEY BELLOWS: Yes, always willing, but not wanting. That's all the questions at this time your honor.
JUDGE LEMERY: Court will take a short recess and convene in one hour.

Court later convened in the afternoon session

WITNESS FOR THE STATE, DOCTOR TOOLE:

STATE: Tell the Court you name please and occupation.
WITNESS: My name is James Toole, I am a physician and surgeon.
STATE: Where do you now live and where did you live in 1898?
WITNESS: I presently live in Caribou, Maine. I lived in Bucksport in 1898.
STATE: Doctor Toole, did you examine the skull in the box marked as States exhibit # 4?
WITNESS: Yes, I examined the skull at that time in Mr. Ware's undertaking rooms in Bucksport. I testified at the Coroner's hearing but the skull was not present. I then again examined the skull yesterday as States exhibit # 4.
STATE: Did you testify at the preliminary hearing in Bucksport?
WITNESS: I was not called upon to testify at the preliminary hearing in Bucksport. I originally examined the skull at Silver Lake Cemetery. The purpose of the examination was to ascertain the cause of death.
STATE: Please, describe to the court what you found at that time.
WITNESS: The lower jaw was loosened entirely from the skull and fractured on the left side. The right side of the skull was cracked and part of the lower jawbone was missing. The lower part of the left eye socket was gone, as was the upper jaw and roof of her mouth and some other bones. On the forehead were three marks that did not show on the skull. The left side of the skull had a circular crack with a depression in the center, and the crack extended down from the circular one. None of these appear on a normal skull. A heavy blow would have been necessary to cause the wound on the left side of the face. Unconsciousness would follow and result in death eventually, perhaps immediately. A blunt instrument would have caused the circular

wound. It would also have caused the contusion on the forehead. A person would have had to fall from a great height to have caused such wounds on the head, like a fall from a second or third story building.

STATE: Would you, in your opinion, think the head would have fallen from the body when being removed from the site?

WITNESS: I should not have expected the head to fall from the body when being moved, even though it had been out of doors for about two weeks. The vertebrae would have had to have been badly damaged.

ATTORNEY BELLOWS CROSS-EXAMINATION DOCTOR TOOLE:

DEFENSE: In your opinion what sort of instrument could have caused the injury to the right side of the head.

WITNESS: One like that of a policeman's Billie club.

DEFENSE: Are you convinced this was a murder?

WITNESS: Absolutely!

DEFENSE: Why did you move out of town so shortly after the preliminary hearing?

WITNESS: A better position was offered and I accepted.

WITNESS FOR THE STATE, JOE MANK:

STATE: Tell us your name, where you live and what relationship you have to Joe Bogg.

WITNESS: My name is Joe Mank, I live in Orland and I am Joe Bogg's Uncle.

STATE: Did you live there in 1898?

WITNESS: Yes, I did.

STATE: Were you at the Orland fair in 1898?

WITNESS: Yes, I was.

STATE: Did you see your nephew, Joe Bogg, at the fair?

WITNESS: Yes, I saw Joe Bogg there.

STATE: What day was the fair on?
WITNESS: The fair was the Wednesday, before the finding of Mrs. Ware's body.
STATE: At the fair did you and Joe Bogg discuss helping Mr. Tekworgy move the body?
WITNESS: No! I had nothing to do with the moving of any body!
STATE: When did you find out that Joe Bogg helped Mr. Tekworgy move a body?
WITNESS: It was the following Sunday that Joe Bogg told me he helped Mr. Tekworgy move a body. I thought he was fooling me!
STATE: Thank you Mr. Mank for this information.

CROSS-EXAMINATION OF WITNESS JOE MANK:

DEFENSE: Mr. Mank, didn't you go to the State Prison?
WITNESS: Yes, I did go to State Prison.
DEFENSE: Did you finish primary school?
WITNESS: Yes, I finished primary school.
DEFENSE: Tell the court what you were in prison for.
WITNESS: I was incarcerated for attempting rape on my half sister, Rosemary.
DEFENSE: When you were in prison, didn't you say to Attorney Bunker it was Joe Bogg who had something to do with Mrs. Ware's murder?
WITNESS: No, I never said Joe Jr. had anything to do with Sarah Ware's murder! I only said he helped to move a body with Mr. Tekworgy. I don't know who it was or what it was all about!
DEFENSE: Thank you Mr. Mank.

Court adjourned for a brief afternoon recess.
Crowds waited outside the Ellsworth Hancock County Courthouse in the blistering hot sun. Many felt sure that the person who committed this horrible crime would finally be convicted. Some discussed why some crucial information was not

presented from certain individuals who testified at the lower court. Were they left out with intention? It was said by one individual, "Maybe tomorrow other witnesses will be presented."

The crowd outside the Ellsworth Courthouse grew larger and larger. Men and women alike were reading the local newspaper of the previous day filled with the news of the now infamous murder of the Sarah Ware trial. Court was to resume with more witnesses. This would continue to be an interesting and confusing day. Very important evidence had been heard from the State. The State was to finish its interrogation of witnesses in the afternoon session.

It had been another day for William Tekworgy in the Hancock County Courthouse. He had already listened for days with great composure as the State Prosecution had sought to weave damaging evidence in hopes of a conviction by the jury.

WITNESS FOR STATE, MR. LAUREL SPAULDING:

STATE: State your name and where you live.
WITNESS: Laurel Spaulding. Presently I live in Foxcroft, Maine, but I lived in Bucksport in 1898.
STATE: Did you ever hear a conversation between Joe Bogg and Mrs. Ware?
WITNESS: I had always heard kind words between Sarah Ware and Joe Bogg over money matters and just general conversation.
STATE: You lived in Bucksport in 1898, tell us where please.
WITNESS: On the corner of Oak and Pine Street, nearly opposite William Tekworgy.
STATE: What was your relationship with Mr. Tekworgy?
WITNESS: We were just neighbors.
STATE: Did you remember having a conversation with Joe Bogg on September 17, 1898 in the evening, concerning bees in a tree in your yard?
WITNESS: Yes, I was in Bucksport on that evening. Joe Bog came along and talked with me about the bees in my tree. He hung around for a long time and then he proposed

	we cut the tree down for the honey. I told him I didn't want to do it. Joe Bogg then walked up Pine Street to Pond Street. I saw him get on Mr. Tekworgy's jigger sometime in the evening hours.
STATE:	Are you sure it was Mr. Tekworgy and his jigger?
WITNESS:	Yes, I know them boys. I had worked on Mr. Tekworgy's jiggers. He had two, one being bigger than the other. Mr. Tekworgy drove the jigger up Pine Street toward Pond Street. Mr. Bogg jumped on the jigger and rode with Mr. Tekworgy.

It was at this point that the witness pointed to Mr. Bogg and said, "that is him, Joe. Bogg, right there!"

STATE:	Did Mr, Tekworgy ever visit you at your home?
WITNESS:	Mr. Tekworgy had visited my house frequently since September 1898. My wife, Mr. Tekworgy and myself often discussed the Ware case.
STATE:	What did Mr. Tekworgy tell you concerning the Ware case?
WITNESS:	It was during one of our conversations Mr. Tekworgy told me that he could throw a stone into the yard of the murderer. He also said he thought Joe Bogg did the handling of Sarah Ware but he could not remember who helped Joe. Mr. Tekworgy then said to me, 'I thought of offering a reward for information about the murderer, but that it was a bad idea. It might result in the conviction of an innocent man.' I thought this a peculiar thing for him to say at the time. He didn't appear to want to discuss that statement, so I never pursued it.
STATE:	Were you in Mr. Tekworgy's store two weeks before the disappearance of Mrs. Ware?
WITNESS:	Yes, I was in Mr. Tekworgy's store two weeks before Sarah disappeared. Sarah Ware was also in the store. She and Mr. Tekworgy seemed to be having a discussion

over money matters. I heard Sarah Ware say to him. 'Just pay me the money you owe me!' Mr. Tekworgy seemed to have been provoked and angry at the time.

DEFENSE ATTORNEY BELLOWS CROSS-EXAMINES MR SPAULDING:

The witness heated up during the cross-examination by Attorney Bellows. He leaned forward on the arm of the chair in the witness stand and volunteered information. "I want to say right here, that I don't know anything about where Joe Bogg and Mr. Tekworgy went when they left on the jigger or got back or what they did!"

DEFENSE: Thank you, Mr. Spaulding, but I prefer to ask my own questions. I do appreciate your kindness in volunteering information. Now, about the jigger! The jigger used the night Sarah was murdered had a dropped axle. Is that correct?

WITNESS: The jigger might be a dropped axle or might not. There were sides on the jigger, but I don't know if they had boards on them. I couldn't say how high they were. I did not measure them.

DEFENSE: I did not ask you if there were sides on the jigger, I asked you about the dropped axle!

WITNESS: I already answered that question!

DEFENSE: All right Mr. Spaulding let's resume. Are you sure Mr. Tekworgy told you a stone could be thrown from the Tannery Bridge into the yard of the suspected murderer?

WITNESS: Look, I told you that! Mr. Tekworgy told me that he could stand in his own back yard and throw a rock into the yard of the murderer, and stand on the Tannery Bridge and do the same, I know what he told me!

DEFENSE: You are not on friendly terms with Mr. Tekworgy because Mr. Tekworgy repeatedly beat his horse over the head with a club, isn't it so Mr. Spaulding!

WITNESS: No, I am not on unfriendly terms with Mr. Tekworgy. Mr. Tekworgy is on unfriendly terms with me!

DEFENSE: Mr. Spaulding, when he told you that the stone could be thrown directly across the street, whose property was he talking about?

WITNESS: The lot across the street from Mr. Tekworgy belongs to a Mr. Carlton Bellows, a relative of yours!

At this point it caused a laugh from Senior Counsel Bellows, who then turned and walked away.

WITNESS FOR THE STATE, MRS. ARVILLA BOGG:

STATE: State your name, address, and what relationship you have to Joe Bogg.

WITNESS: Mrs. Arvilla Bogg. I live in Bucksport. I am Joe Bogg's mother.

STATE: Did your son speak to you about moving a body with Mr. Tekworgy in 1898?

WITNESS: Yes, the Sunday before Mrs. Ware's body was found, my son was at my home and told me that he helped Mr. Tekworgy move a body, but Joe said he did not know who or what it was at the time. It was a week before the Orland Fair.

STATE: Does this time frame tie in with the time that Mr. Mank said Joe Bogg told him at the fair about the murder?

WITNESS: Yes, because my son told me he had told Mr. Mank a week before finding the body.

STATE: Did Joe ever mention to you any disagreement that Mr. Tekworgy and Sarah Ware might have had?

WITNESS: Joe told me Mr. Tekworgy took something from Sarah's room at Mrs. Files home.

STATE: Do you know what Mr. Tekworgy took?

WITNESS: Joe told me Mr. Tekworgy and Sarah argued about what was taken at the poker game. I am not sure what it was though.

If the State had pursued Arvilla Bogg's last statement about the poker game, then one might have known what and where the game was held!

DEFENSE CROSS-EXAMINATON, ARVILLA BOGG:

DEFENSE: You say you are the mother of Joseph Bogg and what was your maiden name?

WITNESS: I am Joseph Bogg Jr.'s mother. My maiden name was Mank.

DEFENSE: Do you feel your son could be capable of the murder of anyone?

WITNESS: Certainly not! However it is my understanding Joe did not know who or what was in the canvas.

DEFENSE: I understand schizophrenia runs in your family, is that correct?

WITNESS: Well yes, but that has nothing to do with what Joe told me.

DEFENSE: No more questions at this time, you may step down.

Hancock County Courthouse 1896
Destroyed in fire. 1929
Old Jail house on left,
Today it is the Ellsworth Historical Society

CHAPTER EIGHTEEN

DEFENSE

It was 8:30 Wednesday morning July 27, 1902 in Ellsworth. It was sweltering hot and muggy. It was almost 80 degrees, but that did not stop a large crowd from gathering in front of the courthouse. It was the day that Mr. Tekworgy was to take the stand in his own defense. People were prepared to sit in the hot, stuffy courtroom. A considerable amount of young ladies fearful of losing their seats had induced one of the court officials to secure empty pint bottles and fill them with ice water and attach them to strings, and hoist them to the gallery. It was stifling!

The room had been filled to capacity. Every available seat had been taken. It was the largest crowd attending the trial as yet. Many ladies brought lunch with them. It seemed they came intent, not to be left out from viewing the case. It resembled, at noon on the lawn in front of the courthouse, a female seminary student's picnic. The morning session consisted of more witnesses for the State.

The defense came prepared to put a large number of people on the stand to show that the reputation of Joe Mank and Joe Bogg Jr's veracity for truthfulness was not of the best and that their reputation was well known beyond the confines of Bucksport.

Mr. Pall's testimony given was to repute things said about him. He faced the ordeal nervously with apprehension of the pending cross-examination by the Attorney General. One could tell from his constant shifting position several times during the questions being asked of him.

DEFENSE WITNESS, STEADMAN E. PALL:

DEFENSE: State your name, where you live and what you did.
WITNESS: My name is Steadman E. Pall. I live in Bucksport. I was a Town Selectmen in 1898.
DEFENSE: It has been stated that you went to where Joe Bogg was living after the preliminary hearing. Can you tell us if you did?

In a loud, clear voice that could be heard all through the courtroom, he answered the following questions that were propounded upon him.

WITNESS: Yes, I went to Joe Bogg's residence but he was not home, so I left word for him to come by my office the following morning.
DEFENSE: Mr. Pall, as Selectman of the town of Buckspsort, did you tell Mr. Joe Bogg you would pay Mr. Bonsey, his father-in-law, from town funds for Mrs. Joe Bogg and their daughter's board while Joe was in jail?
WITNESS: Well, when Joe Bogg and his wife called at my office I did tell Mr. Joe Bogg, as he had testified, that I would pay Mrs. Bogg's father Mr. Bonsey, for her and her daughter's board but he refused to accept help.
DEFENSE: Mr. Pall how did you find out about Joe Bogg's retraction of his first statement?
WITNESS: I found out about Joe's retraction by a newspaper reporter that afternoon.
DEFENSE: Did you then ask Joe Bogg about this retraction he made?
WITNESS: Yes, I did.
DEFENSE: What did Joe Bogg tell you?
WITNESS: Joe Bogg told me, 'I was forced to retract my statement by Mr. Heyworth, Mr. Tepley, and Detective Hacey. If I retracted my statement, they would give me half the reward of $250.00, which I was offered. That if I did not they would arrest me. They had the warrant

in their pocket.' That was when I asked Joe Bogg to my private office in my store. That happened in March of 1899.
DEFENSE: What happened in your private office?
WITNESS: I told Joe about the penalty for perjury and that he could go to State Prison.

STATE CROSS-EXAMINES MR. PALL:

STATE: Mr. Pall, did you ever tell Mr. Bogg that his family would be looked after?
WITNES: As a town officer, I had the means to meet their needs by Bucksport Town vouchers but Mr. and Mrs. Bogg refused to accept the offer.
STATE: You said, you would bet Joe Bogg would retract his statement within the first 48 hours, on the night Mr. Tekworgy was first remanded, didn't you?
WITNESS: No, I made no such statement!
STATE: Did you not say, there had been a new arrest and that Mr. Tekworgy would be released?
WITNESS: No, I made no such statement!
STATE: So you did not make these statements to the press?
WITNESS: Well, I may have said something to that effect, I can't remember.

WITNESS FOR DEFENSE, NATHAN MCKAY:

DEFENSE: Tell us your name and where you live.
WITNESS: Nathan McKay. I live in Bucksport.
DEFENSE: Mr. Mckay, tell the court how long you have known Mr. Viles.
WITNESS: I have known him for about 20 years.
DEFENSE: Did you see him on the 17th, of September 1898?
WITNESS: Yes, he came to see me at the place where I still work. It was after one in the afternoon when he came in. Mr. Viles took a piece of oak, oh about 2 to 3 inches thick

and about 6 inches long or a little longer and made a sort of Billy club with it. He drilled a hole in the end and filled it with lead.
DEFENSE: Did Mr. Viles say what he was going to do with the Billy club?
WITNESS: Yes, he said that he meant to whack Mr. Tekworgy over the head.
DEFENSE: Why, in your opinion, did he want to do this horrible thing?
WITNESS: Because he blamed Mr. Tekworgy for Sarah Ware's death.
DEFENSE: Do you, in your opinion believe Mr. Viles to be a violent man?
WITNESS: I have seen him very, very angry!
DEFENSE: That is all for now, you may step down.

Defense Attorney Bellows quickly dismissed his own witness. The judge interrupted to say, a lunch break will then be taken, and the afternoon session will resume in one hour.

The streets of Ellsworth that afternoon were filled with many people. The newspaper reporters were anxious to get the story first hand. They were scurrying around interviewing individuals on the sidewalks, in front of shops and on the steps of the Ellsworth courthouse. Their notebooks were full of scribbles, notes and statements.

It was one of the busiest afternoons the city had seen in a long time. Men and women were discussing the fact that Mr. Tekworgy would be taking the stand in the afternoon session. Would he get off? Would the jury of 12 men believe his story? They had heard part of his story before. Would he have anything new to say at this time? They were about to find out, as court began to resume session in one half-hour, and he would tell his whole story this time, some of it not new to those who had been following the trial. Children played on the grass as their parents chattered with one another about the trial.

Young Almena had gone to the trial that day with her parents. She was sitting on the plush green lawn outside the courthouse on a soft brown blanket, which her mother had brought. They all were eating lunch. She had been watching the people and listening quietly to conversations when the lady in white reappeared. It was the same lady she saw at the barbershop two years ago.

The lady asked her if she remembered who she was? "Yes I do," answered Almena.

"Are you listening to what people are saying?" said the lady.

"Yes, I am," answered Almena.

"Listen carefully," said the lady. "Many years from now you will understand, why and what happened. It wasn't only that Sarah Ware died, but it was about the injustices of society. Life and death have many meanings."

Not knowing why at her young age Almena felt a great deal of empathy for the lady in the white dress. With this, the lady softly said, "Goodbye," and gently faded away. Shortly after this one could hear the announcement that court was about to begin.

A NEWSPAPER REPORTER WHO LIVED IN BREWER AND VISITED BUCKSPORT ON OCTOBER 17, 1898 WAS THEN CALLED TO THE WITNESS STAND FOR THE DEFENSE, SAM O'CONELL:

DEFENSE: State your name sir.
WITNESS: Sam O'Conell.
DEFENSE: You are a newspaper reporter and went to interview Mrs. Files about the Sarah Ware murder, is that right?
WITNESS: Yes, I am a newspaper reporter and yes I did interview Mrs. Files.
DEFENSE: Tell us what the interview was about.
WITNESS: Mrs. Files said, she did not go to bed the night Sarah went away as she worried about her whereabouts. She also said, Mrs. Ware feared Mr. Tekwogy and did not want to be alone with him. I also visited Mr. Tekworgy and asked him where he was on the night of September 17, 1898. His reply was, "Ask my family!"

CROSS-EXAMINED BY STATE, MR. O'CONELL:

STATE: What did you think about Mr. Tekworgy's remark when you asked him where he was on the night of September 17, 1898?
WITNESS: Well, I thought it a rather queer thing to say.
STATE: There is more to this interview, isn't there, Mr. O' Conell! Tell the court the rest of the interview.
WITNESS: Mrs. Files talked a lot about her poor Sarah and asked me if I didn't think the man who killed her was a wicked man.
STATE: Did you ever interview Mr. Tekworgy?
WITNESS: Yes, I talked with Mr. Tekworgy and he said, 'It would be wicked to KILL Sarah Ware.'

STEADMAN E. PALL RE-CALLED BY STATE:

STATE: There is no need to tell us your name, you have been sworn in. Just tell us what your occupation was in 1898 and what you know of this case.
WITNESS: I had been first selectman in 1898 and 1899. I had first heard of Sarah Ware's disappearance on September 20th at four in the afternoon from Deputy Sheriff Genn. I later heard that she was found dead. I had employed Detective Odland who was from Waterville to look into the matter. Detective Odland arrived around October 5, of 1898, then again in 1899 for further investigation.
STATE: After she was found dead what action did you take?
WITNESS: I went at once to Mrs. Files, to examine the house. Later I went to the Dogett Tannery; there I spoke with Mr. Bolder. I also spoke with her brother-in-law, George Ware and he told me how they had organized a search party.
STATE: Did you go to the place where her body lay?
WITNESS: Yes I did and saw a quartz rock weighing about one to three pounds at the site where Mrs. Ware's body was found.

STATE: Mr. Pall, where did you next see the quartz rock?
WITNESS: I next saw the quartz rock at the coroner's jury. Then Deputy Sheriff Genn put it on display in his store in Bucksport. It was thought to be the weapon used to kill Mrs. Ware.
STATE: Were you at the preliminary hearing in Bucksport?
WITNESS: Yes I was there.
STATE: What did you hear Mr. Joe Bogg testify to at this hearing?
WITNESS: I heard Mr. Joe Bogg tell his story and also heard Joe Bogg testify in regard to helping Mr. Tekworgy move a body.
STATE: Did Mr. Joe Bogg and his wife come to your store on March 14th or 15th?
WITNESS: Yes, Mr. Joe Bogg came to my store with his wife. It was about two in the afternoon and I had asked Joe Bogg to go to the back room. Mr. Bogg asked if his wife could accompany him.
STATE: Did you ask Joe Bogg about his testimony?
WITNESS: Mr. Bogg said to me, 'Mr. Pall, I lied about helping Mr. Tekworgy move the body, and that I was induced by Mr. Heyworth, Mr. Tepley and Detective Hacey. I was offered half the reward money and if I didn't take it they would arrest me.' Joe Bogg went on to say that, 'Detective Hacey had a warrant to arrest me because of my retracted statement.' Joe.Bogg also said to me, 'When I was testifying at the preliminary hearing I saw you, Mr. Pall, write something in a book, I got scared and I almost broke down and told the truth.'
STATE: Mr. Pall, when was Mr. Joe Bogg arrested for perjury?
WITNESS: It was that selfsame night.
STATE: Mr. Paul, didn't you make a statement saying Mr. Joe Bogg would retract his statement within 48 hours!
WITNESS: I do not remember telling anyone that Mr.Bogg would retract within 48 hours.

STATE: Didn't you move to have Joe Bogg arrested through the detectives?
WITNESS: No, I never knew who moved to have Mr. Bogg arrested.
STATE: Didn't you have a warrant for his arrest and you and Detective Hacey go to Joe's home?
WITNESS: No, I don't believe that is true.
STATE: Mr. Pall, be careful how you answer. the questions there is a fine line between the truth and perjury.
WITNESS: I have answered your questions as I recall them.
STATE: When and why did you go to Mr. Bonsey's house, Joe Bogg's father law, where Joe Bogg was residing?
WITNESS: I went to the Mr. Bonsey's home on Sunday the day before he came to my store. At that time I said to Joe, 'I heard you were lying about Mr. Tekworgy on the stand.' This was the day before Joe Bogg came to my store and was later arrested.

DEFENSE ATTORNEY CROSS-EXAMINES MR. PALL:

DEFENSE: When did you say you first saw the quartz rock Mr. Pall?
WITNESS: At the place where Mrs. Ware was found.
DEFENSE: Where did you next see the quartz rock?
WITNESS: In the Sheriff's possession after Mr. Tekworgy's hearing.
DEFENSE: Mr. Pall why did you not ask Mr. Bogg for all the details of what he knew?
WITNESS: Because at times Joe is not responsible for all that he says. He many times fabricates stories.
DEFENSE: Which story do you believe?
WITNESS: I don't rightly know. I respect Mr. Tekworgy, I don't respect Mr. Bogg!

WITNESS FOR THE DEFENSE, WALLACE WORTHLEY:

DEFENSE: Tell us your name and where you live.
WITNESS: My name is Wallace Worthley and I live in Bucksport

DEFENSE: on Bridge Street. That is I live at Bridge and Franklin Streets, at the corner.
DEFENSE: Please, tell the court how you know Mr. Tekworgy.
WITNESS: Being in the butcher business, he has helped me move animals in the past.
DEFENSE: Were you a butcher in 1898?
WITNESS: Yes, In 1898 I was a butcher. On October 17, 1898, I had killed two pigs and started for my slaughterhouse when the axle on my jigger broke. I asked Mr. Tekworgy if I could hire a jigger and borrow a piece of canvas. I covered the hogs that were in the jigger with the piece of canvas. His canvas was about eight to ten feet long and the same in width. The next day I returned the jigger and the canvas and put it in his carriage shop.
DEFENSE: Did you notice pig blood on the canvass when you returned it?
WITNESS: I didn't notice if the canvass was stained because it was not clean when I borrowed it. I suppose it would be stained, since I used it to cover two slaughtered pigs.

THE STATE CROSS-EXAMINES MR. WORTHLEY:

STATE: Mr. Worthley, in your opinion would there be blood on Mr. Tekworgy's jigger?
WITNESS: Yes, I guess the body of the jigger would be covered in blood after hauling the two pigs, which had been slaughtered!
STATE: Are you sure no blood was on the canvass or jigger when you borrowed it?
WITNESS: Like I told you it was dirty when I borrowed it so I can't say as I did!
STATE: Is there anyone who can verify that you borrowed these items?
WITNESS: I didn't go around telling people I was moving my slaughtered pigs, but I suppose Mr. Tekworgy could.

MRS DEEHAN RECALLED BY STATE:

STATE: Mrs. Deehan, did you ever talk with Mr. Worthley about him using Mr. Tekworgy's wagon for his slaughtered pigs?
WITNESS: Yes, being neighbors I had a talk with Mr. Worthley and he told me he never borrowed Mr. Tekworgy's canvas and wagon. Mr. Wrothley said, Mr. Tekworgy came to him and asked him to say that he borrowed the jigger to move his slaughtered pigs and that Mr. Tekworgy would make it worth his while.

MR WORTHLEY RECALLED BY DEFENSE:

DEFENSE: Please Sir, clarify the issue of Mr. Tekwowrgy's borrowed wagon and canvas.
WITNESS: The canvas I identified is the one I borrowed from Mr. Tekworgy. I never told Mrs. Deehan the story she just told. It is a lie! I did borrow Mr. Tekworgy's jigger and I did use his canvas for my slaughtered pigs.

DEFENSE WITNESS, MRS AGATHA ELBRIDGE:

DEFENSE: Tell us your name and where you live.
WITNESS: Agatha Elbridge, I live on Mechanic Street in Bucksport. I lived there in 1898.
DEFENSE: Do you know Mr. Viles?
WITNESS: Yes, I know him.
DEFENSE: Did he board with you September 17, 1898?
WITNESS: Yes, Mr. Viles boarded with me then.
DEFENSE: Did Mr. Viles go out that night?
WITNESS: I saw Mr. Viles leave the house earlier that evening. I saw him come in around 10 o'clock that night and hang up his coat.
DEFENSE: Did you notice anything unusual about him?
WITNESS: No. I did not.

DEFENSE: Could you be mistaken as to the time Mr. Viles returned?

It was then that Mrs. Viles, his mother, jumped out of her chair and shouted, "Are you trying to frame my son?"
The judge at that time had the bailiff remove Mrs. Viles from the courtroom.

DEFENSE: Let us continue. Would you like me to rephrase my question?
WITNESS: No, it is not necessary, I am not mistaken about the time. My clock chimed 10:00 O'clock!

EX-SELECTMAN STEADMAN E. PALL RECALLED BY THE DEFENSE:

DEFENSE: Did you hear a conversation between Mrs. Joe Bogg and Mr. Danvers?
WITNESS: Yes, when I attended the preliminary hearing of Mr. Tekworgy in Bucksport. I saw Mrs. Joe Bogg there and I heard her tell Mr. Danvers that Joe's story was a damned lie!
DEFENSE: What precisely was she calling a lie?
WITNESS: She was referring to the testimony of Joe Bogg, when he denied knowing anything about the murder of Sarah Ware.

William Tekworgy had sat all forenoon with his head resting upon his right hand with his index finger over his mouth. It seemed to have looked as if his hands and face had a nervous twitching. That was not strange behavior, even if innocent. The man who would not find himself nervous would be indeed a man of steel. Mr. Tekworgy did not appear to be so smug as he was at the beginning of the trial. Though his self-possessed demeanor seldom indicated that he had any great interest beyond the close, careful, watch he had kept upon the witnesses, as they had taken their places upon the stand and told their stories.

DEFENSE WITNESS, WILLIAM TEKWORGY TAKES THE STAND:

DEFENSE: State your name to the court.
WITNESS: William Tekworgy.
DEFENSE: Where do you live?
WITNESS: In Bucksport on Pine Street.
DEFENSE: Tell us about yourself and your life up to this point.
WITNESS: I was born in Ellsworth where I became orphaned at an early age. I lived there for about 12 years with various families during that time. Later on, I moved to Surry where I stayed four years. Then I moved to Bangor for about one year with my wife and two daughters. After that, I moved to Bucksport in 1885 and went to work for John Buck. In 1886, I went into business for myself, principally in tin ware and stoves.
DEFENSE: Tell us what you know about Sarah Ware.
WITNESS: I knew Sarah Ware for about 10 years. She came to work for me doing domestic chores after my first wife's death. I don't recollect the exact date. Mrs. Ware had spent four or five weeks while my oldest daughter was ill. Sarah became almost a surrogate mother to my two daughters. My children were young when Sarah Ware took care of them. I paid her for the work.
DEFENSE: Can you tell us where Sarah Ware lived?
WITNESS: I know that Sarah Ware boarded at Mrs. File's house. In return for board, she cooked and cleaned and did various chores for Mrs. Files. I had frequently stopped by with my children to visit Mrs. Files and Mrs. Ware, we would often have Sunday dinners together. I never had a crossword with Sarah Ware.
DEFENSE: Did you keep a vegetable garden at Mrs. Files?
WITNESS: Yes, in 1898 I had a garden in Miles Lane. I had a young man work for me. I planted all kinds of vegetables there.

DEFENSE: When were you last in the garden prior to Sarah Ware's death?

WITNESS: I was in the vegetable garden on September 17, 1898. I had gone into the house to see Mrs. Ware and Mrs. Files. I knew what time I had been there because the whistle at the Dogett Tannery blew at 4:00 o' clock as I was on my way home. I had talked with Mrs. Ware about the weather and getting Mrs. Files' share of the beans from the garden. That was the last time I saw her alive.

DEFENSE: Tell us about the incidents prior to the disappearance of Sarah Ware.

WITNESS: My daughter and her friend had stopped by my house September 17, 1898. I retired to bed about nine and did not go out again. I went to church on Sunday and then to Mrs. Files. I was there most of the day. My daughter had been with me. On Monday, I first worked in my shop for a while, then I went to the Blue Hill fair and later I went to a group meeting in Blue Hill. I stayed the night with a friend. Tuesday, I returned home.

DEFENSE: Did you see Joe Bogg on Tuesday or Wednesday night as he testified?

WITNESS: No, I did not see Joe Bogg on Tuesday or Wednesday night.

DEFENSE: Did you and Joe Bogg use your jigger the evening of September 17, 1898 and go up Miles Lane as he testified?

WITNESS: No, he did not get on my jigger and go up Miles Lane. I did not go there! He never helped me to move a body!

DEFENSE: Did you go to see Mr. John Bolder in reference to Sarah Ware?

WITNESS: I went to question John Bolder about Sarah after Mrs. Files told me Sarah Ware was missing. There was no one at Mr. Bolder's. I was very busy and thought Sarah

Ware went home, so I did not tell Mrs. Files that I failed to see Mr. Bolder.

DEFENSE: When were you and your daughter at Mrs. File's house?

WITNESS: My daughter and I were at Mrs. Files on the day the body was found. I went up to the lane that night with a lantern to help move the body. I followed the wagons down Pond Street and then went back to Mrs. File's home. The coroner and others were with me. My daughter and I stayed at Mrs. File's house for four nights seeing she was so distraught!

DEFENSE: Where did Detective Odland and Mr Hacey find the canvas?

WITNESS: Detectives Odland and Mr. Hacey came to my place many times. The piece of canvas they found and took was from my adjoining carriage house. The piece they took was the piece of canvas Mr. Worthley borrowed to cover his slaughtered pigs.

DEFENSE: Tell us about the hammer.

WITNESS: There was a hammer in the wagon that I always took with me on various jobs. I used it on occasion when necessary.

DEFENSE: Did you go anywhere after your release from jail?

WITNESS: I was in Bucksport all the time between my release from jail in 1899 to my arrest last April. I was sick in my cell in Ellsworth when Joe Bogg was brought to jail. He visited me in my cell and asked me to forgive him and I told him that I would not want to die without forgiving him or anyone else.

DEFENSE: Do you know who killed Sarah Ware?

WITNESS: I have always tried to find the murderer of Sarah Ware. I have spent money and employed a detective to work on the case. I did this because I have been accused of the murder and my character has been questioned.

DEFENSE: Why would you employ your own detective?

WITNESS: I have heard rumors as to who did it and I have talked with a lot of people I know and I have been accused of her murder! I never murdered Sarah Ware! I never had any altercations with her!

WILLIAM TEKWOWRGY, CROSS-EXAMINATION BY STATE:

STATE: Mr. Tekworgy, you have been married twice, when did you marry your wives?

WITNESS: I married my first wife when I was 29 years old, she is deceased. My second wife and I got a divorce. I do not know where she is.

STATE: You had a vegetable garden at Mrs. Files. How long did you have it?

WITNESS: Mrs. Files and I shared a vegetable garden for many years. We shared the work in the garden.

STATE: So you had the opportunity to visit with Mrs. Ware while attending your garden, is that right?

WITNESS: Yes, we were friends.

STATE: Where is your daughter now, Mr. Tekworgy?

WITNESS: Sir, I have three daughters. My youngest daughter, Georgia lives with her mother. My oldest daughter Mary lives in Sedgwick, however she is not very well. My middle daughter Abbie lives in Danbury, Massachusetts, she just left to go home.

STATE: Joe Bogg worked for you, isn't that right?

WITNESS: Joe Bogg never worked for me prior to September 17, 1898 or since then!

STATE: Where were you precisely on the night of September 17, 1898?

WITNESS: My daughter can answer that question!

STATE: Your Honor, please have Mr. Tekworgy answer that question.

JUDGE: Mr. Tekworgy, please answer the questions addressed to you.

WITNESS: I was with friends playing a friendly game of poker.

STATE: Mr. Tekworgy, please tell us who these friends were.

WITNESS: Mr. Mank and Mr. Joe Bogg. And, of course you know, Joe Bogg's various testimonies.

STATE: Yes, the State does, and we also know that the one he testified to at this hearing is true. You may step down.

Mr. Tekworgy stepped down after his testimony.

DEFENSE WITNESS, ELIZABETH GRAY:

DEFENSE: Please, tell us your name and where you are employed.
WITNESS: My name is Elizabeth Gray, but I go by the name of Lizzie. I am a resident of Ellsworth. I work as a waitress in the Hancock House Hotel just across the bridge on the West Side of town. I was waiting tables several times when Mr. Tekworgy was in the dining room at the hotel.
DEFENSE: Was he alone when you were in the dinning room?
WITNESS: No, he had a companion dinning with him. They were sitting near a window that faced the street.
DEFENSE: Did you overhear any of their conversation?
WITNESS: I overheard Mr. Tekworgy say to his companion, 'The man who committed the murder passed this window twice while we were eating dinner.' I also heard Mr. Tekworgy say, 'I could find the murderer.'
DEFENSE: Did you know the man that Mr. Tekworgy was dinning with?
WITNESS: I did not know the man Mr. Tekworgy was dining with.

Why didn't the State cross-examine and try to find out more information about who the dining companion was and who the man was that passed the window?

WITNESS FOR THE DEFENSE, MR. BRIDGES:

DEFENSE: Tell us your name and where you live.
WITNESS: Moe Bridges and I live in Bucksport.
DEFENSE: Do you know Mr. Tekworgy and can you give us any information?

WITNESS: Yes, I do know Mr. Tekworgy. He told me, 'If people would give me five minutes, I would make it plain to them who killed Sarah Ware.'
DEFENSE: What else did Mr. Tekworgy tell you?
WITNESS: Mr. Tekworgy at another time asked me if I knew where Gerald Viles was because he had been missing since Sarah Ware's body was found and still has not returned.
DEFENSE: Did Mr. Tekworgy tell you anything else concerning Gerald Viles?
WITNESS: Yes, that Mr. Viles wanted to whack Mr. Tekworgy over the head.
DEFENSE: Why would he say he wanted to whack Mr. Tekworgy over the head?
WITNESS: Mr. Tekworgy did not give me a reason as to why.
DEFENSE: Mr. Bridges, do you know where Mr. Viles is?
WITNESS: Mr. Tekworgy told me that he knew Mr. Viles had run off on a schooner headed out of the country.
DEFENSE: Mr. Bridges, don't you consider this incriminating?
WITNESS: Sure do, Sir!

STATE CROSS-EXAMINATION OF MR. BRIDGES:

STATE: Mr. Bridges, did you see Mr. Viles on the night of September 17, 1898?
WITNESS: I met Mr. Viles on the night of September 17, 1898 at the Finson and Brown Store. He had been with his mother and Mr. Harth, the driver of the team.
STATE: Did you see Mr. Viles later that evening?
WITNESS: I saw Mr. Viles again when they passed my house on Pond Street at exactly 8:15 P.M.!
STATE: Did you see Mr. Viles after September 17, 1898?
WITNESS: I saw Mr. Viles when he went up my street to Franklin Street the next day. He lived on Pine Street and had no reason to go up Pond Street. Mr. Viles went by once a day from that time to the day Mrs. Ware's body was discovered. Soon after finding the body, I heard

that Mr. Viles and his Billy club went away on a schooner to South Africa.

WITNESS FOR DEFENSE, REVEREND STEPHEN T. RICHARDSON:

DEFENSE: State your name sir and your occupation.
WITNESS: Reverend Stephen Richardson. I am the clergyman of the Methodist Church in Trenton.
DEFENSE: Do you know Joe Bogg?
WITNESS: Yes, I heard him testify at the Tekworgy hearing in Bucksport. I heard Mr. Bogg say he knew the date when he supposedly helped move the body with Mr. Tekworgy. Mr. Bogg said he knew the date because it was the day he had returned from his trip to Rockport.
DEFENSE: Do you know Mr. Tekworgy?
WITNESS: Yes, he was a member of the Methodist Church in Trenton and attended occasionally. He also was a regular member of the Methodist Church in Bucksport in 1898.
DEFENSE: Do you consider Mr. Tekworgy a reputable citizen?
WITNESS: Yes, I certainly do.
DEFENSE: Have you had occasion to meet Mr. Bogg?
WITNESS: Only on one occasion and I did not think him very reputable.
DEFENSE: Do you know of Mr. Bogg's story of retraction?
WITNESS: Yes, I recollect that he appealed for mercy. I also recollect that he stated Mr. Tepley, Mr. Heyworth, and Detective Hacey induced him to tell the story which he told during the first testimony in Bucksport.

The State did not choose to cross-examine Rev. Richardson.

WITNESS FOR DEFENSE, MR. DENNIS REMMICK:

DEFENSE: State your name and where you live.

WITNESS: Dennis Remmick, I reside in Bucksport.
DEFENSE: What is your occupation?
WITNESS: At present I am a storekeeper, however in 1898 and 1899 I was the recorder for the Western Hancock Municipal Court in Bucksport.
DEFENSE: Did you ever issue an arrest for Joe Bogg Jr.?
WITNESS: In 1899 I issued a warrant for the arrest of Joe Bogg Jr. under the direction of the law officials. Attorney Bunker and I talked, he told me to meet him at Sheriff Genn's house on March 15th about issuing the warrant. The sheriff then asked Joe Bogg and his wife to come to his house. It was there that Joe Bogg told me the story he told in court was a lie and that he wished to retract it. I then asked him if he wanted counsel. He looked bewildered and said, 'No.'
DEFENSE: Did he have anything else to say at that time?
WITNESS: Yes. Joe Bogg said, 'I cannot sleep or eat since I told the story of Mr. Tekworgy moving a body. If I don't tell someone quickly I will go crazy! Now, I am going to tell the truth!' He further stated that Mr. Heyworth, Mr. Tepley, and Detective Hacey induced him to tell a false story. That he would be arrested and sent to prison if he did not retract his statement. They promised him money if he would comply.
DEFENSE: Mr. Remmick, do you really think these men would try to bribe Joe Bogg?
WITNESS: It is not for me to say! However, I did tell Mr. Bogg of his rights and strongly suggested he secure counsel. I recall his wife had urged him to confess what he knew before Mr. Tekworgy's hearing was concluded in Bucksport.
DEFENSE: Mr. Remmick, are you completely comfortable with the way Mr. Bogg changes his stories?
WITNESS: Well, I am sure one of his stores must be true.

STATE CROSS-EXAMINES MR. REMMICK:

STATE: Mr. Remmick, why did you go to Sheriff Genn's house?
WITNESS: Because Attoney Bunker sent for me.
STATE: Where did Joe Bogg go after he left Sheriff Genn's house?
WITNESS: He was taken to Ellsworth by Sheriff Genn and put in jail to be held until the Grand Jury hearing.
STATE: Were you called at the Grand Jury?
WITNESS: I was not called as a witness before the Grand Jury. I did not know anyone who was. Joe Bogg was sent home after the April session. An indictment was not found against Mr. Bogg.
STATE: Mr. Remmick, how long have you known Mr. Bogg?
WITNESS: About six or seven years.
STATE: Have you ever known him to lie?
WITNESS: Well, I've known him as a great talker, but not for his untruthfulness.
STATE: Did Joe Bogg tell you anything?
WITNESS: Yes, Joe Bogg told me 'I did not see Mr. Tekworgy on the night the body was moved.'
STATE: Thank You Mr. Remmick, no further questions

SEVERAL PEOPLE WERE RECALLED AND CROSS-EXAMINED BY THE STATE AND THE DEFENSE:

The first to be recalled by the DEFENSE had been *Elizabeth Gray*. She stated again that she did not know the man that Mr. Tekworgy had been dining with or the man whom he had referred to.

The second to be recalled was *Joe Bogg Jr.* by the STATE. He said after assisting Mr. Tekworgy in moving the body, and before the body had been found, he had told his mother and Joe Mank of moving it. He told his mother on the following Sunday that he had helped Mr. Tekworgy move the body. That he did not know that it was a body at the time. That he had seen Joe Mank at the Orland fair soon after helping Mr. Tekworgy.

Then the STATE recalled *Joe Mank*, Joe Bogg's uncle. He repeated he lived in Orland in 1898 and that he was at the Orland fair at that time. He stated that he saw Joseph Bogg Jr. at the fair on Wednesday before finding the body of Sarah Ware. The body had been found on the following Sunday, after Joe Bogg had told Joe Mank that he did help Mr. Tekworgy move a body.

Joe Mank admitted on the stand he had been convicted and was sent to Thomaston Prison where he served his time for assault and attempt to rape his half sister. He had a conversation with Attorney General John R. Bunker in jail.

DEFENSE ATTORNEY BELLOWS RECALLS MR. BRIDGES:

DEFENSE: Mr. Bridges, have you ever heard Mr. Viles make threats against Mrs. Ware or Mrs. Files?

WITNESS: Yes, I have. Three or four weeks before the death of Mrs. Ware, I heard Mr. Viles make a threat against both of these ladies.

DEFENSE: What did you hear Mr. Viles say?

WITNESS: Mr. Viles asked Mrs. Files if she had a room for rent and she replied, 'No, I only rent rooms to women such as Sarah Ware.' It was at that point that I heard Mr. Viles call them two bitches and he said, 'I will get even with you women!'

DEFENSE: Mr. Bridges are you sure it was Mr. Viles you saw on the night of September 17, 1898?

WITNESS: Yes, I am sure it was Mr. Viles.

DEFENSE: Do you know if Mr. Viles went home after you saw him?

WITNESS: No, I do not.

It was at this time the two attorneys concluded their interrogations and the Judge announced court was convened for the day and that summations would be presented tomorrow morning.

Mildred Ware by Silver Lake

CHAPTER NINETEEN

IS THIS THE CONCLUSION?

CLOSING ARGUMENTS, DEFENSE ATTORNEY BELLOWS:

I say to you, the jury, that there is no credence to the evidence of Joe Bogg; that he is an admitted perjurer. Evidence has been shown that someone other than Mr. Tekworgy murdered Mrs. Sarah Ware.

Sarah Ware was killed where her body was found and that all evidence points to that conclusion. The team of horses that had been heard driving furiously down Pond Street and across the Tannery Bridge had not been identified as those belonging to Mr. Tekworgy. Sarah Ware had been brought to that gloomy place. Evidence has been shown that the wagon belonged to Mr. Viles. Mr. Viles had made threats against both Mrs. Files and Mrs. Ware. I have brought forth witnesses that have shown Mr. Viles to be of an unsavory character.

Before Attorney Bellows had concluded his summary a pathetic incident occurred. Mrs. Viles again had interrupted by exclaiming, "You are a liar! You shan't talk about my son that way!" She had been greatly affected by the references to her son. She sat weeping throughout the remainder of the session and her tears touched everyone there.

Sorrowful as it was, it was only a play of life. It had been another note in the history of criminal justice. It was Mr. Bellow's duty to defend his client; it was no wonder that he had thrown another suspect into his argument.

Attorney Bellows continued with, would the jury prefer a community made up of the likes of Joe Bogg or of men like William

Tekworgy? Would the jury take the word of a man who went to church every Sunday, as Mr. Tekworgy did, or take the word of a man who had willfully committed perjury, like Mr. Joe Bogg, Jr.!"

Mrs. Ware lived in Bucksport for a number of years and lived with Mrs. Files, so Mrs. Files says. No doubt she helped Sarah Ware out. Sarah Ware stayed there until September 17, 1898. It had been said that her children had forsaken her. This was here say by citizens of the town. It has been insinuated that Mrs. Files has done wrong, but do you believe that this woman who took Sarah Ware in, would do wrong?

John Bolder didn't go on the searching party because he was at work. Mr. Tekworgy also had been at work. Had it been worse for Mr. Tekworgy to work and not go on the search? It had been John Bolder's house where Sarah Ware had been last seen in life.

The State has gone into details to show that Sarah Ware was possibly last seen in front of Mrs. Cosby's residence on School Street. If she did come down that way, why and where she went, no one knows. Did she go that way? Why is it no one knew where she went after she bought the cheroot at William Bogg's General Store?

If, after she left the Bogg's store did someone that she had known take her in his wagon to the place where she was found; possibly where she was killed? Had that man been on Pond Street that night? Was it Mr. Viles Sarah saw that night? Mr. Bridges noted that he saw Mr. Viles at that same time! It is questionable whether Mr. Viles was at his own home on the night of September 17, 1898.

The evidence has shown that the grass had been trodden down around her body and the quartz rock that lay near by had been the weapon Sarah Ware was killed with. The rock was at the Coroner's office, but then mysteriously disappeared. Where did it go? If the canvass had been pulled out from beneath her body, her body would have toppled over in an unnatural position? It was said that her hat was under her body when she was found.

The next spring Mrs. Angelina Bogg, Joe Bogg's mother, went there and dug up a piece of human bone. It was the missing jawbone of Sarah Ware. Why would Angelina Bogg do that?

It had again been another black mark against Joe Bogg. What was she trying to prove? Why would she even go to the site of Sarah's dead body?

Three years ago Joe Bogg testified that he and Mr. Tekworgy walked Miles Lane. Has his memory improved? He now says they rode the jigger up the lane.

You have heard witness after witness tell that during the preliminary hearing it had been a Tuesday night Joe Bogg helped Mr. Tekworgy. You've also heard him tell you now that it was on a Thursday! Why the discrepancy?

Was it perhaps because Joe Bogg had since found out that Mr. Tekworgy had been in North Orland that Tuesday night? Mr. Bogg had been well trained in the art of lying, for I think he has a factory where he manufactures stories.

Law Officials arrested Joe Bogg after his retraction; but they did not hustle him to a trial. They waited and advised him of his rights and asked him if he wanted counsel. If anything, his rights were protected. Mrs. Joe Bogg Jr. signed a statement in defense of her husband. It is natural she should try and protect her husband.

Mr. Bogg had made the statement that the detectives were after him and if they kept it up, he would tell a lie. This man had pleaded guilty to perjury! Is the jury going to take his word against an upright citizen?

Mr. Tekworgy didn't run! He stayed here until he was arrested. His name has been tainted. He had hired a detective from Massachusetts, which his daughter arranged. He stayed in Bucksport to fight and will continue to fight until the finger of scorn points to someone else.

Mr. Viles had made threats against Mrs. Files and Mrs. Ware. Mr. Viles had a Billy club made on the very day the crime occurred. What was the necessity for a Billy club? Soon after, he left the State and the Country and to our knowledge has not returned.

The State has wasted a lot of time trying to show that this man William T. Tekworgy committed this horrible crime. Why then, did they not produce the hammer at this trial, which they say was used as the weapon?

They have used a lot of time in producing witness after witness to identify the skull of Mrs. Sarah Ware. There was one man who could tell whether it was or was not. This man was Dr. Lemerson. Why then did they not put him on the stand? Why, because of the expertise of Dr. Toole! This witness' testimony proves that they are not sure of Dr. Lemerson's testimony because of the condition of the skull. Dr. Lemerson's testimony, a dentist and medical practitioner, could not disprove that of Dr. Tool's Ph.D.

The State of Maine, so the Attorney General will tell you, demands redemption for this taking of a life, that this murderer must be stopped. The State of Maine's laws are not intended to punish an innocent victim.

Joe Mank, as people have told you, never spoke a word of truth since he was born. You couldn't believe him and yet they put him on the stand to substantiate the story of Joe Bogg. This man attempted to rape his own sister. This man, who is unfit to associate with man or beast! Will you believe him?

I ask you, as I close, to carefully consider all the evidence presented to you. The responsibility now rests upon you as a jury. Shall I send word to the daughter in Boston, Massachusetts, that her father is convicted on the evidence of Joe Bogg? Shall I say to this daughter your life has changed forever? Shall I say to this daughter Mary, who is sitting here in the courtroom, go home, that Joe Bogg has convicted your father? Shall I say to this man William Tekworgy, go to State Prison for Joe Bogg's lies have put you there?

Gentlemen will you go home and say we have convicted William Tekworgy on Joe Bogg's story of lies? I expect to read in the papers again that he retracted his story and lied. Gentlemen, I thank you and leave this case in your hands.

CLOSING ARGUMENTS FOR THE STATE, ATTORNEY GENERAL SEIDER'S SUMMATION:

This brutal murder was committed four years ago in September. This is the most remarkable case that has ever been tried in the State of Maine.

There have been many hearings on the case before the Coroner's Jury, Municipal Judge and the Grand Jury, but the ghost of Sarah Ware's *echoes from the past* should not go unjustified. The case has been known, written about, and talked about for years. Not only in Hancock County, in the State of Maine, but its publicity has reached as far south as the Commonwealth of Massachusetts.

A persistent demand has been made that the case should be tried before a competent jury in this County. It has been the duty of State Officials to present this case to the jury. In the interest of social morals and solid government, this case was reheard introducing new evidence.

Nothing would detach the County, City and Community Government, such as covering up and ignoring this crime. There is but one result, which can follow in such a course. The crime in this community has been unsatisfactorily examined and consequently brought to a higher court.

It is the duty of every good citizen to tell the truth in this matter. The State and County have a dual capacity, that is, to give the offender the advantage of being innocent until proven guilty.

There are four points to consider in Corpus Deliciti. First, it is the death of a person. Secondly, when a body is found and is suspected of homicide or murder by suspicious circumstances, followed by the decision of a Coroner's Jury. Thirdly, a human agent is responsible and the act is unlawful. Lastly, the person on trial is presumed innocent, until proven guilty. This has been shown. A body was found dead, that of Sarah Ware, found on the second day of October 1898. Looking at the nature of her wounds, it seems there is no question that her death was caused by human means. It is the fourth and last point that we have to consider completely in this case which connects William Tekworgy to this crime.

Sarah Ware left the Files home for the last time on the evening of September 17, 1898. She went to John Bolder's where she paid a visit and cleaned house for his poker guests. It had been proven by the State that Sarah was seen going to Mr. John Bolder's home. There were a number of people that said they saw Sarah Ware stop at the William Bogg General Store after she left Mr. Bolder's, to purchase a cheroot. Mrs. Cosby saw Sarah pass her home assuming she was returning to Mrs. Files, but was never seen alive again!

I point out to you once again, that the witnesses who heard the outcries on the evening of September 17, 1898 fit the time frame of when Sarah disappeared. One witness testified that it sounded like a muffled human cry. This of itself would cast doubt on the defense that George Viles was responsible. It is conclusively known that Mr. Viles was boarding at Mrs. Agatha Elbridge's home on the night of September 17, 1898.

Then comes the two weeks gap and the finding of the body in the lonely secluded Nicholson Pasture. The nature of this place alone tells us why it was selected. It was not a place where a wagon could have easily been driven.

It is evident that the person who chose this place to lie the bruised and battered body of Sarah Ware, found a place of entrance and exit, then left. Was that the place where this poor woman met her death? Had the body been moved to this place after the terrible deed had been done?

In the alder bushes, to the south side of the trail there was evidence of where a wagon had gone. Although there was no sign of a struggle, this was Sarah Ware's final resting-place! The wounds on the body were so severe that she must have bled to death or otherwise been killed instantly, although no objects were found that could have inflicted such wounds.

Mr. Tekworgy said it was Joe Bogg who informed him of how the body came to where it was found. The story of Joe Bogg was first given before the preliminary hearing at the Municipal Court in Bucksport and then the retraction of Joe Bogg came out after the repeated visits of ex-selectman Samuel Pall to Bogg's house. There is no doubt in the mind of anyone who has listened to the evidence that influential forces were used to convince Joe Bogg and his wife to sign the retractions. Mr. Pall's statement that Joe Bogg would retract within 24 hours was followed by the fact that Joe Bog did retract his story within that time. This in itself would be significant to show he was threatened.

Evidence shows the truth of Joe Bogg's first story, for he went directly to where the body had been found when he first heard it. He went right to the place where Sarah Ware was, instead of going up the lane like he would have done if he did not know where she lay.

Joe Bogg told James Mank, his grandfather, long before the body was found, that he helped Mr. Tekworgy move a body. The statement of Mr. Tekworgy that he believed Joe Bogg was the man that moved the body only showed that Tekworgy was not a man to tell the truth. There is the testimony of one, Mr. Spaulding, that shows that he saw the jigger of Mr. Tekworgy and saw Mr. Bogg get on it the night in question.

Joe Bogg told his first story in truth, but it was beaten and pounded out of him by the Chairman of the Board of Selectman. He had no friends to counsel him. Then when threatened by ex-Selectman Pall he blindly did as he was told and made the retraction. When under arrest he reassured officials that his first story was fact, that of moving a body with Mr. Tekworgy.

The matter of the missing money, which was found in one of Mrs. Ware's trunks, after the trunks had several times been searched by experienced detectives who were looking for the money, is something which no word of the defense can smooth away. How did the money get into the trunk and the handbag under the commode? Now let us see how that might have come about. They did not find a handbag behind the commode the first time. How did it get there when it was searched a second time? Who had better access to this? It was the person who occupied the next room to Mrs. Ware's room. It was Mr. Tekworgy, and there was no lock on the door between his room and Sarah Ware's room. Mr. Tekworgy himself said he stayed at the File's house five nights that week. Then there is the testimony of another witness who went for shingles that proves Mr. Tekworgy stayed there longer. He said he saw Mr. Tekworgy sleeping in a chair when he went to see about the shingles not being delivered in late October.

What about Sarah's waterproof coat? You know from the evidence of Mrs. Files that Mrs. Ware did not have one on when she went to see John Bolder. Yet, Mrs. Files said she had one over her arm when she left. However, one was found beside her body, which would explain the discrepancy of the clothing she wore on the night of the disappearance. That brings us back to the handbag behind the commode. Mrs. Files testified that it is not the handbag as shown in evidence! She adamantly denied that it was not the same handbag that Sarah had with her on the night of her disappearance.

What about the mysterious fire in the field when there was no reason for one. Is that why the correct handbag and some of her clothing cannot be found?

Who put the Macintosh where it was found beside Sarah's body? Was it someone who was familiar with the premises? Is Mr. Tekworgy the man who took the Macintosh from the Files house and put it with the body?

Where was Mr. Tekworgy on the night of September 17, 1898? That is something he has never been able to explain, but we hear from a number of witnesses that he was not home. Mr. Tekworgy's daughter, Abby, who was home at the time, knows of his whereabouts on that night, which she won't disclose. On the day the body was found, he knew he was a suspect. Mr. Tekworgy could have easily stated where he was that night, but he did not. He preserved a singular silence regarding his movements on that night, at the same time protecting his innocence.

There have been a number of witnesses who have testified that they had conversations with Mr. Tekworgy saying, "Mr. Tekworgy had knowledge of the crime." I close my case!

The judge then instructed the jury that it is not enough for the State to convict a man. It must be shown that there cannot be a shadow of a doubt as to who killed the woman.

At midnight the jury was still out. The judge retired leaving word that if a verdict was reached he was to be summoned. If not, he would return in the morning.

* * *

As you, the reader, have undoubtedly noticed, there were incidents referred to, which you did not read about. Approximately 61 pages of witness testimonies were burned in a fire at Attorney Bellows office in Bucksport some years after the Supreme Court Trial. Unfortunately this leaves a gap in some of the information that has been presented.

THE FOLLOWING MORNING AT THE ELLSWORTH COURT HOUSE:

It was a dramatic scene in the trial chamber of the Hancock County Court House at 9:44 A.M. on July 25, 1902, a scene which one is likely never to forget. It was impressed upon the minds of many people that day.

The jury remained out all night until the hours of early morning. With the prolonged absence of twelve men it had begun to cause a feeling of suspense. It cannot be denied that it made the people satisfied with their ultimate decision, for it was a long debate.

There were a lot of rumors that circulated around that the first ballot vote was 9 to 3 for acquittal and held so on the subsequent ballots to about midnight. At this time two of the jurors who voted for a guilty verdict, swung over to the other side. This made the vote 11 to 1. This stayed so until the last juror voted for acquittal. This was only rumor reported by a newspaper reporter; and discussed publicly after the acquittal.

Shortly before 11: 00 a.m. the jury announced that it had made a decision. There was a hasty gathering of officials in the courtroom. The expectancy soon gave way to knowledge after a few minutes had elapsed when Mr. Tekworgy was brought into the courtroom. He took his seat in front of the Hancock County Deputy Sheriff. This was the seat where he sat and listened to the evidence for and against him.

Both attorneys were in their places and Judge Lemery took his seat upon the bench. The stillness of death almost filled the room.

Shortly after 11:00 a.m. the Clerk of Courts rose and asked the foreman, "Have you reached a verdict?" "We have sir," replied the foreman." There was a constraint in the way he said it. It made one wonder what the verdict was. Then expectancy soon gave way to knowledge.

The Judge asked the defendant to stand. The clerk of courts handed the verdict to Judge Lemery, whereupon he said to the jury, "And so say all of you gentlemen?" They all answered, 'Yes,' to Judge Lemery's question with concerted nodding of twelve heads. The Judge then said, "The court finds the defendant NOT GUILTY," and the Tekworgy verdict was a matter of legal record! Mr. Tekworgy leaned to speak to his Attorney, whispering in his ear, "We did it!" Then he turned to the jury with a look of satisfaction!

It was the announcement that, after having listened for nine days to the testimonies in the court and the jury deliberated for 16 and ½ hours, the jury was convinced that the State had failed to make its case and that William Tekworgy was to go free. Justice Lemery thanked the jurors for their service to the State in words well chosen and the formal discharge of the prisoner took place.

Mr. Tekworgy left the courtroom in the company of his daughter Mary and Counsel Bellows. They went to the Hancock House in Ellsworth where they had lunch and remained for some time. Then they left from Ellsworth on the 2:30 train, the New York Express for Bangor, then to Bucksport. Also on the train were Mr. Bellows and Detective Haskell from Massachusetts who had been in the employment of Mr. Tekworgy for some time. No one except Mr. Tekworgy knew that Detective Haskell was in his employ. Mrs. Files recognized Detective Haskell as the man that came to her house and said he was a detective and questioned her extensively but she thought he was an imposter.

All the way up the street they were followed by people who thought the government failed to establish the guilt of the prisoner. Those who thought he was not guilty also received William Tekworgy and his daughter with good wishes. His daughter Mary, a good-looking buxom young woman, received many words of praise for standing by her father throughout the ordeal as well as his daughter Abigail.

Through generations some citizens of Bucksport did and still continue to believe Mr. Tekworgy guilty and questioned where and what happened to Mr. Viles. Some people believed that some men of the jury and some witnesses were bought off. To the best of my knowledge neither Sarah's Bible nor her diary were ever found. Rumor has it that Mr. Tekworgy sold Sarah's Bible and that it does exist in Searsport, Maine however, I have been unable to locate it. No further information could be found on what happened to Mr. Viles and his Billy club.

Joe Bogg was absolved of any crime connected with the murder of Sarah Ware. However, Bucksport townspeople shunned him from then on. Three years hence he mysteriously disappeared.

Mildred knew she would visit her mother's grave later that day and tell her the sad news as she watched intently and listened quietly to Mr. Tekworgy's response as he answered a question propounded by a Bangor Daily News reporter. Mr. Tekworgy said, "I am not a bit surprised at the verdict because I am not guilty! I had expected it all along. I am glad that it is over and I want to resume my business, to show the people in Bucksport that I am an honest man. I want to regain my honor and the people's confidence, which I feel they have always had in me!"

Mildred walked away heavy hearted from the scene that she had just witnessed and went to Silver Lake Cemetery to visit the site of her mother's lonely pauper's grave. Quietly sitting there she said, "I will always love you mother."

Mildred gasped, and caught her breath; she could not believe what had just happened. Surely she did not hear her mother answer her saying, "I love you too Mildred." She was sitting by her mother's lonely secluded grave quietly talking to her about childhood memories. Mildred had talked about the night Ex-Selectman Pall came to their home uninvited and she saw her mother attempt to hit him over the head with a frying pan. It was a short time after that they were sent to Canada to stay with Aunt Catherine. With father dead, she knew now that her mother had done the best she knew how for herself and her brother.

Suddenly a calm peaceful feeling seemed to come over her. Mildred listened acutely as her mother told her what she knew about why and who killed her. "You must never reveal what I have just told you, it has to be our secret! There is other information in my Bible and diary, which is pertinent to my life. Find Mrs. Files she can help you find them. You must keep what I told you and what you will find in them to yourself until the right time. Your life will be in danger if anyone finds out you have this information. I will come to you again when the time is right and you can reveal our secret."

Mildred promised her mother she would tell no one of her conversation. With this, she calmly and slowly walked away saying, "Until another time mother, when the time is right, I then will let all know your secrets. We may not have lived together as mother and daughter while I was growing up, but we have maintained a closeness, a love that a mother and daughter share."

EPILOGUE

SARAH'S FREEDOM

This, I say to you, learn to forgive and love.
But first love yourself. I forgive you. I love you.
Let us give this love to others; let it be worldwide.
Love is the greatest gift we should not hide.
There is no room for violence.
Now I am released from this bondage,
My head and my body are now joined
As one, thought some.
My head held captive for over 100 years.
There are no more tears!
    I AM FREE, FREE, YES I AM.
My head was put in a box, not fancy just plain,
Carried to a lonely lower pauper's grave
My body interned without any name.
The Silver Lake Cemetery was my home.
No small service over my body was known.
In Ellsworth Court House Safe, was kept my head.
Still, separate for 100 years.
There are no more tears!
    I AM FREE, FREE, YES I AM

When Silver Lake Cemetery was to be flooded
It was decided by a few that my box be uncovered.
With the Ware family my body went
In Oak Hill Cemetery, Except for my head,
Some chose to keep me separated instead.
I am still separate.
There are no more tears!
    I AM FREE, FREE, YES I AM
100 years have passed. A kind person did a good deed.
I should be whole again they all finally agreed,
From Ellsworth Court House Safe, came my head
To Oak Hill Cemetery to be put with my body instead.
Did my head and my body become as one, I think not.
Below sits my body, my head still in a box, on top
I am still separate.
There are no more tears!
    I AM FREE, FREE, YES I AM